THE TART'S FINAL NOEL

GRAVESYDE VILLAGE MYSTERIES
BOOK THREE

PATRICIA RICE

PLEASE JOIN MY READER LIST

Please consider joining my newsletter for exclusive content and news of upcoming releases. Be the first to know about special sales, freebies, stories from my writer life, and other fun information. You'll even receive a thank-you gift. Join me on my writing adventures!

To Join, Please Visit —
https://www.subscribepage.com/ricewebsite

AUTHOR'S NOTE

In the Gravesyde Priory Mystery series I introduce readers to the heirs of Wycliffe Manor, who turn a derelict manor into a home. Each of the novels has its own romance and mystery to solve and those characters continue to appear in this Gravesyde Village spin-off series. There's a list of which couples star in which book at the end.

The history of the village is wrapped around the manor, the ancestral home of the Earls of Wycliffe, built on a former priory. In the way of medieval fiefdoms, the earls resisted district boundary changes, so the estate, in 1815, is an exclave of Shropshire, although south of Birmingham and surrounded by Worcestershire, creating legal havoc when it comes to crime. As appointed executor of the trust operating the manor, Captain Huntley has been chosen as the local magistrate.

The manor has been empty, or nearly so, for decades. The village has been left to die. With the return of the manor's inhabitants, and spurred by the end of war and the industrial revolution, the locals are gradually returning to their homes.

As a side note, I have referenced the town of "Stratford" where the bankers and solicitors reside. Although there is a Stratford in London and the famous Stratford-on-Avon nearby, this Stratford exists only in my mind. Birmingham, however, is completely real, an industrial and technology center akin to today's Silicon Valley.

In this holiday work, I thought readers might enjoy seeing how the various couples from earlier books are getting along. The story stands alone and those who haven't read earlier volumes can still enjoy my romantic protagonists, a bit of heartwarming, festive joy, and a mystery to savor!

CHARACTERS

VILLAGE (in order of importance):

Sgt. Rufus Russell (Rafe): retired army; innkeeper; bailiff
Verity Russell: teacher, Rafe's wife
Paul Upton: curate, carpenter
Minerva Upton: librarian, curate's wife
Daniel and Daphne Turner: orphans, eight and five
Margery Bartlett Turner: orphans' *deceased* mother
Major Thomas Turner: orphans' *deceased* father
Widow Rosemary (Willa) Willoughby: *deceased* baker
Bartletts: Margery's parents, former owners of bakery; moved to Virginia
Geoffrey Cooper: distant cousin of Margery and Willa
Brighid (Brydie) Calhoun: Kate's sister, Damien's fiancée
Damien Sutter: solicitor and landowner
Caitlin (Kate) Calhoun Morgan: widowed with three children, **Arthur** age 14
Rob age 12, **Lynly** age 8.
Jed Jasper: setting up hardware store
Cratchit: ex-soldier works in carpentry shop

Sgt. Major Fletcher Ferguson (Fletch): retired army; Rafe's friend and business partner
Benedict Bosworth Jr: banker in Stratford
Garret Browning III, esquire: lawyer from Stratford
George Dryden: young law clerk from Stratford
Ralph Parsons: Willa's half-brother
James Elton: employed by orphans' family
Jacques Rousseau: Damien's French valet

MANOR:

Captain Alistair (Hunt) Huntley: US Army engineer, magistrate
Clarissa (Clare) Huntley: wife of Hunt and secret novelist
Arnaud Lavigne: Hunt's artist cousin, former French comte
Henri Lavigne: Arnaud's younger brother, tavern owner, peddler
Patience Upton Lavigne: Henri's wife; gardener; curate's sister
Lady Elsa Villiers de Sackville: manor cook
Honorable Jack de Sackville: stable owner; Elsa's husband
Lavender Marlowe: young seamstress
Daniel Walker: Hunt's friend, steward; Meera's husband
Meera Abrams Walker: physician/apothecary; Clare's best friend
Dorothea (Thea) Reid Talbot: haunted interior decorator
Henrietta (Nettie) Upton: housekeeper; mother of Patience and Paul Upton
Terrence Birdwhistle: tutor
Laurence, Viscount Chatham; Mr. Shaw; Mr. Watson: visitors
John Gillespie: visiting manservant

MONDAY

DECEMBER 18, 1815

ONE

"OLD RED HAS GONE MISSING AGAIN," MISS BUTLER CALLED FROM the inn's kitchen. "We're short of eggs. We need more good layers."

Good layers. The irony pierced her heart. "I'll look in a minute." Clutching her polishing rag, Verity Russell swiped at tears with her shoulder.

If she rubbed the planks any harder, she'd wear a hole through them. Solid walnut and her husband's pride and joy, the heavy Jacobean trestle table suited the derelict medieval inn they were restoring. Making the boards shine was probably a waste but she needed an excuse to be alone.

More good layers, indeed. That hurt. That hurt a *lot.*

Verity had been telling herself that she cried because she would no longer be teaching in here. Starting a school for the village children in her husband's pub had been her very first accomplishment after escaping her narrow London life, and she had a right to be proud.

But the late Earl of Wycliffe's heirs had rebuilt their medieval tower to allow local children access to the manor's schoolroom. Verity's students would be taught there after the first of the year.

She didn't fool even herself with that blatant fustian. She wasn't crying over the change. Children had no place in a public inn, and she actually looked forward to working with Mr. Birdwhistle at the manor. The students would benefit from having two teachers, a better library, and more space.

She selfishly cried for herself and the child she thought she would bear by summer. She hadn't realized how very much she wanted a child of her own. Foolish of her. She and Rafe Russell had only married a few months ago. They had too little money and too little time as it was. Thank goodness it had been too soon to tell Rafe. With all his other worries, he didn't need to share this sorrow. For him, she had to keep smiling. Sometimes, she simply needed to be alone with her grief.

Having rubbed every stick of furniture plus the centuries-old bar, she ran out of beeswax. Her students were all home, preparing for the Christmas festivities. Even the dour old women in the kitchen were singing hymns in merry rounds. Having exchanged wintry tents for cozy chambers at the inn, their new staff had reason to be joyful.

Time to hunt Old Red. Avoiding the merriment in the kitchen, Verity slipped into the inn's lobby, donned a cloak, and set out in the chilly wind to search for the recalcitrant old biddy who wouldn't stay penned. Best to make a stew for dinner than let a fox have good meat. The biddy was too old to lay much longer anyway.

At twenty-five, was *she* too old to carry babes? Verity fought a fresh spurt of tears, although now she could blame the wind for making her eyes water. With no family and all the women in the manor busy with holiday plans, she had no one she dared ask. Besides, it was too personal, and given her lonely upbringing, she wasn't accustomed to sharing.

As if sensing her distress, her marmalade kitten pounced from nowhere to circle her ankles. She leaned over to pet Marmie's furry head, then tucked him into the warmth of her cloak. Well-fed these days, the once-abandoned kitten was now almost too large for her pocket.

At this early hour, frost still lingered in the shadows. The old hen most likely had retreated to the warm stable. A city girl, Verity had never learned to cook or wring chicken necks, but she might learn for this foul fowl. Not a charitable thought for the holiday season.

Perhaps she should think about pleasantries, like how to make a kissing bough. She'd been a child when she'd helped her mother decorate for Christmas, but it shouldn't be difficult. Rafe had pointed out the mistletoe in the trees behind the inn. She had no notion of how one harvested it.

Once they reached the large, drafty stable, Marmie jumped out to chase mice. When the manor had an excess of guests, they sheltered their carriage horses in the inn's extensive stable. The income hadn't covered costs as yet, but it was a good start. The inn's bedchambers were scarcely ready for more than a few guests.

She was more comfortable with counting pounds and shillings than cooking. Food was Rafe's domain, but as bailiff, he often had to be out and about, which meant someone else had to prepare meals.

The hen wouldn't go near the horses at the busy end of the stable. She preferred the empty stalls in need of repair. Verity stalked down the hard-packed dirt floor, listening for the old biddy. Red usually roosted on a grain bin, but a rustle in one of the old stalls gave her away. With grim triumph, she eased open the sagging door, prepared to pounce.

Two small shapes dived into a meager haystack that hadn't been there yesterday.

Startled, Verity almost slammed the stall door, but the wriggling rearends attempting to hide in loose straw were too ridiculous to fear. She'd spent these last months dealing with children from five to fourteen and knew when they were avoiding authority. She probably knew these two. The only problem here was why they were in the stable. Some idle game to while away the holiday hours? Or were they hiding from something or someone?

She'd spent many years hiding from her fears. No longer.

She crouched down to a child's height. "Where are you Old Red? I need eggs for my breakfast. The rashers are almost ready. And I have toast browning. I just need your eggs." Promises of food usually lured children faster than yelling.

No whispers. Just more rustling as they burrowed deeper. Shouldn't they have recognized her voice? Were they *not* some of her students? That would be decidedly worrisome.

At the sound of her wheedling tone, Marmie returned to sniff for food.

"I do wish I had someone to share tea and toast with," she said wistfully. "Eating by myself is lonely."

A single whisper. No reply.

"Well, if I can't find those eggs, I shall just have bacon on toast, I suppose. Maybe if I leave the door open, Old Red will wander in later." She stood and eased from the stall. Did she go inside and hope they took the bait? Or wait and pounce? She didn't wish to terrify them. "I wish I had children to share my meal."

She hid behind the door but peered around to watch.

A tousled towhead with big violet eyes popped up cautiously from the stack. A moment later, another towhead, this one smaller, wearing bedraggled blue ribbons in her pigtails, joined him. Verity's heart tore at their tear-stained, dirty, frightened faces. They were so very *young*. . .

Marmie leaped into the pile of hay, lost his footing, and slid down in front of startled blue eyes. Verity used that excuse to return. "Oh, my, Marmie you naughty kitty, you were supposed to find a chicken, not children! Hello, you two. Did the Christmas angels send you to share my breakfast?"

Two children in a stable at Christmas—angels might possibly be involved. For the first time in a week, a shaft of joy pierced her gloom. She had never really believed in angels, but. . .

The smallest child reached for the kitten, cuddling the spoiled creature before crawling out of the straw. Verity thought the girl couldn't be much more than five. Her pinafore was filthy and wrinkled but not ragged. Her gown fit, and her shoes were muddy but solid. This was no neglected child—but Verity had never seen her before. Those huge violet eyes watched her warily.

With an irritated sigh, the boy crawled out. He looked too much like the younger to be anything but her older brother. The only difference was that the girl's hair was silky straight and his curled in ringlets. Men got all the looks.

"Oh, my, definitely sent by angels," Verity declared. "I am Mrs. Russell. And you are?"

"Daniel and Daphne," the boy said curtly. "Do you really have toast?"

"I most certainly do. And rashers and milk, and if we can round up a few eggs, we can have those too." They watched her so hungrily that her heart broke all over again. "Do you know how to look for eggs? Old Red sometimes hides them in here but we'll find more in the henhouse."

The boy nodded. The girl clung to Marmie and simply followed them out.

Mrs. Hatter stepped out the kitchen door. The elderly servant had probably seen them from the window. Verity held a finger to her lips, then gave a shooing gesture. Smarter than most, the stout old woman limped inside and probably continued to watch from the window.

Verity handed Daniel a basket and showed them how to look around the outside of the henhouse. Someone would have already searched the inside. By the back fence, Old Red, the stubborn old biddy, clucked from wherever she'd been hiding and scampered. The little girl released Marmie to crouch down and uncover the nest and an egg. Either the child knew how to find eggs or she was capable of hearing. She simply didn't seem to speak.

The children happily rummaged in weed patches, robbing Rafe of the eggs he was probably counting on for cakes or other dishes. Her husband loved cooking. . . and eating. But he could go without eggs for a day.

Once they had a nice supply, Verity signaled for the pair to follow her to the kitchen door. She put a finger to her lips and gestured for them to stay behind and to one side. Children loved games, and these two were already prepared to be sneaky. She leaned inside and whispered to the servant watching her as if Verity had taken leave of her senses. "Clear the room, please. I don't want to frighten them."

Too new to this employment to be anything but obedient, Mrs. Hatter hustled everyone out. It was time they started cleaning upstairs anyway.

Verity held a finger to her lips again and gestured for the children to enter. "The kitchen is all ours," she whispered.

In exaggerated stealth, they crept into the warmth of the enormous inn kitchen. Rashers were, indeed, keeping warm by the fire. Verity couldn't cook much, but she knew how to fix eggs. Bread was already sliced, so she had each child take a fork and toast slices over the fire while she scrambled their find, adding cream and cheese and just a bit of salt, having learned that most children liked their food bland.

She hadn't had servants since she was a young girl. She hadn't forgotten how to do for herself in these last few months of being pampered by Rafe and the new staff. She dished out the bacon and eggs, buttered the toast, and boiled fresh tea for herself while the children dug forks and spoons from the drawer under the table. Marmie had followed them in and curled around everyone's ankles. Once a starving alley cat, he was always ready for a meal.

The table was much too tall. Verity poured milk and had them sit on the hearth while she confined Marmie to her lap by feeding him bits of bacon. She hadn't eaten this morning, but for the first time in a week, she was finally hungry. Perhaps she had simply needed a bit of intrigue to distract her.

"Well, Daphne and Daniel, this is so much better than eating alone, thank you! Did you fly in on angel wings last night?"

The little girl giggled, so she could make sounds. Captain Huntley at the manor had hired a deaf-mute boy as an assistant. He mostly grunted, possibly because he'd never heard a laugh.

Daniel was all but inhaling his food. He washed down a huge bite with milk, then frowned. "The carriage had a pony. It will be hungry too."

"I will have someone look for the pony," she said reassuringly, hiding her concern. "Do you know where you left it?"

"Nanny fell asleep and it went off the road," he said matter-of-factly, tearing into his toast. "We were cold, and Mama said we can always find help at the church, but no one was there."

The chapel was just down the road from the inn, on the east end of the village, which meant they'd come from Stratford—or London. The carriage shouldn't be difficult to find. It rather sounded like the driver had passed out drunk, though. Shouldn't this nanny be awake by now and frantically hunting the children? Why in the name of heavens would she be driving children about in the dark on a wintry night?

"The curate was visiting his parishioners," Verity explained, not wanting to discourage them from seeking churches—although it was more likely that Paul Upton and his new wife, Minerva, were dining late at the manor. "Do you know where you were going?"

"Nanny said we was a burden on the parish and we was to be sent back to where we belong." He wrinkled his freckled nose. "We're not very big. How much is a burden?"

Evidently listening, Daphne pushed her eggs around, and a single tear trailed down her dirty cheek. Still, she said nothing. She certainly looked old enough to talk.

But Daniel's explanation was all Verity needed. The children were orphans with no one to take them in, so "Nanny" had been driving them to a workhouse.

"A burden is what someone doesn't want to carry. I am sure

you weren't a burden to your mother or father. Do you know where they are?" Verity let the kitten jump down now that the pair had nearly cleaned their plates.

"Mama died." Daniel said it bravely, as if he'd had to repeat the story more than once, but his eyes looked bleak. "She was sick. She said she wrote our family and they was to take us in. But no one came." Hiding tears, Daniel tried to tempt the kitten from his sister by holding up a tiny piece of bacon, but Daphne had buried her face in the kitten's fur and wasn't letting loose.

His simple statement induced a cyclone of emotions that Verity couldn't quite manage. Tears returned to her eyes, but hope rose in her heart. If their family didn't want these two precious babes. . .

Gravesyde wasn't a real village with taxes and all. They had no money to pay for a workhouse or orphanage. And she wasn't about to allow these children to be abandoned in an awful place like Birmingham, the only town where they could possibly be taken.

Perhaps, when they found the nanny, she could tell them more. Verity wouldn't get her hopes up. Yet.

"Well, then, we must find your family like your Mama wanted, mustn't we?" she said cheerfully. "There must have been some delay on the road. I am sure they are missing two beautiful angels already. Let us get you washed up and tidy and we'll see about finding your nanny and the pony."

And if no one claimed these babes, she would. Relief swelled her heart at that decision.

TWO

MINERVA UPTON HUMMED AS SHE PICKED HER WAY PAST THE parsonage drive's half-frozen mud puddles. She'd been practicing Christmas carols with her sister-in-law and the other ladies at the manor last night and the joy still bubbled. All of Gravesyde Priory had reason to celebrate this year, and she could not remember ever loving the holiday so much. She'd spent the early part of her life following her father's half-starved troops across the Continent and these last few years moldering in a duke's library. Now, newly married, she was enjoying her freedom entirely too much.

She truly loved being married, perhaps because she dearly loved Paul. No stiff, formal gentleman, he was a Renaissance man of a sort—kind-hearted enough to handle his wayward parishioners with a gentle hand, talented enough to repair the crumbling chapel and parsonage, intelligent enough to have graduated Oxford and meet her bookish barbs with humor and understanding. How could anyone not love a man like that?

But the foolish creature insisted on eating. Having grown up with pan bread and grease and the occasional overcooked quail wing, Minerva had never developed much interest in food. Not married a month, and she was already failing as a wife. She wished to please her new husband with a nice meal in the morning, if nothing else. Even genteelly-raised Verity could fix breakfast. Of course, Verity's husband did the baking.

Minerva had to waste the few coins of her meager librarian's salary on buying bread. Rafe's inn wasn't set up for a bakery, but fortunately, the Widow Willoughby provided. She had ancient ovens left over from when there had been a busy village and a real bakery. The bakers had moved away with everyone else, but Willa, with her hermit habits, had remained. She turned out delicious breads and buns and anything else requested. Minerva told herself she was helping a poor widow by providing her with an income.

Unfortunately, her weekly bread-buying meant Paul wouldn't have a new shirt at Christmas. Even if she might afford the fabric, she wasn't much at sewing beyond hems and buttons.

She turned off the main road to traverse what could barely be called an alley behind the village shops. Once-lovely thatched cottages, with large yards for pigs and chickens and vegetables, were scattered along this winding pathway. After the earl and viscountess died, the village had died, too, abandoning the cottages to the bank. Minerva wondered how the widow held onto hers all alone. A bakery selling a few loaves of bread a day couldn't pay a mortgage or even rent. But the lady was reclusive and Minerva didn't like to pry. Well, not too much.

Oddly, no smoke rose from the great ovens on this chilly morning. Had she arrived too late? Was the baking all done for the day? Or had the widow decided to take a holiday? What on earth would she feed Paul if she couldn't buy bread? Perhaps Rafe had some extra?

She supposed there was always porridge, but she had no fruit to make it special. What else could be added to ugly, gray porridge to make it appealing?

Well, perhaps Mrs. Willoughby had something leftover from yesterday. Minerva knew how to soften old bread. She knew how to make-do with almost anything, but she was as partial to fresh, hot bread as her husband. She'd learned to eat well since returning from the war-torn Continent.

Bypassing the baker's unused front door, she turned down a worn flagstone path to the overgrown backyard, and knocked at the kitchen shutters. Age had stripped them of any paint except a few blue flakes in the cracks where the bare wood had weathered. No one answered.

She tried the door, which matched the peeling shutters. Still no response.

Minerva frowned. She'd only lived in Gravesyde since June, but she had never seen Mrs. Willoughby leave her house. She supposed she must. A baker had to buy supplies. But she never attended chapel and one never saw her about. Presumably, a baker had to rise early in the morning and must go to bed before the tavern opened in the evening, One of these days, Rafe would open the inn's pub, but for now, the tavern was the only neighborhood gathering place besides the church. There was no real excuse not to attend church once the bread was baked, though.

She tested the latch, and to her surprise, the door swung open. "Mrs. Willoughby? It's just me, Minerva Upton. Are you well?"

Middle-aged but still attractive in an overblown sort of way, the baker had never been talkative, but she always replied. The house echoed empty.

"Mrs. Willoughby?" She entered and called louder. *Yes*, she was meddlesome.

The kitchen appeared neat as always, the ingredients for breadmaking set out on the old oak table, The two giant baking ovens, however, barely emitted any heat. That was concerning. The stink caused her to peer in. What had she been burning? Old clothes? Had she run out of kindling? Minerva poked at the embers to stir them and called, "Mrs. Willougby?"

Was that a groan? Swallowing hard, she gripped the fire iron and swung around to search the kitchen. She didn't dither for long. She'd lived with war. Sometimes, lives depended on speed, and she wasn't timid. "Mrs. Willoughby? I'm coming in," she cried louder.

She didn't want to face a shotgun. She'd give any intruder a chance to run out the front, but who would rob a poor baker? She suspected the woman must be ill.

She had never gone past the kitchen before. She peered into the front room. The parlor seemed a little disturbed, but the furniture was sparse. A dog having a romp could have made it look messy, not that the widow had a dog. Feeling ridiculous, she continued gripping the poker.

That was definitely another groan. Heart pounding, she made her way past an ancient wooden settle, a faded sofa, and a spindly writing desk, working her way toward the front door and stairs.

Sprawling across the parlor hearth was a gentleman in a fine caped greatcoat attempting to crawl up on hands and knees and slipping on a saddlebag. "Will you cease that caterwauling, woman?" he muttered, righting himself.

Minerva had seen plenty of drunks in her time. She didn't smell alcohol, but she'd wager there was an empty bottle of gin about somewhere. She didn't offer her hand. He wasn't a large man but still twice her size. "Where is Mrs. Willoughby?"

He sat up on his haunches, then caught a worn, upholstered chair and shakily hauled upright on his own. He blinked at her. A head taller than her petite stature, with fashionably cut, mud-brown hair and muddy eyes, he wasn't imposing. She hid the fire iron in her cloak.

"Willa? Didn't she come home?" He rubbed the back of his head and grimaced. "Devil take it, did she hit me? I told her I was coming."

This was a little too much oddity for this hour of the morning, and Paul would be looking for his breakfast soon. But Minerva's instinct for danger had gone on full alert. "And you are?"

Unsteadily, he dropped into the upholstered chair without bowing or waiting for her to sit. "Distant cousin, of a sort, Geoffrey Cooper, Miss. . ."

"*Mrs.* Upton. It looks as if Mrs. Willoughby took your letter for a warning and left. Hold your head down, let me take a look at it." Minerva's father was a colonel. Telling people what to do was in her blood. She set the poker aside as he followed orders.

He turned his chair to cross his arms on the sofa back, letting his head sink onto them. "Can't hold it up anyway. I quit drinking, I swear. I haven't touched a bottle. . ." He grunted as she found the matted, bloodied bump on the back of his head. He'd smeared blood on his linen, probably from rubbing the wound.

"Mrs. Willoughby is strong if she's the one who struck you," Minerva said, almost in admiration. She couldn't have managed to concuss a man like that. "I can send for a physician, but she'll tell you the same thing. You need to stay awake for a while, don't try to do anything strenuous until the nausea and dizziness settles."

She glanced around for a weapon, but she held the most likely one. She checked the ends but saw no blood or hair. Of course, she'd had it in the oven. "Are you sure you didn't say something rude to her? I've never known her to strike anyone."

"Don't remember a blamed thing. I was supposed to attend a funeral but I was too late. Story of my life. I used to visit my cousins here in summer, many years back. I'd written Willa, asking if I could stop on a night or two after the funeral. I didn't hear from her, but that's not unusual. She doesn't write. I figured she'd find someone to read my post. She has no reason to hit me. May be the only person in the world who doesn't, mind you. . ."

Hospitality required that she provide hot tea, at the very least. With the fires out, the usually cozy cottage was freezing. Caution said this man could be dangerous—but the expensive greatcoat. . . Well, wealth did not a gentleman make.

But concern for the baker was paramount. "Did you look upstairs?"

He rubbed his no-doubt aching head, frowned, and glanced down at his coat. "Doesn't look like I had time."

Definitely signs of concussion if he couldn't remember what

happened. Or a hangover. "Start a fire and I'll make tea in a bit. I'm going up."

The baker had once had a prosperous home, far larger than the parsonage, Minerva observed as she ran up the stairs. A small sitting area with a threadbare carpet graced the hall at the top of the stairs. Two closed doors at the rear, one open overlooking the front. . . very nice. Minerva chose the front first.

And entering—gagged on a scream.

THREE

BRYDIE

"Lynly, remember not to disturb Mrs. Russell. She's sad and doesn't want to hear about your quilt, all right?" Brydie didn't bother steering the pony cart. The poor old beast made the trip into Gravesyde nearly every day and simply followed the ruts.

"Why is she sad?" her eight-year-old niece asked.

Well, Brydie should have anticipated that. She didn't have an answer.

"Wouldn't you be sad if you were a long way from home with no family at Christmas?" Arthur answered. At fourteen, Lynly's brother considered himself a man and an authority on almost everything.

The real man riding behind them had encouraged Brydie's nephew to think for himself lately. The boy would be going off to boarding school after the first of the year, so she supposed he needed to grow up a bit, but she'd always remember her nephew as a baby—

A nearly incoherent shriek froze that thought and had her sawing at the pony's reins. A moment later, they heard a cry—

"Brydie, thank all the heavens!"

Rob, her twelve-year-old nephew, was the first to point out the woman in the upper window of the baker's cottage. *Minerva?* What was the curate's wife doing. . .

Damien rode into Minerva's view before Brydie could even think to respond. The curate's wife shouted again. "Mr. Sutter, fetch Rafe, please—and hurry! Someone better fetch Dr. Walker. It's early. She should still be at home."

If Minerva needed a physician and *bailiff*—something bad had to have happened to the baker. *Not at Christmas, please Lord!* They'd had so many tragedies this past year. . . Brydie handed the reins to Arthur. "Leave Lynly and Rob and the pony cart with Mrs. Russell. It will probably be faster if you run for Dr. Walker."

She set the reins aside before anyone could protest. Damien, her betrothed, rode around to help her down. "Stay outside," he warned. "Minerva would not be screaming if Mrs. Willoughby is just ill. Persuade her down here until we return."

At thirty, Brydie had finally found a man to love, one who loved her back. But she was too old to change her managing ways now. Her beloved was accustomed to meek ladies. He needed regular reminding that she'd never be one.

"Don't go all protective on me, Damien Sutter." Brydie picked up her heavy woolen skirt, revealing the boots and trousers beneath. "I've seen my fair share of death."

Damien *knew* that. But apparently now that she was about to be his wife, he'd lost his wits.

Scowling, he leaned from the saddle to kiss her hair. She wasn't a small woman. "Take my crop." He handed her the leather he kept for shooing sheep from the road.

Relieved they needn't argue, she clutched the grip, lifted her cloak and skirt, and ran down Willa's overgrown walk, stalky weeds and shrubs scattering seeds as she brushed against them.

Damien cantered off, leaving the cart under Arthur's guidance. The boy urged the pony into its version of a gallop, leaving Brydie with the colonel's imperturbable daughter and whatever had her screaming.

The few times Brydie had visited the baker, she'd always gone to the kitchen door, but Minerva had called from the front. That door was closer. She brushed past the untrimmed holly and privet and reached for the handle. The door opened before she touched it.

A weary stranger blocked her way. In his caped greatcoat, he appeared broader than Brydie but not taller. From the looks of his pale face, she could probably topple him if necessary.

"Does that woman do nothing but shriek?" he asked grumpily. Not waiting for an answer, he staggered up the front stairs.

Oh, well, if that's the way he meant to be. . . Wrapping her cloak around her, glad for her gloves since the cottage was chilly, Brydie shoved past the unsteady gentleman and raced up to the front chamber. The manor's librarian had always been somewhat reserved, but one couldn't marry a curate and remain standoffish. Minerva knew how to ask for help.

The casual habits of the manor's inhabitants had filtered down to the general populace. Minerva may have taken the name Mrs. Upton when she married, but she was Minerva to most of the village—especially since the original Mrs. Upton, the manor's housekeeper, was the curate's mother.

The petite librarian barred the door to the front bedchamber. "We can't do anything. It's too late. If Mr. Sutter has gone for Rafe, then start a fire. Fix tea. This looks very bad."

Acknowledging not just the status of the curate's new wife, but also her wisdom in a crisis, Brydie did as told. Sometimes, the only adequate response to a problem was tea.

She had to assume Mrs. Willoughby was dead. The baker couldn't have been more than forty as far as Brydie knew. Willa had been an adolescent working in the bakery when Brydie was a little girl. They used to buy hot cross buns, and Willa had wrapped them up to keep them warm. They'd been so delicious. . .

Hurrying downstairs, she passed the stranger still dragging

himself up. He didn't even express bewilderment at her hasty retreat but continued his trudge.

Kindling had been added to the stove and a fire was catching when she reached the kitchen, so she had a kettle heating by the time Rafe arrived, accompanied by Damien. Mr. Upton followed shortly after. All three ran upstairs. Minerva the General could sort them out.

Walking from the far end of town, plump, short Dr. Walker arrived next. Brydie pointed the lady apothecary/physician up the stairs, then turned Arthur away. "The place is full to bursting. Go help Mrs. Russell and keep an eye on Lynly and Rob, please. I'll be over shortly."

"I'm supposed to help Mr. Sutter set up an office," the boy protested.

"And you will do that when he's ready. Sometimes, we must think of others before ourselves. See if Mrs. Russell needs any help. Rafe may be here awhile." She watched her tall nephew lope past the hedges, away from whatever grim scene was above. Children should enjoy Christmastide. He was off to school next month. This might be the last one they shared with him as a child.

Brydie found the tea and started a pot. She hadn't known Mrs. Willougby well enough to mourn more than the loss of her sweet buns. Both Brydie and her sister baked. Since they had few coins, they'd never bought bread, but they liked an occasional holiday treat. She'd have to learn to bake buns on her own.

How had Willa kept those great ovens fired up? Shivering in the drafty cottage, she peered inside one and found a fresh fire crackling. Had Minerva done that? Or possibly the grumpy stranger.

Damien came down first. "Meera says it's too late for a solicitor and I am unnecessary."

"But if the death is not natural. . ." Brydie waited expectantly. If they meant to marry, he must learn to share.

Her intended ran a hand through his thick, golden-brown hair. In this dim light, the silver threads weren't visible.

"Someone stabbed her while she was sleeping. It's not pretty, and you're not needed any more than I am. Dr. Walker has a blood-thirsty nature and experience with corpses. She's sending Minerva down. Have you found anything she might eat? She looks queasy."

"Then it truly must be bad. Minerva has patched soldiers on battlefields." Brydie began opening cupboards.

Damien grimaced. "Dr. Walker said bleeding copiously means the victim was healthy. Rafe wants to arrest the stranger who claims to be a cousin, but the man hasn't even the strength to stand straight much less drive a knife through anyone. It's more likely the killer bashed in his head."

Brydie found a biscuit tin and opened it. . . to a stash of coins, some gold. She held it out to show him. "It wasn't robbery then, or the thief was incompetent."

Damien uttered an impolite word. "I'll start searching the front room. You take this one."

Searching for something edible for Minerva, Brydie opened another tin that actually contained a few biscuits. The larder was nearly empty since all the flour and whatnot were on the table, ready for the morning baking.

The cottage had a cellar. Feeding people came before clues. Brydie lit a lantern and dared the rickety stairs. Potatoes, eggs, carrots, butter, a container of milk. . . It was so cold upstairs at the moment, the milk might keep up there, until those ovens heated, anyway. She found a currant cake and a barrel of apples. That would have to do.

Minerva had fixed her own tea by the time Brydie carried up a pitcher of cream, a pocketful of apples, and the cake. The librarian did look a trifle pale. Brydie cut her a slice filled with currants. "You haven't eaten, have you?"

The curate's wife shook her head. "I was here to buy bread for Paul's breakfast. How will I feed him now? I can't ask his mother to send down loaves."

Brydie eyed the bread makings on the table. "I can start the dough, but it needs to rise. You'll have to eat before that. Peel and slice those apples, and we can make a skillet bread."

She heard Damien rummaging through the front room but didn't feel guilty for not hunting for something she didn't know to look for. He'd eventually remember that she didn't take orders well.

"I haven't made skillet cakes in years! I've let my meager kitchen skills go to waste while living in the lap of luxury." Minerva grabbed a paring knife—then stared at it. "Was she killed with one of her own knives?"

"Not a paring knife, I assume. Was the weapon not in the room?" Brydie had experience at balancing death with practical reality.

"It was still in her," Minerva muttered, returning to peeling, apparently also stifling emotion with action. "But the handle on the weapon was different. I suppose only in places like the manor do handles match. I need to think about anything but poor Mrs. Willoughby. . ." She peeled furiously while studying the room. "This kitchen is almost as large as the one at the manor."

"Not quite, but years ago, the Bartletts hired a lot of people to help with the bakery, especially this time of year. They needed space." Setting an iron skillet on the hot stove, Brydie mixed the apples and butter into it. "I assume they must have been reasonably wealthy during the earl's time, maybe before. They weren't a large family, if I remember rightly. The elder Bartletts gave up the bakery and moved away. . . ten, fifteen years ago, maybe? After their only child married."

With the apples sliced and cooking, Minerva began opening and closing cabinets and peering at shelves of baking pans, continuing the search Brydie had abandoned. "Why would anyone kill a lonely widow who obviously had nothing?"

"Willa might have hoarded more blunt than in that tin. Who is the grumpy stranger? I hope Rafe is questioning him." With the skillet bread cooking, Brydie began on the loaves. She set the yeast starter warming and began mixing flours. Willa apparently used the fine white flour sparingly since there wasn't much of it on the table.

Brydie had been making bread since childhood and didn't measure, but she'd like the recipe for those hot cross buns they used to buy, when they still had coin. She glanced around for a notebook—then remembered Willa couldn't read.

From her perch on a chair, Minerva answered, "He says he's a Geoffrey Cooper and a distant cousin who was in the area for a funeral. Gravesyde hasn't had any lately, thank all the heavens, so it must have been elsewhere. He doesn't seem to remember what happened."

Damien reappeared in the doorway holding a thin sheet of stationery. "This appears to confirm his claim, unless he placed this here after he killed her. I doubt he could hit himself on the head though."

With her hands coated in flour, Brydie let Minerva read the letter.

"It just says what he told me—he means to attend a funeral and might he stay the night. Curt, to the point of unkind."

That sounded like the curmudgeon at the door. Brydie dismissed the letter. "Does it look as if someone searched the house?"

"The house is large and she's stuffed it with everything she was ever given, found, or bought from the looks of it. Searching will take days, but it does appear as if drawers were opened." Damien looked uncomfortable and left before he could be questioned more.

"He's not telling us something," Brydie said. "How did she buy anything on the price of a few loaves of bread?"

"Perhaps her late husband left her an annuity?" Setting aside the letter, Minerva climbed back on the chair to search the top of cabinets.

"I don't think she ever actually married. We called her Willa when she was just a girl because her uncle called her Willoughby. I'm not even sure what her birth name is. *Was*. The title was just a politeness." Brydie checked the skillet bread before starting on the loaves.

Minerva ran a long-handled spoon to the back of the top shelf and exclaimed in triumph as she snagged a thick book, nearly tumbling it onto her uncapped dark hair.

Brydie watched as the librarian opened the crumbling leather notebook with reverence, then wrinkled her nose. "Ancient recipes. The ink is faded to nearly illegible."

"Hold it for me so I can see." Working the flour mix, Brydie studied the tiny, spiky, hen-scratching on the stained pages. "I wonder if I could have someone copy it fresh? I'd love to have those old recipes."

"I'll ask around. Maybe there are some simple ones I might follow." At a knock on the back door, Minerva set the book aside.

Rafe's partner, the disturbingly large and grim Sgt-Major Fletcher Ferguson filled the doorway with his bulk and his frown. "I just heard. Something happened to Willa?"

At the sound of Fletch's deep voice, Damien immediately returned to the kitchen to grab the former soldier and haul him back outside.

Minerva and Brydie exchanged looks, then as one, eased open the door and blatantly listened.

"It's none of anyone's damned business," Fletch was protesting.

"A copper fine for cursing," Minerva whispered.

Damien kept his voice lower and forced Fletch to do the same. A moment later, Fletch's glare broke into sorrow. He shook his shaggy head in vigorous denial.

They couldn't hear his reply.

Brydie closed the door. "Willa and Fletch? That seems an unlikely match, poor soul."

Minerva wrinkled her nose and didn't reply.

FOUR

VERITY

AT THE INN, VERITY HAD ARTHUR HAUL TWO SMALL BEDS FROM THE room of castoffs she and Rafe hadn't sorted yet. They'd spent more time in furnishing rooms for themselves and staff than setting up guest rooms. It wasn't as if travelers were pounding at their door. Gravesyde was well off everyone's beaten path.

Which was why it was exceedingly unusual for unknown children to arrive in this backwater.

"The boy said their carriage had an accident and they left their nanny and a pony on the road," Verity told Brydie's nephew. "Since the children found us first, they most likely came from the direction of Stratford. Can you look for the carriage?"

She had been waiting for Rafe to return, but whatever business he was on must be complicated.

"If little ones could walk here, it's probably not far. May be easiest if I walk. Old Tess doesn't move fast these days." Arthur helped her straighten the sheets while the children watched warily from a corner. "Reckon we have some of Rob and Lynly's old clothes we can bring over that might fit them."

"I was hoping they might have a trunk in the carriage, but

since the driver hasn't shown up. . ." Verity wrinkled her nose and whispered, "I'm afraid they may have been abandoned."

More likely, she was *hoping* they had been and was setting herself up for heartbreak. But she needed a little hope, just for a little while, until the sadness went away. Rafe didn't deserve her gloom.

"Anyone who loses little ones isn't trustworthy." Arthur nodded knowledgeably. "I should have brought Mr. Sutter's carriage if there is a trunk."

"We only had a bag." Daniel spoke up. "Elton wouldn't let us take more."

Daphne looked ready to cry again. Verity had scrubbed their hands and faces, but with no clean clothing, hadn't tried to do more. She scooped up the little girl, hugged her, and set her on the freshly made bed. "We will send Arthur to look for your bag now, and then we will go back to your home for anything else. Do you know where you lived?"

And where to find this Elton so she could slap him? Hard.

"Beanblossom," Daniel said, testing his new bed. "Mama said if we got lost, to tell people we are the Turners from Beanblossom. Daphne wants her doll and I had important schoolbooks."

Verity was from London and not familiar with all the villages in the area. Why would anyone call a town *Beanblossom*? And Turner. . . the name was too common to be of any use. She glanced at Arthur, who shook his head.

"Well, we shall find your home," she replied with a confidence she did not feel. She was having significant doubts about her wisdom on any of this. Children weren't kittens to be scooped off the street like Marmie. There had to be someone, somewhere, looking for these two. They had obviously been well brought up, even if they were orphans now. After whatever had happened, they still trusted adults to make things right.

Verity wished it were only that easy. "Arthur, why don't you run up to the manor and ask whoever is about if they might help you find the carriage? They'll have a horse you can ride."

The boy brightened and raced off on his errand, leaving Verity to decide what to do with two grief-stricken children.

As if conjured by magic, Brydie's eight-year-old niece wandered in holding one of her patchwork pieces and a needle. "The thread knotted. Can you fix it, Mrs. Russell?" She studied the children with curiosity.

Ah, a solution of sorts. "Daniel, can you read?"

The boy nodded. "I'm eight and go to school. Daphne is only five."

"You're my age!" Lynly exclaimed with interest. "Rob's twelve and bigger than me but he says sewing is girl work. He's cutting currants for cake."

Brydie's sister, Kate, had brought up her children to help wherever they were. They were a joy to have around. Verity tested this new pair. "Daniel, would you like to read a book to Daphne and Lynly? Lynly is sewing a Christmas gift for her mother. Daphne, can you sew?" At her head shake, Verity continued, "Lynly, do you think you might show Daphne some of the things you first learned? And Daniel can read to you while you work."

They didn't appear enthused but children needed occupation as much as adults did, especially when dealing with grief and strangers. She remembered the emptiness after the death of her parents far too well, and she'd been half grown by then. This way, she could keep an eye on the heartbroken waifs while she did the inn's accounts. Listening to children would be less depressing than summing the books. She already knew the inn's expenses far outweighed the income.

Her heart lightened a bit while she listened to the boy's voice sing-songing one of the simple books in her library, while Lynly whispered to the youngest. Verity wondered why the tyke didn't talk. She'd ask Dr. Walker if she knew any reason for not speaking at this age.

Verity wished Rafe would hurry up and finish his business. She didn't want to raise her hopes too high if he hated the idea of taking in orphans. Or if he insisted on taking them wherever they belonged. She didn't want to give them to a family who neglected them—or an orphanage!

The newly installed bell over the lobby door clattered. That wouldn't be Rafe. He entered through the kitchen. Putting down her pencil, she told the children to stay put. Passing the kitchen, she asked Rob to keep an eye on the children. He was up to his eyeballs in chopped fruits and his mouth was suspiciously full. Half-blind Miss Baker seemed serenely unaware of the hungry thief.

"Give some to the others," she told the boy as he stood and appeared ready to stuff his pockets.

Brydie and her sister obviously didn't have time for fancy Christmas baking. Kate worked at the manor, sewing for others. Brydie looked after the children and helped anywhere she was needed, usually at the inn. Verity wondered what she had found to do that she hadn't arrived yet to supervise. Perhaps she was stealing some time with her fiancé. Brydie worked hard and deserved a bit of fun.

In the lobby, a skinny young man in a short top hat and shabby coat waited. Rafe really needed to be here to greet strangers, but actual guests seldom strayed this far off the main highway.

"May I help you?"

He hastily removed his hat and twirled it nervously between his fingers. "Are you the innkeeper? I was told I might find a room for a month or two while we set up the new hardware store." He bobbed a belated bow. "Sorry, I'm Jed Jasper. I'm to be the clerk."

All the men were eagerly awaiting the new hardware. Finally, the village would have more than Oswald's antiquated mercantile.

"Mr. Jasper, welcome, I'm Mrs. Russell. My husband is out at the moment. Let me fix you some tea while I send for someone to show you what's available." She had no idea what was available to rent for *months*, but she led him into the newly cleaned pub.

A paying guest! For months. . .

They had never talked about letting rooms as a permanent abode, as they did in towns. The inn had room to spare, of course, but their staff and facilities were limited. Having grown up in a mansion, she knew nothing of such arrangements.

She asked Miss Butler to prepare tea for their guest, then hurried outside. Rafe hadn't returned. Neither had Mr. Sutter. Fletch should have been here while Rafe was out, but for some reason, he must have left for the stable where he trained horses. What on earth was happening that they'd abandoned incompetent her to handle an entire inn? She couldn't show men to their rooms.

Hammering in a shed off the stable drew her in that direction. Mr. Upton was establishing a carpentry shop in the shed, but the curate wasn't around either. His assistant, Nate Blackwell, and one of the ex-soldiers from the manor were working on shutters. She'd met the soldier with the peg leg. . . *Cratchit*. That was it.

"I have a dilemma, gentlemen." She waited until they politely put down their tools. Rafe was going way into debt keeping them employed. They had to be respectful. "There is a stranger seeking rooms to let. I need someone to show him about. I really don't know what a gentleman expects—"

Blackwell was the silent sort. Cratchit, however, set aside his tool and wiped his hands. He had blood on his shirtsleeve and a bandage on his arm. "Needs a place to heat his water unless you want to be carrying up hot water twice a day. Has no valet, does he?"

She hoped Meera had seen to his injured arm, but that wasn't her concern. "No, Mr. Jasper says he's just a clerk. We have braziers in some rooms. . ."

Still struggling with his coat, Cratchit limped for the door. "The shutters ain't in bad shape in that new wing." He pointed out the stone section extending behind the Elizabethan half-timbered main structure. "There's only two rooms up and two down, but there's a solid chimney between them."

They'd had the chimneys cleaned when they started the restoration. But they hadn't even talked about opening that wing. They didn't have enough staff to run all the way to the far end of the inn, especially in bad weather. So they'd not furnished anything. But a room by the week. . .

"I can find a bed and linen, maybe a washstand, in the castoff room." She was thinking aloud as they crossed the dirt yard. "But no dressers that I remember."

"Hooks, shelves. I can do that. What do you want me to tell him you'll charge?"

Anything at all was better than nothing, but she had to be professional. She erred on the low side, just until they learned how much work this involved.

He nodded. "Charge extra for washing linen and housekeeping. Include breakfast but anything else is extra."

A customer for Rafe's pub! "It sounds like you've done this before." Verity had no difficulty keeping up with his limping stride as they strode down the back hall.

"Been taking rooms most of my life. Better than a tent when I have the coin."

Wondering where he slept now, Verity introduced Cratchit to Mr. Jasper and left them to talk.

Renting rooms! Of course. Gravesyde might not have travelers, but childless workers who lived here might afford a room easier than renting one of the many vacant, run-down cottages.

By the time she settled the orphans in her private dining room for lunch, she'd heard no more from Cratchit and their new guest than furniture scraping against the attic floor.

They were still eating when Arthur's loud shouting from the lobby caused the little ones to cringe and Verity to hastily shove from the table. Kate's eldest was usually a polite lad.

She waved Rob and the orphans back to their seats, picked up her skirt, and hurried to the lobby. Arthur had Brydie's height, but with his golden-brown locks, he didn't look much like either of the auburn-haired sisters. His tanned cheeks red with the wind, he twisted his cap apprehensively. "Mr. Russell isn't back yet?"

That was worrisome but Verity tried to act as if all were well. "Not yet. Is aught wrong?"

He swallowed and sought words. "We found a buggy that went off the road. The wheel is bent. Mr. Henri is bringing it in. I brought the bag." He stepped aside so she could see the tapestry satchel. "But—" He gestured helplessly. "The person. . . the driver..."

Arthur had never been erudite but this nervousness was unusual. Before she could draw him out, carriage wheels rattled into the unpaved yard.

"I'll fetch Mr. Russell." The lad took off as if the hounds of hell were on his heels. He galloped off on one of the manor's horses with the expertise of one who'd been riding a horse that size all his life.

What on earth was going on that no one was telling her about? She was feeling decidedly left out.

Well, she had found the children. No one knew about them yet, either.

She watched from the window as Henri drove a two-wheeled —wobbly—vehicle into the yard. Henri owned Monk's Tavern and lived at the manor with his wife, the curate's sister. Verity rather enjoyed the eccentric connections of the village, but right now, she wanted a town crier to tell her what was happening.

If this was the pony Daniel worried about, it seemed sturdy and unharmed. The hood of the buggy was turned so she couldn't see any passengers. She had thought she'd glimpsed another occupant beside Henri when he drove in, before he turned it sideways. Should she be nosy and step outside, or just take the bag back to the children?

Having spent these last ten years raising herself in a mansion's cellar, she'd never quite learned social niceties. That made her timid. But she'd promised herself that she would be brave and learn to put herself forward—if only she knew what was rude and what wasn't.

The children were fine. They were eating. They didn't need distraction. She donned a cloak and stepped into the windy yard. Presumably summoned by Arthur, Rafe and Damien Sutter raced from the alley behind the shops just as she stepped outside. Short-legged Dr. Walker, escorted by Mr. Upton, followed in their wake. Fine, if Meera could be here, so could she—even if Meera was a physician. Arthur galloped past, off to return the manor's mare, apparently unwilling to return to whatever was in that buggy.

Henri swung down to intercept Verity before she could reach him. "Don't," he warned. "Let Rafe handle this."

"Handle what, sir?" she demanded with indignation. "What, exactly, is going on?"

Rafe swung up on the far side of the carriage, expressed his anger and dismay in language not fit for anyone's ears, and swung down again. "I quit. I cannot do this. Battlegrounds are bad enough, but they usually do not involve women."

Tall, barrel-chested, and muscular, her husband was the largest, strongest man in the village, which was why the magistrate had probably made him bailiff. Rafe could handle drunks with one hand, but in reality, he was a gentle, ginger-haired, soft-hearted giant. He wanted to be the genial host of an inn and a pub —but the lack of population demanded that they all hold several positions.

Verity put her arms around him and rested her head against his chest. "Who else could do the job better than a man who cares?"

He hugged her hard and buried his face in her hair and she forgave him for leaving her ignorant. He must have his reasons. As she did hers. Suddenly protective of those two innocent children, she didn't mention them.

After taking a quick glance in the buggy, Damien left the yard and hurried inside the inn, most likely to look after Kate's children. Or take notes in his new office. Solicitors took lots of notes.

Even Dr. Walker seemed a little green after inspecting whoever was inside the carriage. She stepped down, shaking her head. "I can't tell anything until she is taken to the manor. I don't yet have the space or equipment for this kind of work at home."

"Fox and rats?" Henri asked, rubbing his nose as if to be rid of a smell. Darkly handsome, he was strong from his years as a peddler, but even he looked unsettled.

"Most likely," Rafe agreed. "I'll go over the buggy after she's removed."

From that, Verity gathered the vehicle held a dead woman. No wonder the nanny hadn't come looking for the children.

The curate shook his head and ran his hands through his auburn hair. "Two coffins instead of the nativity scene I meant to build. Will it ever end?"

Two? Verity didn't wait to hear more. She lifted her skirt and fled into the inn to be certain the children were safe.

FIVE

MINERVA

"Why us?" Minerva demanded angrily, scrubbing the skillet from which they'd eaten the delicious apple bread. She felt better now that Paul had come looking for her and they were both fed with the impromptu breakfast.

Paul and Damien had left when young Arthur warned of still another body. It was almost *Christmas.* She wanted to be preparing wassails and plum puddings. Well, maybe evergreens and gifts. Cooking wasn't her forte. "Why must people come here to die?"

"Well, Willa was already here." Brydie pointed out pragmatically. "And it is quite cold. People die of cold, especially if they're not healthy. We lose more people in winter than summer. We have a lot of old folk here."

Despite her thirty years, village born and bred Brydie was very naïve. Minerva hated to be the one to force her to see the world's ugliness. She'd let her continue believing Willa was just a baker, but whatever had drawn the men away this time would be public knowledge soon. They hadn't run off to find an old lady dead of pneumonia.

"I don't think your nephew would look quite so green or

called for Rafe, if this corpse died of cold." Minerva slammed the iron skillet on the hearth to dry. "Paul will be making coffins instead of sermons. How much room can be left in the cemetery?'

"We could start piling them up in the Priory's crypt," Brydie said with dark humor, taking the second batch of bread out of the oven. "Where is Mr. Cooper? Did the men leave him alone upstairs?"

Minerva remembered grim jests from her days of following the troops. That was how one dealt with constant death. But Brydie had never seen stacks of corpses dumped in an impromptu grave. It wasn't amusing.

"Last I saw, the curmudgeon took himself out to tend his horse. If he's a suspect, he could just ride away." Still disgruntled, Minerva peered out the kitchen window, but there was no view of the old shed that probably hadn't held a horse in years.

"Or if he is a killer searching for something, then he'll stay and look after we're gone. Did the men search upstairs?"

Brydie might be innocent, but she was also exceptionally clever.

"They did, but they're not women. We should look." Minerva winced at sight of the elderly figure in black rags inching up the back walk. "Mrs. Essex. Don't sell all the bread, leave me some."

That was selfish. The village was made up of people incapable of baking due to age, infirmity, or lack of equipment. Willa had provided a valuable service. Brydie might be occupied making bread and dealing with customers the rest of the day.

Brydie answered the knock on the kitchen shutters and Minerva lingered, just in case.

"I saw all the toing and froing," the old widow said at the opening. "Is Willa well? I been to the tavern last night and brought her the king's shilling for Saturday night, if you'll tell her that, please, and give me my bread." She held out her towel-covered basket.

The king's shilling? Whoever said such things? And why was

she expecting bread in return for the message? Maybe she should ask Fletch, Minerva thought suspiciously.

Brydie took the basket and wrapped a hot loaf in the towel. "Did you see anyone come by last night. . . when Willa was ill?" Brydie asked misleadingly.

Minerva managed a sardonic smirk at her friend's deviousness. She couldn't have done better herself.

"There's always summat comin' and goin'," the old lady grumbled.

"But you didn't see anyone in particular last night? I'd like to warn them, if I can." Brydie handed out the basket.

"Warn them?" Mrs. Essex asked in alarm. "She has that grippe came around last winter? Didn't see who was here last night. I was down to the Monk's, listening to Miss Patience. She's the voice of an angel."

"Mrs. Lavigne sings beautifully, doesn't she? What time did you come home, do you remember? And you saw no one after that?" Brydie waited with puzzlement for payment that Minerva assumed wouldn't be coming.

The elderly neighbor apparently acted as Willa's go-between with her customers at the tavern was Minerva's assumption.

"Ten's when Monk's closes. No one's out and about after that, though I may have heard a horse oncet I was in bed. But I'm a bit hard of hearing, y'know. You tell Willa to get well soon, all right?" Mrs. Essex wandered back down the path.

Brydie shut the door and wrinkled her nose. "That's an odd way of doing business. So, there may or may not have been a visitor after ten. . ."

"Probably Mr. Cooper. Whoever hit him may have arrived earlier, while everyone was at the tavern. Willa's yard is a veritable forest of old bushes. I doubt we'll find out much from the neighbors." Minerva would have preferred Brydie's company in searching the corpse's room, but people might go hungry without bread. She needed to stay in the kitchen.

Someone had drawn a sheet over Mrs. Willoughby, thank all

that was holy. She'd seen battlefields and knew gruesome, but a woman's peaceful sanctuary shouldn't be a bloody battleground, no matter what her profession.

The wardrobe revealed a few silk robes that might have been gifts, but no dinner gowns, just plain dresses a baker might wear. Among corsets tied with new ribbons—more gifts from her. . .suitors?—she located a pair of knotted stockings. Since the other pairs were carefully darned and laid out, the knot seemed odd. She untied it and removed a small collection of gold trinkets and a silver spoon. If Willa's clients came from Gravesyde, they weren't wealthy, so these might be stolen to pay for her services.

Minerva's suspicions always leapt to extortion, but if Willa couldn't write, how would she extort her victims? And really, why bother? Gravesyde scarcely had a society open for scandal broth, unless one of the married gents at the manor was involved.

Fletch apparently was. He didn't have much coin but he wasn't married either. He might keep their relationship quiet out of respect, but he had no other reason to hide it. What men and women did in their own homes was no concern of hers. Minerva had lived in a man's world long enough to know that much, even if she didn't respect their immorality.

She returned the knot of jewelry to the shelf and continued hunting, with little success.

Mr. Cooper's voice carried up the stairs. He must have returned from the stable and be talking to Brydie. She shouldn't leave an unmarried woman unchaperoned. It could take weeks to work through all the victim's hoards. Minerva suspected Willa had hidden her valuables from any thieves among her customers. Whoever was here last night might have robbed her, but they couldn't have possibly found everything. Perhaps they were only after one particularly valuable item. Or a personal one.

At least, she didn't have to search books this time. Those were generally the only valuables in Gravesyde. Minerva traipsed back down the stairs.

"She kept hay and oats in the shed," Mr. Cooper was saying. "She must have had visitors."

"Any one of whom could have killed her? But why?" Brydie sliced one of her hot loaves and buttered it. Apparently the gentleman was regaining his appetite.

"I haven't seen Willa in years. I cannot imagine." He sat down at the table with the tea Brydie poured for him.

Minerva could imagine, but she saw no reason to speak of it in front of the stranger. There were undoubtedly lonely men all over the countryside who may have availed themselves of Willa's services.

"Does she have family?" she asked instead. "Is this cottage hers? Money or passion are the usual motives." Although, if their assumption about the deceased's occupation was correct, she may have entertained an unscrupulous man who killed because he could. Did murderous urges constitute passion?

Killing someone while they slept seemed more contemptible than passionate.

Minerva glanced out the window and wished this cottage wasn't so far off the main road. She should probably see if anyone lived in the neighboring houses, but they were scattered and mostly vacant. If killers were still about, she'd prefer an escort—or at least, a weapon.

"I assume the house still belongs to my Uncle Bartlett. I don't even know if he's still alive. I'll have to write my mother. She keeps up with family better than I." Mr. Cooper tentatively touched the bandage on the back of his head. "Of course, Willa doesn't have writing paper. I can't stay here. I need to be on my way."

"You're in no condition for riding anywhere, and I'm thinking Rafe will not approve of any witness to murder leaving town." Brydie slapped eggs in front of him to go with the bread. "They have stationery at the inn and the mercantile."

The stranger squinted at Brydie. "He can't keep me here. I have business to tend to. I only brought two changes of linen."

"Tell that to Rafe, and he'll lock you up. The inn has wash women," Minerva said callously, wrapping up the last bread loaf Brydie had baked. She could make it last a week, possibly. Could she learn to bake in a week? "If Willa is your cousin, it's your duty to stay and help us find her killer."

He rubbed his forehead and ate his eggs, obviously working his way through their demands. "All right, I'll need stationery and a pen. Since I missed her funeral, I suppose I need to write my other cousin's solicitor anyway."

Minerva frowned. "Two cousins died? Willa had a sister?"

He started to shake his head, grasped the wisdom of holding still, and wrinkled his nose. "No. Uncle Bartlett, from my maternal grandfather's side, is the one who owned the bakery. After his only daughter married well, and business here grew bad, he left for the Americas. Meg's only my second cousin or whatever. She's the one who died recently. Willa was a distant relation to my Aunt Bartlett, not actually any relation to me except by marriage. She was orphaned young, my aunt took her in, and the girls grew up together. Willa was probably ten years older, and I assume my uncle left the bakery in her hands because his daughter wasn't interested. I doubt there is any connection in their deaths. I was told Meg has been ill and her death is no surprise. I've been sailing and am only recently home."

He didn't look like a sailor, but Minerva supposed now that his pain was lessening, he wasn't as pale.

"Does Willa have any other family? You should probably also write your Uncle Bartlett to tell him of her death and warn that the house is empty. It's a shame to let a nice place like this go to ruin. Although a letter to the Americas and a reply could take weeks." *Leaving the town without bread,* but Minerva tried to think beyond her own needs.

Mr. Cooper sighed. "I don't even know if he's still alive. Let me write my mother first. She has little better to do than harass the family for information and tell them what to do."

"Is she nearby?" Minerva asked hopefully. "Perhaps she might take over the cottage?"

He almost snorted up the tea he'd just sipped. Patting his mouth with a napkin, he winced. "She's in Edinburgh, married to some fine scholar these days. I apparently have a gaggle of younger siblings and step-siblings who must be reined in and trained to leap and obey her wishes. I admit, I only stopped in once or twice in summer breaks at school and haven't been there in years."

"I don't suppose you know how to bake bread?" Minerva asked, more wistfully than hopefully.

"I know how to stoke a fire and shovel loaves in and out. That was the extent of my lesson the summer I stayed here, many years ago."

"What can you do, then?" Brydie asked in her usual blunt manner, setting another bowl of dough to rest.

"Drink and gamble," he said flatly. "I'm very good at both and not much good at anything else."

Paul walked in at that point, heard this last, and raised his eyebrows. "Well, you'll not find much gambling around here, so I hope you have enough coin to buy food." He turned to Minerva. "Henri is coming with his cart to collect Willa, and Verity has found children hiding in the stable. She wants to keep them."

Causing the injured Cooper to flinch, Minerva and Brydie both dropped everything and rushed for the door.

SIX

BRYDIE

Bypassing the men gathered around a hooded buggy, Brydie and Minerva raced into the inn.

Damien met them in the lobby. He caught Brydie and hugged her, while holding up a hand to halt the curate's wife. "The children are fine. Verity has them in hand. She thinks they're orphans being transported to the parish of their birth, when some unfortunate accident occurred. She wants to keep them, but we need to verify facts first."

Brydie had been raised to believe hugs and kisses belonged behind closed doors, but the manor folk were more forthcoming, and so she resolved to be. Not minding changing her ways for this, she kissed her betrothed's freshly shaven jaw, loving the right to do so, then pushed away his restraining hold. "Kate's children? Are they with Verity too? I really need to meet these new ones. If they're street ruffians—"

Damien shook his head emphatically. "They're very well raised, claim to have come from Beanblossom. There is no such village of which I'm aware, but it may be the name of a cottage."

Brydie only wanted to rush to the children she'd helped raise from infancy.

Minerva, however, was a librarian and a curate's wife first and foremost and caught Damien's concern. "If this is their parish, we have no records for the last fifteen years. They cannot prove the children came from here if they are younger than that."

"As far as we can ascertain, the girl is about five and the boy is eight. No parish records?" Damien asked in dismay.

Minerva shook her head. "Paul's stepfather sent the records to the rector fifteen years ago and abandoned Gravesyde after the viscountess's death. If they were born here. . . they may have been baptized elsewhere. We'll have to ask the rector or check with the clerk in Stratford. If they were being transported to Gravesyde, someone must believe their families are from here. Should we write the manor's solicitors in Stratford, as well? They may have been informed of deaths or estates. . ."

Brydie hesitated but had to add, "We should ask Mr. Cooper if the cousin who died had children."

Damien dragged the stationery and inkpot from the lobby counter to begin dashing off correspondence. "He didn't mention any but we can ask. Minerva, if you'll inquire about birth records, I'll write the solicitors and bank. We might have time to make the morning post. I cannot imagine that buggy traveled far. I'm amazed it made it down that rutted lane at all."

"Mr. Cooper needs to write his family about Willa and the bakery. We will have a collection for the post this morning." Minerva took some of the stationery and ink and carried it away, presumably to Mr. Cooper.

"What happened to the driver?" Brydie had learned recently that not everyone was as they seemed. She hated thinking like that, but one must wonder why the driver had been out at night with small children. The unpaved road was dangerous. Only thieves and kidnappers would travel it in the dark. Or the occasional madman.

Coming on top of Willa's death. . . She really hated thinking in circles.

"All Dr. Walker can tell us is that the driver most likely died sometime last night. Animals. . . I'm sorry. I'd rather not say more. We need to learn what we can from the boy. The youngest, a girl, does not speak."

"Frightened," Minerva said curtly, returning to the lobby. "I have seen it before."

Frightening a child into not talking? What horrible. . . "I cannot do this. The two of you may discuss facts and laws and letters. I must see Verity and the children. She will be in a state by now." Brydie hurried to the back of the inn where Rafe and Verity had taken up residence.

She heard Lynly chattering and sighed in relief. Her eight-year-old niece had a heart condition and was frail as a result. That didn't prevent her from taking charge when she could.

She found Verity in a small bedroom, sorting clothes from a tapestry bag, while Lynly and two young towheads watched with interest. Rob, her twelve-year-old nephew, was apparently taking notes. He glanced up at Brydie's entrance. "We're making a list of what Daphne and Daniel need. They might fit in some of our old clothes."

Brydie studied the pair of blond heads, one who had hidden behind the bed upon her entrance. They were enchanting enough to come from a fairy town called Beanblossom. The beribboned little girl seemed several years younger than Lynly. Built sturdier, she might fit her niece's old clothes. The curly-haired boy was some years younger than Rob, but also more robust than her nephew. He would quite likely fit last year's trousers if the hems were adjusted.

Except the pair wore *velvet*, of considerably better quality than anything Kate's children had ever worn.

"They must have family to have such nice attire," Brydie said bluntly. The hope on Verity's face fled, followed by determination.

Verity was strong. She'd cope, eventually. "Excellent idea, Rob. They'll need rough garments for playing in."

She lowered her giantess frame to the floor so as not to tower over the fairy-like newcomers. "You miss your mother, don't you? I lost mine when I wasn't much older than you. Want to tell me about her?"

Daphne ducked her head. Daniel attempted to appear brave and shook his.

Lynly sat on the floor, too, holding one of her quilt patches. "She sewed, like me."

She'd have to leave interrogations to her niece. Brydie smiled at the shy pair. "Did she make those lovely clothes Mrs. Verity is unpacking?"

The little girl climbed on the bed and nodded eagerly.

The boy frowned. "Mama made my shirts, but I go to school and need a proper coat. I went to a grown-up *tailor*. And the bad man told Elton I couldn't bring my new coat."

A *bad man*? Brydie felt a cold chill. "Who is Elton?"

Daniel shrugged. "He carries stuff for mama."

A footman? Some sort of servant, most likely. "Does the bad man have a name?"

Both children shook their heads vehemently. Odd. "Can you tell me what he looks like?"

Daphne hid under the covers. Daniel shook his head and appeared ready to cry. "He came when Mama died. Elton said my daddy sent him to send us away."

Poor Lynly looked ready to cry too.

Good schoolteacher that she was, Verity intervened. "I have told them we will find Beanblossom and their clothes, if we can. Do you know any tailors?"

A *tailor*—a clue. Even Verity was hunting clues. Rightfully so, it seemed. Some cruel, lying thief or servant could be selling off everything these children owned. "There is one in Stratford and several in Birmingham. Perhaps one of the men can make inquiries?"

She turned back to the eager boy. "Who is your teacher?"

"Mr. Clapper. He has a school in the front of his house! It's full of books and a globe and he reads to us from Shakespeare!" Daniel bounced on the bed. "Can I go back to school?"

Brydie refused to tell them they had no home. She knew they were welcome here.

"Maybe not with Mr. Clapper," she cautioned. "But after Christmastide, we will have a school in a grand manor house. If you stay, I think you will like Mr. Birdwhistle, the tutor. And Mrs. Verity also teaches." Brydie smiled at the little girl watching warily from the bed. "Maybe Daphne could go to school too."

That started a riot of voices, since Rob and Lynly both attended Verity's school and wanted to tell all about it.

Reassured that the children were fine, uncertain about Verity, Brydie rose and tugged her friend and sometimes employer into the hall. "Damien and Minerva are writing letters to rectors, solicitors, and bankers. I'll have them ask about Elton, the tailor, and the school as well. Did you ask about their father?"

"As best as one can with children that age who lack understanding. They say their father went to fight bad people and can't come home. That might mean their mother didn't want to say he died in battle. They wore black for a long time, according to Daniel, but they outgrew the blacks, which means *someone* has been dead at least a year. If their father can't take them, who else? Except, apparently, their *father* sent Elton. It is a puzzle."

"Surely, their mother didn't lie about their father, but the servant saying their father wanted them gone, argues elsewise. That's just not right. Someone has to know them and their mother —or at least where Beanblossom is." Brydie grimaced. "It's just. . . it's Christmas. People go visiting. Banks and solicitors may have closed their offices early."

"Not Bosworth." Verity wrinkled her nose. "He's likely to show up at the manor expecting to join the festivities. He's a very hard person to like, but he has a good heart, I believe."

Bosworth was the banker who handled funds for the manor

and others in the village. Bridey had never had funds to put in a bank and only knew him by reputation. "Bosworth was orphaned and adopted, himself, if the earl's family is correct. That may work in our favor. He'll know who to write or ask. This mystery should be easily solved." Brydie hugged Verity. "We'll give them a jolly Christmas while they're here. Did Rafe start a plum pudding?"

Verity offered a weak smile. "He did. I haven't celebrated Christmas since childhood. I'm not at all certain what I should be doing. Won't the children expect gifts?"

"A cloth doll for Daphne. A book for Daniel, if you can part with one. We could make a kissing bough, if that's not too naughty. I don't know how the manor is celebrating. This is the first time in years that Gravesyde will have any celebration. Will the manor allow us to cut holly and ivy for the inn? Although the parsonage grounds have plenty. We can ask Minerva. I'm sure she or Patience will be decorating the chapel."

Rafe stormed in before Brydie could return to Damien. They were supposed to be setting up Damien's legal office in one of the inn's empty rooms. A solicitor needed to be available in town and not out at the bleak house he'd inherited.

From the rage in Rafe's usually genial features, the office wasn't opening today.

"Oswald says the post won't be coming through anytime soon! They took apart the bridge that flooded, and the rider refuses to cross downriver, says we don't pay enough. Everything from Birmingham is going directly to Stratford, but they have no rider. If we want mail, we'll have to ride there to pick it up until the bridge is rebuilt. I'll have to act as post rider."

Verity uttered a cry of dismay. "But there's so much for you to do here. . ."

"What about Fletch?" Brydie asked quickly, remembering the scene earlier today. Rafe's partner had a drinking problem. He needed to be kept busy. "Won't he be eager to hear answers to our questions? He could go directly to the source instead of waiting on letters."

"Fletch isn't too good with people." Rafe stopped to think about that. "I suppose he might take the post, though. We ought to set up our own posting inn, put some of Jack's horses to better use than eating oats."

"If we can prove Mr. Cooper's innocence, you could employ him to run it. He doesn't seem to have much occupation," Brydie said dryly. "But I doubt he can ride anywhere today with his aching head."

"I'll look for Fletch. Don't know if he can make Stratford and back for tonight's delivery. He can deliver our post in time for the afternoon coach, but he'll have to stay the night in Stratford and carry two days' post when he returns." Rafe strode off to consult with his partner.

"Thanks, Brydie," Verity murmured. "I need Rafe here. We even have a guest who wants to rent by the *month*. I had to send one of Mr. Upton's helpers to show him about. I don't know what they decided."

"A paying guest is good!" Brydie wanted to wipe the sadness from her friend's eyes. "It's sometimes hard to find joy when faced with so much death, but you saved those precious angels. That's a blessing. Rafe may have found additional income. There's another. If we can only find a baker—"

"Don't suggest Rafe!" Verity replied in alarm. "Perhaps Lady Elsa will know someone. Or you could do it. I know you and Kate bake."

"First, we'll have to see who owns the cottage." But the idea of her own bakery—would it pay more than her sister earned by sewing? Not if they had to pay rent and give bread to a nosy neighbor. Oh well.

Brydie went in search of Damien and Arthur. She loved the people and promise of a future in Gravesyde and was thrilled Damien had decided to settle here so she needn't desert her family.

But instead of a post office or bakery, they would have to find an undertaker if people didn't quit getting murdered.

SEVEN

VERITY

VERITY KNEW SHE WAS FORTUNATE THAT HER HUSBAND LOVED TO cook. Growing up with servants until she was fifteen, she had never learned. In hopes the inn might actually have guests some-day, they were gradually acquiring a limited staff to assist with cooking and cleaning—women no one else might hire. Miss Butler was half-blind. Mrs. Hatter was arthritic and better at sweeping than dicing. And Mrs. Mayfield had a sickly cough, which meant she was mostly relegated to washing pots, not heavy cleaning or carrying. None of them had experience with the ancient fireplace. The kitchen had no stove.

Verity thought she might have to buy one. Rafe didn't want her throwing away her limited funds on a project that might never support them.

But as dinner approached, she gazed in dismay at the burnt chickens, half done potatoes, and gravy that might be good for plastering the hole in the ceiling. Something had to be done. In the wake of all the tragedy and excitement occupying Rafe, their staff had tried to learn the fireplace. They'd really *tried*.

"Perhaps add a little water or milk to the gravy?" she

suggested. "If we remove the burnt parts and chop the chickens into pieces, could we put them in pies with the gravy and potatoes so the potatoes will finish cooking?"

"And some carrots," Miss Butler agreed. "But we'll need pie crust."

Dinner would be very late. And they had the new tenant and Mr. Cooper sitting in the pub with coins in hand, waiting to be fed. And the children should have supper before bed.

It was enough to make one weep, but Verity had seen true disaster, the kind that still gave her nightmares. Burnt chickens weren't the end of the world.

"Toast cheese on the old bread, then cut it up. Bring out the pickled onions. Can we fry up some apples? I'll serve those with Rafe's ale to the guests to hold them until the pie is ready. The children won't mind a picnic for their supper." Although she had wanted them to be happy, not hungry. Some old scones and jam for pudding might be filling.

She had once led a lonely, boring existence sitting in a cellar, reading. Her father's books had not exactly prepared her for the chaos of life, but they'd taught her to think and imagine. If only she knew how real, live people would react— She didn't.

She was simply incapable of standing about, wringing her hands.

By the time she had the children and two guests happily drinking and munching toasted bread and cheese, Rafe returned to take over pie preparation. She stood on her toes and kissed his stubbled cheek. "I can't join you. I must put the children to bed. I am sorry about dinner."

He grabbed her for a proper kiss, then set her down so he could wash his hands. "We need more help, especially if we're raising children. You must look after them first, I understand."

"You don't mind?" she asked anxiously. They'd scarcely had a moment's peace all day to talk. Taking on two terrified young children when they had so many other tasks. . . It was asking a great deal.

"They can't go to an orphanage," he said firmly. "More than that, I cannot promise. And neither can you. We'll talk later."

Perfectly content after completing their meal of cheese and apples, Daniel happily splashed in the iron tub while Verity combed Daphne's wet hair into a braid. The children had instructed her, explaining what their mother did for them, as well as they were able. In Daphne's case, she spoke with gestures.

They chose a book for Verity to read after they crawled between the covers. Daphne whimpered for what Daniel said was her rag rabbit, so Verity tied a towel into a knot with ears. It wasn't the same, but the child had something to cry into.

By the time she was done, Rafe had dinner on their private table.

"It smells delicious." She took the chair he pulled out for her. "How do you do that? All I smelled was burnt chicken."

"Herbs and spices, onions, little things. I suppose I was fooling myself thinking I can cook and tend bar and run an inn, plus be bailiff, no matter how small the village. I had no idea how much work is involved." He dumped half their pie on his plate.

"And now you think you'll be postmaster?" Verity savored the pie. Despite all the upsetting events the day had brought, she was hungry.

"Fletch doesn't want to be postmaster any more than he wants to stand behind the guest desk to welcome customers. It means actually talking to people. He does what he must, but he'd rather not. Pity I can't make him bailiff. He'd scare people into talking." Rafe wrinkled his nose as he tasted the results of their make-piece meal.

"But he rode into Stratford, didn't he? We really need to know where Beanblossom is."

"We need to know a lot more than that. For all we know, one of our two guests is a killer. I can't even verify where Fletch was all night. He says he was alone in the stable. Sick horses don't talk. Even Upton's carpenters have no one to vouch for them after they left the tavern."

Little by little, Verity had pieced together what had happened to the village baker. Two women in one night. . . She shuddered. Even if one death was accidental, traveling at night did not make good sense. It spoke of urgency or fear. And Willa. . . She'd had no notion about Willa's extra occupation. With so many new people and single men around. . .

"It could even have been one of the gentlemen from the manor," she said worriedly. "They have guests for the holiday. How do you account for all their whereabouts?"

"I don't." Gloomily, he shoveled up another forkful of pie. "It's always the problem here. Too much space, too few people to act as witness. What I would give for a gossipy neighbor or two! And it looks like he used Willa's kitchen knife, so identifying the weapon doesn't help."

"I just cannot imagine what that poor woman might have done to enrage anyone so." Verity picked at a piece of chicken that might be Old Red. She wouldn't miss the cantankerous old hen but they needed more hens to start raising chicks if they wanted to keep eating eggs. They should buy another rooster too.

Rafe took a swig of ale. "I think the killer was searching for something when Cooper walked in. I'm putting him up here tonight and setting some of Captain Huntley's guards in the bushes around the bakery. Maybe the scoundrel will return to finish looking."

"Lovely thought. You didn't tell Mr. Cooper about the guards, did you?"

Rafe snorted and glared over his mug. "Give me some credit, woman. Even with that knot on his head, he has to be on my suspect list. I've put him at the far end of the inn with our other new guest, away from you and the children. Did you pry any more information out of the orphans? It's odd to have two deaths in one night, but I fail to see any connection. Meera doesn't believe the driver was stabbed. It may have simply been an attack of the heart."

"Other than the names of a tailor, servant, and teacher, I have nothing useful. Daniel called someone a bad man because he made him leave his books behind. But I don't know what that might have to do with the driver they call their nanny. Was she following orders or fleeing the 'bad man'?"

"Driving at night seems a bit ramshackle. They'd have run into the closed bridge if they'd kept going through town. It's hard to believe that Gravesyde was her destination. She had enough coin to take the toll road into Birmingham. Did she get lost? Was she unwell and looking for help?" Rafe frowned as he sipped his ale.

"Is Arnaud sketching the nanny so we can post her likeness in the lobby?" Verity knew the manor's resident artist had done so before, although he didn't care for drawing people.

"I gave his first sketch to Fletch to show in Stratford, if he'll at least talk to the postmaster. I'll place another in the lobby when Arnaud has it finished. I should probably show it to Mr. Cooper. Perhaps the nanny was related to Willa? Would that be too much of a coincidence?"

Verity sighed and set down her napkin. "It might mean the driver was murdered too, so let's say that's too much coincidence. She may have had good reason for driving back lanes instead of the main highway. I simply cannot believe no family claimed such lovely children. She may have been kidnapping them or saving them from kidnappers. How would we know?"

Which meant she ought to keep them out of sight until she knew there was no kidnapper or *bad men* looking for them.

Rafe rose to fetch the pudding he'd made of old scones. "Which is why you are not to become too attached. There must be people out there looking for them."

Verity prayed she could do that, but they'd already lifted her spirits. She wanted Rafe's children, of course, but right now, her nest needed filling, and this pair served nicely. She simply hoped they weren't fairy changelings like in the stories.

TUESDAY

DECEMBER 19, 1815

EIGHT

"I THINK WE SHOULD VISIT THE RECTOR IN STRATFORD." TUESDAY morning, Minerva buttered her toast—leftover from yesterday. The sun wouldn't rise for an hour, but curates and their wives had too many duties to lay abed, no matter how much she enjoyed snuggling under the covers with her new husband.

Who was scribbling notes for his sermon at the breakfast table. Paul had lived alone too long and had developed numerous bad habits. He was a busy man. Would he quit listening to her now? They hadn't married in haste like Verity and Rafe, but they were both such independent people. . .

He lifted his auburn head and squinted at her. "The rector? Why would I do that? I doubt he even knows of my existence."

She sighed in relief. At least, he had heard her. "He knows. Your vicar will have complained of the benefice we've not rented out to explain why he contributes so little to the rectory. I doubt he has mentioned that he claimed gold coins from the manor and used them to feather his own nest rather than include them in the church tithe. He won't introduce you. I know you think you'd rather stay a curate than take on more responsibility, but you have to think of the future. You may be the only Oxford-educated cler-gyman in the entire parish." Minerva had learned strategy at her father's knee.

Paul grimaced. "I had noble dreams in my foolish youth, before my family returned here. Are you saying you would some day prefer to live in town, in the grandeur of a rectory?"

Minerva hid her smile. He listened. He just didn't understand. "After one lives in a duke's palace, no, not particularly. But the fact that you are better educated and better connected than the vicar might open the rector's eyes. It won't hurt to meet him. The chapel needs funds before the roof falls in. You have to balance your calling with fund raising. Besides, he might ignore the letters we've written asking about the children. He won't ignore a personal visit."

"Ah, enlightenment." He beamed at her. "You want to solve the mystery. You're correct. We haven't traveled anywhere together, and we're entitled to a brief honeymoon. I doubt we can reach Stratford, make inquiries, and return home tonight, though. Do you think they can put us up at the rectory?"

"Or Bosworth can," she said with a malicious smile, speaking of the banker who owned mortgages on half the village. "He stays at the manor all the time. He ought to return the favor for manor folk, of which we should be counted."

He finished his tea and shoved from the table. "You have a convoluted mind. I like it. Do you think we might borrow that dreadful buggy the children arrived in? We'll make the rector feel guilty that he leaves his possible successor in such poverty."

Minerva laughed at this preposterous leap of faith. "Far better than arriving in the manor's landau and having him think we don't need funds. The blacksmith repaired the wheel last night. I'll pack a satchel. You ask after the buggy and horse. If people insist on dying in Gravesyde, we should at least acquire public transportation in return for providing their final resting place."

"Which does make one wonder how a nanny would acquire a carriage and horse. It seems unlikely. If we don't identify her, I fear we'll have to use the communal coffin and bury her in a pauper's grave. A most excellent reason for sleuthing." He kissed her hair and trotted off to his study.

She ought to feel guilty for drawing him away from his work, but her supremely intelligent, dedicated husband was in danger of having no life of his own. Minerva decided it was her task to provide him with opportunities to occasionally escape their busy schedules.

Besides, she hated mysteries. She liked facts. And she'd love to have at least one mystery solved before Christmas. Those adorable orphans deserved better than to be abandoned to strangers, even if Verity would be a lovely mother.

Willa. . . She didn't know what to make of Willa. Learning the baker sold more than bread had jarred her from complacency. No woman should have to sell her body. Well, perhaps Willa had enjoyed bed play and was lonely. Who was to know? But there was no reason to kill her!

They reached Stratford a little after noon, buried under blankets and still half frozen but well fed from the basket Lady Elsa at the manor had provided. Minerva hadn't been out of Gravesyde in months. After paying the toll to drive the last mile of macadam highway, she sat back in their bouncy, two-wheeled buggy to study what a real village ought to look like. A stone croft or two and some half-timbered houses with thatching still existed, although these seemed larger and better maintained than most of Gravesyde. The yards had neat hedges, trimmed rose branches, and patches of seed heads that would be flowers by summer.

But in the town center, brick buildings had replaced much of the stone and timber. Several had huge gables with double windows, indicating the attic might be tall enough to stand upright in. There were even several brick buildings three stories high, just like London. The streets were relatively busy with carriages and horses, not as bad as the city, of course, but far busier than Gravesyde.

With expertise, Paul guided their old mare to a stable down an alley, near a substantial granite building simply labeled BANK. "We'll have to walk from here. Do you wish to visit Bosworth first or the rector? I can't be certain where we'll find either of them at this hour."

"Since the bank is right here, let's try that first. I assume the rectory is near that impressive spire in the distance?" Minerva took Paul's gloved hand in hers to step down, then returned her icy fingers to her muff.

"I believe so. I've not visited since my university days." He held her arm to guide her down the cobbled alley, to the main street. "Anything in particular we're asking Bosworth besides a bed for the night?"

"About deaths and wills and trusts, perhaps? Those children didn't come from a poor home. Oh, and Beanblossom. And then, about the tailor and teacher. Elton may be too much to ask." So many things they needed to know. . .

Minerva had far too much experience to be a foolish miss, but that didn't mean she didn't enjoy having a handsome man guiding her into the bank's grandiose marble interior. They weren't fashionable by any means, but her cloak was well-lined and Paul's greatcoat wasn't too shabby, if one didn't look too closely. And he'd even brought out his tall hat instead of the bedraggled wool cap he tended to wear.

A bespectacled clerk behind a large mahogany counter glanced up expectantly. Otherwise, the echoing lobby appeared unoccupied. At their request to see Mr. Bosworth, the clerk frowned and scurried off. Captain Huntley and the bank were engaged in a lawsuit over property lines, while Bosworth had some claim to ownership in the manor, so the relationship between the bank and Gravesyde tended to be. . . diplomatic, at best.

"Perhaps we should have started anywhere but here," Minerva whispered. The ceiling was unnervingly tall and the small windows didn't allow enough light.

"Too late. We beard the dragon now." Paul indicated the banker's approach.

Benedict Bosworth Jr. had a slight middle-aged paunch beneath his immaculate gray waistcoat and iron-gray frockcoat. Even his blond hair had a hint of silver. He was taller than Paul, but not by much. He bowed in greeting. "Mr. Upton, Mrs. Upton, I haven't seen you s-since your n-nuptials. How may I help you?"

They had no money in his bank. He didn't invite them to his office. But Minerva had lived with dukes and earls and an army colonel accustomed to being treated with respect. She squeezed Paul's arm and spoke for him. "It is somewhat of a confidential nature, if you don't mind?"

She could hear Paul chuckling. She loved that he didn't mind her officious nature. He was quite capable of correcting her if so inclined. But the banker bowed and led the way to his office, which suited them both.

"There is n-nothing wrong at the manor, is there?" Bosworth asked, indicating that they take seats in his much warmer, less intimidating office. He didn't actually express concern but the bank handled part of the trust for what the heirs now called Priory Manor. He was interested.

"No, although as magistrate, Captain Huntley has authorized us to make inquiries." Paul sat back in his leather chair and crossed his legs as if accustomed to special treatment by bankers. "The post isn't being delivered until the bridge from Birmingham is repaired, so we thought it might be expedient to deal with this in person. You'll be receiving a letter from him shortly, but we need to know answers as quickly as possible."

Priory Manor was a very large part of the bank's business, and rumor had it that the banker was a baseborn son of the last heir, so Bosworth paid attention and nodded. "I am at your disposal, of course."

"A carriage crashed the other night, killing the driver, and leaving two young children abandoned. They can only tell us that their mother recently died after an illness, and it's possible their father died in the war. They cannot tell us where the driver was taking them, although we suspect it was to an orphanage." Paul gestured with his hat. "Our parish, of course, is too poor to support even a workhouse. We are hoping to find out more."

Nice reminder that Bosworth contributed nothing to their funds. Minerva hid her grin. "They are beautiful children, well kept," she told him. "We feel sure there must be respectable family who possibly have not heard of their mother's death. They say they're Turners from Beanblossom. Does this mean anything to you?"

Expressing no concern for the orphans, Bosworth sat back, pressed his fingertips together, and addressed the facts. "I b-believe there may be a cottage a mile or so out of town with that rather p-preposterous name. I do not think we have any accounts for a T-turner, but I have a vague memory from some years ago when the place was p-purchased. You might ask Mr. B-browning, the Priory's solicitor. His firm handles most of the p-property transactions here."

"Thank you, he and the rector are our next visits," Paul said. "So you've heard of no recent deaths, small estates, anything of the sort?"

Bosworth shrugged. "None of which I'm aware."

This was turning out to be a most distressing visit. How could a widow and her children simply disappear from public view? "The children have also mentioned a Mr. Clapper as a teacher at a small school, and the boy had a tailor, although he did not provide a name. Can you provide any information on anyone of that sort?" Minerva asked.

"T-teachers and t-tailors seldom carry accounts. I'll ask my clerk, but do not hold out hope there. Now, if that is all. . ." He rose, indicating his generosity had ended.

"It seems we will have to stay all day to make these inquiries." Minerva didn't immediately rise. "That means we cannot go home until tomorrow. I don't suppose you know of a respectable, inexpensive room we might take? The parish does not have funds to spare."

Paul rose and held out his hand for her to take. "The captain said we were to put ourselves at your disposal, if that will not be an inconvenience."

Minerva hid her smile. That put the final nail in the banker's coffin.

Bosworth looked pained, hesitated, then finally offered, "I have room to p-put you up for the night. My father is at home, if you wish to leave your b-bags with the servants. He will arrange it."

"That is most gracious of you, sir." Minerva stood and settled her cloak about her. "Christmas is less than a week away. You should attend service with us. Patience has planned a lovely choral interlude. Not exactly Church of England but a chance to celebrate all we have been given this past year. We'd love to have you."

"Thank you. You may tell me what you have found over d-dinner. Good day." He bowed them out.

"Well, that was fun." Minerva chortled as they returned to the street. "Do you think he is shy because of his stutter or just made of cardboard?"

"A little of both, no doubt." Paul indicated a distinguished brown brick building across the busy main road. "Shall we stop with Mr. Browning before returning to the carriage and seeking the rectory?"

Mr. Browning, the lawyer, a vigorous man in his forties, had also visited the manor on different occasions and was much more receptive to their visit. When Paul gave him their story, he nodded and summoned a clerk to fetch a file. "Sad story. Mr. Turner purchased the property through a trust fund, if I remember rightly. When he died, he left a life estate to the property to his mistress. I hadn't realized they weren't married until she died and the estate reclaimed the property."

He took a file his clerk handed him and opened it. "Yes, here it is. Beanblossom Cottage Trust. The file is confidential. I cannot reveal the owners or any other information. The cottage has been placed on the market for sale."

"And the children?" Minerva asked in horror.

He frowned and studied his documents. "Mr. Turner's will was written some time ago, apparently upon his coming of age. It does not mention a wife or even the trust. Admittedly, that is odd. Normally, the property would revert to the eldest son, but if there are no marriage documents or settlements. . ." He gestured to indicate this was the result.

Orphans. . . and abandoned by the family that should have taken them in, illegitimate or not.

NINE

BRYDIE

"I rather love having a horse and carriage and riding out of the wind." With Damien's aid, Brydie's sister climbed down to the manor drive from the barouche Damien had appropriated from a scoundrel who had robbed him of his inheritance.

"Be kind to your new friends and listen to Brydie." Kate hugged her children, who had scampered down first. Then, carrying her sewing basket, she marched up the drive, leaving them in the inn yard.

"We should probably drive her up to the manor when the weather turns bad." Damien helped Brydie out next.

"We are so used to walking, that we don't think twice about it, as long as Lynly is kept warm." She shooed the children toward the kitchen door, but Lynly lingered to feed the horses apples. "Have you chosen a room for your office? Arthur can help you haul furniture, if you're ready."

"I'm in no hurry. Since Rafe has to stay at the inn while Fletch is out of town, I told him I'd try searching Mrs. Willoughby's house more thoroughly. Although, since I am told no one showed up last night, the killer may have found what he wanted." He held the horses as Verity and the orphans approached.

Carrying a basket of eggs from the henhouse, Verity led her two fledglings to admire the animals. "Tomorrow is market day. Willa used to provide bread for the mercantile to sell to the farmers' wives. We might talk with them, see what they know," she suggested.

Brydie brightened. "I could have a baking day, bake a dozen loaves or so, and sell them tomorrow so we don't seem too intrusive? Should we make a list of questions to ask?"

"Excellent idea," Damien agreed. "As long as I'm at Willa's with you, you should be safe in her kitchen, if you don't mind not observing the proprieties. Will you have enough flour?"

Brydie snorted at the idea of propriety. She'd been helping her fiancé clean out his family home all week without any companion. They may have been a little naughty, but Kate's cautionary tale didn't allow for more. They had yet to even cry banns. "If I can use some of Willa's coins to buy more flour, I should have everything I need. Do we donate her treasures to the church for a funeral? I can add what I earn from the bread."

"Tricky question until we learn more. Mr. Cooper is her only representative at the moment. It may be his choice. I have a notion he needs funds, but he doesn't seem anxious to take anything of Willa's." Damien reached into the barouche for the bag they'd brought from the farm and handed it to Daniel, who was daringly stroking a mare's nose. "Play clothes, so you may visit the hens and horses and let Rob lead you astray."

The boy beamed. "Thank you, sir."

Not to be outdone, Lynly pulled out another satchel. "And I brought Sunday clothes and play clothes and Miss Princess. She needs her hair fixed though."

She opened the bag to pull out a rag doll with yarn hair and handed it to the wide-eyed Daphne. "We will make her new clothes and she can be your dolly."

With tears in her eyes, Verity sent all the children off to the kitchen. "That was generous, thank you. I can ask Lavender to sew some simple garments but not knowing if I can keep them, it's hard to know what I should do. They only have the one pair of shoes each, and they're almost too small. I cannot help feeling someone is selling everything they owned. Good shoes might bring a thief quite a few coins."

Verity had lived in poverty for years. She would know the value of such things. Brydie tried not to think badly of people, but she feared the innkeeper was right.

"Paul sent me a note saying he couldn't work on the coffins today," Damien said. "He and Minerva have taken another of Arnaud's sketches of the nanny and gone to Stratford in hopes of finding out more. If they see Fletch, perhaps they can all investigate. Jacques is learning to make small shoes instead of boots. He can practice making them for the children. We'll figure out how to pay him—perhaps he can do charity work in lieu of rent while he's looking for customers."

He led the horses to the stable.

Jacques was Damien's French valet, but he desperately wanted to make gentleman's boots. Damien's father had left a shoe shop, which Damien refused to enter if he could avoid it. The Lord worked in mysterious ways, Brydie decided, especially in Gravesyde.

"I do hope Damien finds enough legal business to keep him busy," Brydie said as she watched him go. "He is keeping occupied by creating plans to renovate Sutter Hall, while he waits to see if he can reclaim his mother's money. But he's accustomed to traveling about, negotiating contracts."

"He's found what he needs here," Verity assured her. "And it isn't as if Gravesyde doesn't offer enough to do. He need only choose his task. I have to take these eggs in so Rafe can make breakfast for our new guests. For him, having guests is almost as good as Christmas."

"Does Mr. Cooper have any plans? Will Rafe let him leave

once we hear from his family?" Brydie followed Verity toward the kitchen.

"Mr. Cooper talked to Henri about trading last night. Now that Patience is increasing, Henri wants to stay home more. But Henri is very clever and knows how to make a profit. I'm not so sure Mr. Cooper does, or that he even means to stay. He told Rafe if he had to pay for being imprisoned in the inn, he's leaving."

Interesting, but none of Brydie's concern. Seeing Damien returning, she waved Verity off. His welcoming smile melted her heart every time. He looped his arm around her waist, and she loved that she didn't feel like a towering giantess beside him.

"It's a pity everyone is so busy. We ought to organize Willa's effects into some order, keepsakes should family ever arrive, charity donations, bits that might be sold to cover expenses. . ." Brydie suggested as they strolled the lane to the bakery.

She had dealt with far too many deaths and funerals in her life. She knew what was expected. "The church ladies are seeing to her laying out once Meera is done with her, but we don't know if her coins should be used for a proper funeral."

"We'll let Cooper decide," Damien concluded. "Although I seriously doubt he knows enough about his family to have any notion of what they might like to keep. I thought my family was bad, but we only had each other to ignore. He has a whole host of siblings he hasn't even met."

Brydie disapproved of an able-bodied man who neglected family. "Isn't it rather odd that he's had two cousins die recently, even if they're distant or not really related? One killed while he was supposed to be attending the funeral of another?"

"The world is full of people and people die. He cannot be in two places at once, so I don't think you can assume he goes about murdering his family, especially since he doesn't seem in any position to inherit anything." At Willa's bush-shrouded front door, Damien produced the key Rafe had confiscated. "We need to have someone trim this shrubbery if we're to come and go for a while."

Brydie glanced at the key he returned to his pocket. "Perhaps the intruder did not return last night because the door was locked. Do you think Willa left it open while she slept? Or did she leave the key outside for the killer to find?"

Damien frowned. "I'll make a note to ask Fletch about her habits."

Had Fletch and Willa been stepping out? Willa had been older than he, but Fletch had no family and was no doubt lonely.

More interested in baking than Major Ferguson, Brydie donned an apron and examined her remaining ingredients. "I do worry that Mr. Cooper is not exactly what he seems. I suppose I don't like coincidence that he just happened to arrive the night Willa was murdered."

"You think someone knew he was arriving and wanted to find something before he did? Since Cooper wrote to say he was on the way, she might have left the door unlocked for him," Damien acknowledged. "And if Willa had Oswald read Cooper's letter to her, the entire village knew."

Brydie puckered up her nose, knowing he was entirely right. She simply rather believe a stranger was guilty.

He gestured at what might have been a butler's pantry in a manor house, but instead, held all the pans and bowls and utensils a busy bakery might need. "Did you and Minerva search all the cabinets?"

"Even on top. But I didn't go too far in the cellar. I was afraid of rats." After lighting the kindling to start the ovens warming, Brydie set out all the mixing bowls she could find and began measuring. Baking for a week would be a lot easier this way than with one bowl that only held enough ingredients for two loaves, at best. When she was married. . . She dwelt on that pleasant dream while Damien clattered down the stairs to chase rats.

She winced at a pistol shot. He carried a small firearm with him, she'd learned the hard way. As much noise as that made, all the rats would flee, which was the point, she supposed.

After he'd been down there a while, she heard him come up

the stairs again. "A cat would be simpler," she called over her shoulder, so she didn't have to see minced rat carcass.

"The spiders down there are probably larger. I'll find the rat holes and fill them. But it looks like she has a trunk full of every letter anyone wrote to her, plus some old family papers. I'll sort through to see if there is anything that indicates a deed or will." He left coal dust behind as he traipsed through the kitchen to heave the rat out the back door.

"You'll mop your mess before we leave," she called over her shoulder.

She'd set aside six bowls to proof near the ovens before Mr. Cooper straggled in around noon. She could hear him talking to Damien in the front room and poked her head around the corner to ask a question that had nagged at her. "Mr. Cooper, did you notice a buggy on the road when you rode into the village?"

He narrowed his eyes as if in thought. "Don't believe I did. It was after dark when I arrived though." His eyes widened again. "If you mean the one that crashed, she was out much too late for driving that road. My horse stumbled in those ruts."

Brydie nodded, satisfied, and returned to her baking. How many loaves did Willa usually bake for market? Brydie seldom paid attention, but she thought she remembered her having buns as well. She'd need eggs for those. Did Willa have a henhouse hidden in the jungle of her yard?

Donning a ragged shawl hanging beside the door, finding a basket in the larder, she stepped into the gray day. Perhaps Willa had an herb garden. She could make savory buns as well as sweet. If she meant to spend the day baking, she might as well make what her own family needed as well.

Weeds and winter-bare bushes overhung the nearly-buried stepping stones, but the path was better than fighting through the underbrush of the rest of the yard. At one time, the family must have had extensive gardens—back when they could afford help.

The henhouse was little more than a tumble-down shack with the roof nearly caved in. She could hear a hen clucking in the tall weeds. The path was cleared, so Willa must have used it. The doorway was a bit low for Brydie's height, but she ducked under the lintel to look for a nest.

A hard arm crossed her throat and dragged her inside.

Before the arm's owner could speak, Brydie shrieked at the top of her lungs and began kicking.

TEN

VERITY

WITH THEIR GUESTS FED, RAFE LEFT TO HELP DAMIEN SEARCH Willa's house. Maybe Rafe might give Brydie some breadmaking tips, Verity mused as she set luncheon on the pub tables for the children. Gravesyde *needed* a baker. Brydie might be a good one. And then she'd be close by to look after her sister's children on days like this.

But for now, Verity didn't mind watching Rob and Lynly. They were good for the grieving orphans. They'd been teaching them to make pomanders out of apples and cloves to give to the inn staff on Boxing Day. The older women had arrived with very little in the way of clothing to need scent, but they'd treasure any gift. And Verity was paying Lavender to make over some simple gowns she and Rafe could give them on Boxing Day. Verity was as excited about that as she was the church festivities.

If only they could settle the question of the orphans. . .

When Rafe raced into the lobby, hollering for his wolfhound and grabbing his shotgun from behind the counter, Verity's heart wrenched in terror. Wolfie bolted out the door and the two were gone before she could reach the lobby to question. Reassuring the wide-eyed children, she stood in the pub's mullioned window to prepare for whatever horror threatened now.

Returning from his mail delivery, Fletch was just riding toward the inn with a loaded mail pouch. At Rafe's shout, he dropped the pouch in the yard and galloped down the back lane —toward Willa's cottage. Verity couldn't relax until she knew what was wrong.

Moments later, Brydie and Damien emerged from the lane. Damien had his arms around Brydie's shoulders, but she seemed unharmed—although excessively agitated, even for Brydie. Her tall, fiery-haired friend was normally genial and smiling, but once her temper was aroused. . .

Deciding this was Brydie in a fury, Verity relaxed a trifle. Telling the children she'd read them a story if they behaved, she left them in the pub with their pomanders and hurried out to greet the pair. She picked up the mail pouch while she was at it. "What happened?"

"Brydie tried to kill a chicken thief," Damien said with a strained smile, taking the canvas pouch and slinging it over his shoulder.

Verity assumed that was a lie but Brydie didn't contradict him. She was too furious, apparently.

"*I have bread rising!*" she shouted. "I need to go back. And I want to make buns. There are eggs. You can collect them if you like, but they shouldn't be left to rot!"

"*He could have killed you!*" Damien shouted back. "Until this monster is caught, you're not going anywhere without me!"

Oh, very bad tactic to take with Brydie. Verity winced as her Viking-sized friend swung a fist at her fiancé's arm. They'd never make it to calling the banns at this rate.

Damien, very inappropriately, grabbed Brydie's fist, pulled her arms behind her back, and kissed her into silence, right there in public. Brydie wriggled futilely for a moment, then subsided, finishing the kiss with vigor.

Chicken thieves were better than the insane arsonists they'd stopped in the past, Verity concluded, waiting for the explosions to end so she could learn what had happened.

Dealing with arsonists didn't make her fearless. Maybe they needed another hound to stay behind while Wolfie was out. She'd hate to have her hens stolen. Although picking up a shotgun to look for a chicken thief seemed excessive. Rafe could pound a man into the ground with a single fist. So they were assuming the thief and the killer were one and the same. Verity shivered.

Damien's kiss apparently served to calm Brydie back to rationality, of a sort. When he finally released her, she leaned her forehead against his shoulder and took deep breaths. "I still want to kill him," she insisted, proving she wasn't composed.

"You nearly did," Damien said with a hint of strained laughter. "By the time I reached you, he was doubled over and hobbling like a cripple. Rafe will find him, and you can kick him again."

"Would you like luncheon and perhaps a draft of ale?" Verity asked dryly, gesturing toward the open door. "Not that I can provide more than bread and cheese."

"That's why I want to go back!" Brydie insisted, reluctantly accepting Damien's nudge into the slightly warmer lobby. "I can make some lovely buns that will taste delicious with your cheese. Add a little bacon or pickled onion. . ."

"You are worse than Lady Elsa." Verity led the way into the pub where the children were pretending to work but listening as hard as they could. "If you're done eating, take your pomanders into the kitchen and ask if there are any currant biscuits you might have. You can work there, where it's warmer."

"But Miss Butler will see our gift!" Lynly protested. "We will take them to the bedroom, then come back and ask for biscuits."

Brydie buried a laugh and cheered up. "There's our Lynly. Rob, as man of the house, why don't you fetch biscuits while the youngers carry your gifts to the bedroom."

"Where's Arthur?" Damien asked as the children traipsed off. "Shouldn't he be the one looking after them?"

Verity liked that he already concerned himself with the welfare of his intended's family. Kate and Brydie were strong, but everyone needed support occasionally. "I sent him off to help the new hardware merchant. He really needs to be working with adults and not children. When he comes back, we'll send him with the mail pouch to Mr. Oswald." There really hadn't been time for responses to their inquiries, so there would be naught of importance in it. "Now tell me about hen thieves while I tap Rafe's ale."

"A vagabond was hiding in the henhouse," Brydie said with indignation, marching toward the kitchen. "I'll put together sandwiches."

In the dim light of the pub, Verity set ale on the table and raised her eyebrows questioningly. Damien waited until Brydie was out of hearing. "The scoundrel tried to choke her. It's a wonder you didn't hear her scream all the way here. My heart nearly dropped to my boots. By the time Rafe and I reached her, she'd kicked his shins and kneed him and was trying to scalp him with her bare fingers until he fought loose and ran."

"Ah, now I know where Lynly learned that. . . very unfortunate maneuver." Verity had been heartily impressed when the tiny eight-year-old had fought a kidnapper by kicking him in his manly parts a few weeks ago.

Damien ran a hand over his disheveled hair and snorted. "Brydie learned it from me and my brother. She wasn't wearing her gloves. Her fingers are turning blue."

Verity shivered. "I need to heat cider then." They both knew that, like Lynly, Brydie got chilblains too easily. "I don't like this at all, mind you. Rafe better catch the mongrel."

She marched off to join Brydie in the kitchen, where Miss Butler was already preparing hot tea and forcing Brydie to hold the mug to heat her hands.

Setting the tea aside, Brydie hacked bread and cheese as if they were the enemy's necks. She'd found the last of the ham and assaulted that while Miss Butler assembled the sandwiches. "He was hiding in the *henhouse*," Brydie said without preamble.

"Waiting for everyone to leave. Damien thinks he was the killer, but he won't say it aloud."

"You read minds? Come along, let us serve you for a change." Verity took a plate of the sandwiches and elbowed her much larger friend back to the pub, where Damien was adding coal to the fire.

Brydie took a seat, still insisting she had to go back to Willa's and finish the bread.

"Let Cooper do it. We need to leave him over there to guard the place anyway. He said he knows how to shove bread into the oven." Damien added more tea to her cup after she swallowed the boiling beverage practically in a gulp.

"He won't know how to knead and shape the dough or the right temperature or when to take it out. And I want to make buns," Brydie insisted truculently. "I've already proved I can take care of myself. You can't stop me."

Before that turned into another argument, Verity intervened. "Why didn't the guards Rafe set there last night find the thief?"

"The guards didn't attempt to hide. I saw them smoking and passing a jug when I went past last night. He probably just waited until they left this morning to return. And then we arrived." Damien quaffed his ale as if he needed it more than food. He seemed pretty shaken, so it wasn't as simple as Brydie tried to make it.

"Hen thieves aren't that smart," Brydie scoffed, sticking to the more innocent theory. "There is no fence to keep him out. He knew Willa had hens. We weren't looking after them. He probably thought he was doing the hens a favor."

Damien didn't argue with that. Verity thought he might ought to so Brydie didn't take more chances, but perhaps she'd work it out on her own once she calmed down. "Is there a rooster? Might I steal him?"

Scowling mutinously, Rafe trudged in before they could argue the morality of "rescuing" poultry from a dead woman's property. He pulled ale and threw it back, then, in disgust, waved his mug.

"He had a horse. Fletch and Wolfie are trying to follow, but Fletch has been riding since sun up. His horse is knackered. By the time I saddle up, or run to the manor for help, the scoundrel will be long gone. We all need to start carrying firearms. Any man who attacks a woman deserves to be shot."

"Then he's gone and I can finish my baking." Brydie glared at them defiantly.

Both men shouted at once. With a sigh, Verity snatched their mugs from the table and held them behind her. "Stop it, both of you! That bread is needed or people go hungry. If you fear the thief was more than a thief, tell us. And if so, then we need people in that house, day and night, searching for whatever a killer might want."

That took the steam out of their whistles. Brydie looked shocked, then pounded her mug on the table and cheered.

ELEVEN

MINERVA

"Church first," Paul insisted as they drove the battered buggy through Stratford in the direction of the steeple. "There's bound to be a curate around. I'll introduce myself, ask if the rector is in. I suspect a curate will know the orphans' family better."

With the promise of the solicitor's young clerk meeting them at Beanblossom Cottage, Minerva was eager to find an end to the mystery. Unfortunately, her husband made sense, as always. They needed to present themselves to the rector, if possible, and learn more about the Turner family.

The gothic spire was the prettiest part of the blocky stone church. They found the curate harvesting the last rose hips in the yard. An older man, with thinning gray hair and a burgeoning belly on his thin frame, the curate nodded at Paul's introduction.

"Heard of you. The rector is visiting in London this week or he'd speak to you. Your vicar complains you are holding back the tithes from the rich manor folk." He didn't appear overly concerned, just interested.

"The manor folk live off a trust they don't control and have few funds of their own. They tithe time, food, and labor for the well-being of the community, as they can and as they should," Paul replied evenly.

Minerva could have added spitefully that the vicar expected a curate to live on goodwill, alone, but these were Paul's fellows. He didn't interfere in her librarian duties. She offered him the same respect.

Although, at some point, he'd have to be curious on how she spent her salary. Well, without Willa, it wouldn't be on bread. He'd soon notice missing toast. She fretted that it might be too late for them to communicate about domestic issues. They had both learned independence as children.

But solving mysteries. . . That's what had brought them together.

"We're actually here at the manor's request," Paul continued. "The carriage we arrived in," he gestured at the drive, "lost a wheel outside Gravesyde and crashed yesterday. The driver died and no one recognizes her. We are hoping someone will identify the vehicle or this sketch." He produced Arnaud's image of the woman.

The curate removed spectacles from his pocket and examined the portrait. "Excellent work, but I can't say I know her, sorry."

"The two children she had with her are also unidentified. They say they are a Daniel and Daphne Turner from Beanblossom Cottage, but no one in Gravesyde recognizes them. We are trying to determine where they belong. Might you know the family?"

The curate nodded toward the graveyard. "We just laid their mother to rest a few days back. Her solicitor paid for a decent burial, but there were no mourners." He wrinkled his nose as if he'd say more but resisted.

"What name was she buried under?" Minerva asked. She hadn't missed Mr. Browning calling her a "mistress."

He looked relieved at the question. "Smith, Peggy Smith. We knew her as the Widow Turner, but I assume a solicitor knows best."

Paul grimaced. "Do you recall the solicitor's name? What firm he represented?"

"Not rightly. He spoke with the rector, and I just followed orders."

Minerva refrained from rolling her eyes. A woman would have asked and remembered. But if she remembered correctly, the rector was a widower. Perhaps the housekeeper. . . ? But they wouldn't be seeing the rector this trip.

"Were the children baptized here? Under what name?" Paul brought out one of his ever-present tools—just a small knife, this time—and began cutting rose hips to add to the curate's basket.

Thankful for her gloves, Minerva snapped off the hips and listened.

"Turner," the old curate answered, sounding puzzled. "After her burial, I asked if I should notify the registrar of an inaccurate entry. The father signed the baptismal papers under Turner. Neither of them were a member of the parish originally, so we had no reason to believe they weren't married. They bought the cottage just before the boy was born."

"Were the records changed?" Paul asked with a frown.

"I believe the rector spoke with the solicitor and was to take it up with the bishop." The curate looked uncomfortable with the notion of changing his records.

"Did the parents ever say where they married?" Minerva inquired, her suspicious mind circling. They needed to ask Browning if it was legal to change the records.

"I really didn't know the couple well," the man said apologetically. "He was often away, a soldier, I believe. She didn't have a carriage and had to walk to services, which didn't happen often enough because she was sickly."

And had babies who fretted and got ill. Mothers without servants had a hard time walking anywhere.

"This is helpful, thank you. Although Smith isn't any easier to trace than Turner. Might you make us official copies of the birth records in case we find their family? That would help tremendously." Paul handed him his card. "We're to meet a solicitor at the cottage, so if you would just send the documents to me when they're ready?"

Brilliant! So even if the records were changed, they'd have a copy of the original documents. Minerva didn't like the path her thoughts had taken.

Paul slipped the curate a coin for the service, then took her arm to steer her back to the carriage.

"Now he will think you are richer than he and start looking for a new position," Minerva murmured in amusement as he handed her up.

"He most likely has the perpetual curacy, as I do. He's unlikely to leave and the rector knows it. I imagine Hunt will reimburse us if we help solve the case." He shook the reins and sent the horse back to the lane.

"Do you find the conflict of information as suspicious as I do?" Minerva settled back in the seat. Jostling wheels had been a part of her itinerant childhood. She accepted the discomfort if it accomplished her task.

"You have a naturally suspicious mind, my love, but yes, I agree. The children called themselves Turner. They had no reason to make that up. The husband apparently claimed them and his name was Turner. It's only this unknown trust solicitor calling her Smith and a mistress, not a wife."

"Thank you. Mr. Turner might be an utter rogue and rakehell with mistresses and children scattered over the countryside, but she believed herself married, so she must have had marriage documents. We need to find them. Do you think Browning's clerk will allow us to search?"

"No, not too obviously. But we could ask *him* to look through desks and such in search of the children's identity—provided any desk or papers remain." Paul hurried the mare into a trot, glancing at the overcast sky.

They didn't have much time before dark. Less, if it rained.

Mr. Browning's clerk had already tethered his horse and gone inside by the time they drove through the open gate. Rose briars covered the cottage wall. They must have smelled heavenly in summer. The yard was merely a square of well-maintained grass. The old two-story stone and thatch cottage sprawled to either side with newer additions.

"Not elegant but, for a young couple, expensive to buy and maintain," Minerva whispered as Paul handed her down.

"We'll need to ask after the staff. They might help." He took her arm to lead her down a flagstone walk.

Wearing a frown, Mr. Dryden, the son of one of Mr. Browning's partners, greeted them at the entrance. A well set-up young man with blondish hair and a round face, he gestured at a cart behind an enormous rhododendron. "It seems someone has started removals, but we have not authorized any. We shall have to write the estate to verify approval."

The young clerk lacked Minerva's worldly experience. She left Paul talking with him and drifted over to examine the cart's contents. Whether it had been loaded legally or illegally, why had it been abandoned? It was obvious no one guarded the cottage. She tested a trunk lid, found it unlocked, and peered in. Silver. She dropped it back and looked under the second. Clothes. No books. Thieves seldom recognize the value of books. Movers from an estate would.

She returned to Paul and Mr. Dryden. "Does the silver belong to the estate or has family claimed it?"

Dryden stared at her in alarm. "It all belongs to the estate! We're authorized to permit removal of personal objects, but the silver— No, no, I'm quite certain that is a part of the inventory to be sold." He rushed to examine the trunk.

"Really, whoever owns the estate is a complete gudgeon to not keep servants to guard the place." Minerva entered the house, leaving Paul to help the clerk haul the trunks inside.

She hastily scanned the front room. Not luxurious but charming, with lively chintz upholstery and a pretty blue velvet drapery. A Chippendale writing desk had been ransacked, the drawers hastily closed, leaving papers sticking out the edge. Minerva sorted through them but found no legal documents. She suspected they'd been stolen if there had been any. Her nose for trouble tingled.

The right-wing addition contained a formal dining room, from whence the silver had been pilfered, if the rings in the dust on the empty shelves were any indication.

The left addition contained a generous study and library. The books about head height appeared scattered and shoved carelessly in place. Searching for a safe? The desk was empty. Mr. Turner's effects may have been removed upon his death.

While the men were otherwise occupied, she hastened up the stairs.

A portable writing desk in the main bedchamber held receipts and a few unopened letters addressed to Mrs. Thomas *Turner*. Unlike Willa, the deceased must have thrown out all correspondence to which she'd replied. There was nothing here from parents or any other family. A quick search revealed no neatly stored letters.

Minerva opened the letters and made note of the signatures, but the names didn't ring any bells. The letters didn't include more than a date and salutation. But they verified she was known as Mrs. Turner, not *Smith*.

The clothing had been emptied from the wardrobe. Any jewel case had been removed. They'd probably find one in the cart. Surely, her jewels were among her personal effects and belonged to the children, but there had been none in their bag.

She could hear the men downstairs by the time she reached the nursery. She should hurry. An open trunk sat between two small beds. Children's clothes and shoes had been tossed in—not neatly folded as a nanny might.

On the pink bed, she found a cloth rabbit and a doll with a porcelain head. Schoolbooks still sat stacked on a child's desk. These thieves really did not value books. She added all of them to the trunk but found nothing that would help locate family.

"I haven't checked the chambers over the wings," she told Paul when he joined her. "I assume she had servants, but they would have packed up their belongings when they left. Do you think they may have returned to ransack the house?"

He lifted the children's trunk and carried it to the head of the stairs. "It's a very real possibility. Have you found any book-keeping journals of whom she may have paid and when?"

That he acknowledged her snooping without criticism made her smile. "Not yet. She doesn't appear to be someone who cared much for writing." She indicated the trunk. "But the children had books. She read to them."

"I'll search the remaining rooms. Go sweet talk Mr. Dryden and convince him we need to remove the children's belongings. He's in a state and attempting to do a complete inventory on the spot."

Knowing the search was in good hands, Minerva trotted downstairs to distract the clerk. He was counting pots and dishes in the kitchen.

"We should take the silver back to your law office," she offered. "And if you don't think the estate will mind, we'll take the children's personal items. Someone has conveniently begun to pack everything upstairs."

He looked at her, wide-eyed. "Do thieves pack clothes? Should I consult the previous staff? Call a constable?"

Mr. Dryden's son was very young and needed to learn cynicism.

"Staff did not heave everything they could lay hands on into trunks, willy-nilly," she informed him. "So, yes, call a constable, if you have one. The estate should be notified. Perhaps they'll hire a guard. I'll write a receipt for the trunk we take for the children and refer them to the church if they have questions." The Stratford church, not Paul's. She didn't want thieves looking for them.

He bobbed his head anxiously. "I don't know who she employed. I'll speak with the neighbors. She must have paid them somehow."

True. "Mr. Bosworth claims it wasn't through his bank. Perhaps Mr. Browning can make inquiries of the other solicitors."

"Yes, I'll do that. We need to take that silver back to town immediately. It should fit on the back of your carriage. If you have what the children need—"

A woman's voice shouted from the front room. "Halloo? Anyone home? The door was left open!"

Minerva lifted her skirt and raced down the passage. The neighborhood busybody might impart useful information. She slowed down to enter the front room in what she hoped was a ladylike fashion. "Yes?" she asked, as if she had every right to be here.

A middle-aged woman with an enormous bonnet concealing her hair, wearing the black bombazine of a matronly housekeeper, studied her expectantly. "Are you the new owner?"

"We are packing Mrs. Turner's trunks. Did you need to speak with her solicitor? He's taking inventory." That was only a little fudge. Dryden wasn't anyone's solicitor as far as she was aware. She simply wanted to establish that she was no thief. And discover the name the lady had been known by.

"Well, that's a relief, it surely is. I'm Mrs. Middleton, from next door. There's been all sorts of coming and going here and I was that concerned, I was. How are the children faring? Do you know?" She didn't exhibit a bit of inhibition at her nosiness—and didn't question the name Turner.

Minerva didn't have time to be coy. "Their carriage overturned and the driver died. We are trying to determine where they were being taken. The solicitor thought the children had gone to the family." Well, she'd learned to lie as a child.

Mrs. Middleton covered her mouth in shock. "Oh, my, those poor tykes! I had my worries. I tried to talk to the people who were clearing out the house, but they were. . . not friendly. Told me to mind my own business, if you will! But I looked after them since they were babes and I was so fearful. . ."

"Then you might know the family? Where we should take

them?" Minerva bobbed a curtsy. "Forgive me, I'm Mrs. Upton. Our church has the children now." She deliberately refrained from saying where. "They are too young to tell us more than their names and the name of their home."

Mrs. Middleton shook her head in sorrow. "Such a tragedy. I had no idea she was so ill. Not well, certainly, but to die so young. . . I'm sorry. I never met her family. She wasn't one to talk much, kept to herself. But you can tell when children are well loved. Their father came home whenever he could, until he was sent to the Continent. She held services for him but there never was any body or burial. He just didn't come home, as so many didn't. The children only stopped wearing blacks this past year. She never did."

Dashitall, she needed names, places. . . "Well, if you learn anything more about the family, let the rector know, please? The cottage's solicitor claims not to be aware of more family. Do you know the names of her servants or where they might be found?"

Mrs. Middleton frowned. "She only had a maid and a man of all work. They packed up and left right after the funeral. There was a fine carriage here, so I thought the family had taken them away. I cannot remember her ever having visitors other than the neighbors. I will ask about. Those poor tykes! I cannot imagine. . ." She hurried off, no doubt to canvas the neighborhood for a lovely morning of gossip.

The widow must have led a very lonely life with no family about—and such a peculiarity did lead one to imagine the worst. Minerva had the sinking sensation that even should they find Daniel's teacher, no one in Stratford knew the children any better, and they had reached a dead end.

TWELVE

BRYDIE

BRYDIE TIED UP THE LAST BATCH OF BUNS WITH BROWN PAPER AND string and added them to her basket. She peered into Willa's front room, where Damien had organized neat stacks of papers from all over the house, holding them down with whatever heavy objects came to hand. She'd heard no cries of success and assumed he'd located nothing to tell them who owned the cottage.

She didn't know where Cooper had gone. He was supposed to be sorting Willa's belongings for his family.

Sgt-Major Fletcher Ferguson, as she knew the tall, surly soldier was properly called, sat on the aging sofa, bending over a square case clock that had been on the mantel. She'd noted earlier that it was running slow. Damien had taken a flask away from him and handed him the clock—a successful ploy, apparently. Brydie was still wary of the major, but he was much too large to be the man from the henhouse. Judging by his grim visage, he'd have snapped her neck in one try. She shivered. Having a killer lurking about was enough to make one stay in bed. . . well, no, that hadn't helped poor Willa.

"I would like to deliver these buns to the neighbors now," she told the men. "If you're busy, you needn't accompany me." She fully intended to bribe the neighbors into talking.

Damien grunted in exasperation and unfolded himself from the stacks of paper on the floor. "Fletch, we're leaving you guarding the house." He picked up the coat and hat he'd flung over a chair and handed Brydie her cloak. "Wear your shawl under that flimsy wrap or you'll freeze. It's almost too dark to do this. Can't interrogating the neighbors wait until morning?"

"I have to be at the market," she reminded him. "I cannot rest until I. . ." She stopped, casting a glance at Fletch, who might or might not be listening since he'd done no more than grunt at them. He was grieving. She didn't want to send him back to his flask again.

Damien nodded and followed her into the kitchen, donning his outer garments. "I understand. I just don't think you ought to be the one investigating."

"You can read legal documents. I can bake and talk. Rafe can chase egg thieves. Division of duties. If Minerva were here, I'd have her go with me. The curate's wife is supposed to visit the parish." Brydie donned a shawl and tugged on her gloves.

Damien threw her cloak around her. "We'll only traipse about until dark. Kate has no doubt taken the children home already. You should be with them."

She patted his stubbled cheek, enjoying his masculine familiarity. "I have been walking these lanes in the dark since childhood. You cannot change my ways now that you've decided to return here." She hoped this wasn't an argument they must repeat for a lifetime.

He brushed a kiss against her hair before pulling up her hood. "If you love me, you won't give me any more attacks of the heart. I'm an old, old man and cannot take much more."

She snorted inelegantly and cast him a sideways glance. "Yes, old and doddering, I see that now. I shall knit you a shawl for Christmas."

Her beloved stood nearly a head taller than she. Well-muscled, although not as broad as Fletch and Rafe, he'd once lifted her as if she were a sack of flour. Definitely doddering. And intent on having his own way. She hoped he enjoyed fighting.

They strode through the shadows of the winter hedges as the sun lowered behind the manor hill, outlining the Priory towers rising above the trees. Most of the small cottages along the lane had been abandoned decades ago, their thatch rotted and fallen in, their yards a bramble of overgrown weeds and shrubs.

Mrs. Essex lived in the one nearest Willa. Smoke drifted from her chimney. They'd already talked to her. She no doubt knew by now that Willa was dead and she wouldn't be receiving more free bread. Brydie strode on.

"There's smoke coming from that chimney." Damien nodded to a house further down and across the lane. "Shall we just stop where there are signs of life?"

The task was daunting enough that Brydie agreed. "Winter is a very bad time for investigating, but I suppose the holiday is good excuse for being neighborly."

This house appeared as abandoned as the others, with an overgrown yard and rotting thatch, although the roof did appear to be in one piece, with no obvious holes. Little more than a shepherd's stone croft, it probably hadn't been improved since it was built a century ago. A horse whickered in back. Someone was home.

Damien knocked on the cracked wooden door. Brydie held her breath, expecting the leather hinges to fall in.

No one immediately answered but the aroma of roasting meat carried through the cool air.

"Vagabond?" Brydie offered.

She shouldn't have said anything. Damien's expression grew grim and he pounded harder.

Eventually, they heard a rustling in the front room, followed by muttering and rattling on the other side of the door. It dragged open with a loud creak of swollen wood. An unshaven man with untrimmed dark hair peered warily through the crack. "What d'ya want?"

Trying not to be too suspicious, Brydie beamed and held up one of her packages. "Merry Christmas, sir! We are trying to meet the neighbors before the holiday, invite everyone to chapel services. We'll have a choir and spiced cider. I'm Brydie Calhoun and this is Damien Sutter. He's just returned to Gravesyde." She bobbed a curtsy.

Damien removed his hat and bowed. "Have you lived here long?"

The man accepted the package of buns still warm from the oven. They smelled delicious and Brydie's stomach rumbled. She didn't eat while baking. Perhaps she should have.

Reluctantly, the man muttered, "Ralph Parsons, just moved in. Place belonged to my granny. Thank ye, kindly." He started to close the door.

Damien inserted his boot. "Do you know any of the other neighbors? It's late, and we don't want to stop at every house if they're empty."

"Just got here, I said." He eyed Damien with suspicion. "Don't know nobody."

"Well, come down to the tavern later and you'll find good company. I don't suppose you knew the lady across the lane?"

"Don't know no one. People been back and forth all day. Got supper cooking. Need to get back to it." He tried to shut the door again.

"Did you notice anyone last night?" Brydie asked cheerfully. "We're trying to find her family."

Parsons eyes narrowed. "Didn't notice nothing. Her family lost?"

Damien returned his tall hat to his head. "That's what we're trying to ascertain. Good evening to you, sir, hope to see you in church." He tugged Brydie's elbow to turn her back to the lane.

"I suppose it's not polite to punch the neighbors," she said thoughtfully. "Perhaps I can wish that the uncleaned chimney burns the house down around him."

He glared down at her. "You burn down houses for rudeness?"

She could practically feel his glare through her hood. "He's our hen thief. He's the right size, I remember the beard, and he's roasting chicken."

Damien swung his glare to the ramshackle cottage. "A vagabond thief who assaults women, charming. I'll send Rafe out in the morning. But we have no proof of anything."

"We could ask to see his shins, see if they're bruised." Brydie was too tired to go back and punch him. The fellow had probably been hungry and she'd interrupted his breakfast. He must know these lanes if he escaped Fletch. The sergeant-major was unfamiliar with much of the village. "Is Fletch guarding Willa's tonight? If Parsons is the killer, he's likely to break in again and be gone by morning."

Brydie started up the walk of the next house showing smoke in the chimney.

"Fletch, Cooper, and another of the captain's ex-soldiers, one who swore off drink, are guarding it. But unless the killer is after Willa's trinkets, I can't see that there's anything there to be found besides a trunk full of letters from family. A hen thief and a killer aren't necessarily the same."

"Which is what I've been saying all along," she sniffed. "How does anyone ever catch wrongdoers?"

"Not easily," he concluded wearily.

They repeated their performance at a few more houses without any more success, although the older inhabitants were far more hospitable than Mr. Parsons. They all had tales to tell of Willa but none added to their limited knowledge beyond reminiscences of the Bartletts and buns.

"We're halfway home," Brydie noted as they emerged from the last cottage on the lane. "Do you need to go back to the inn to fetch your horse? I'll be fine walking on." She had one bundle of buns left she thought she'd earned after this day's work.

"The horse will be fine with Rafe. Chicken thieves and killers roam the night. We need to find a horse for you." Damien took her arm and led her over a stile to the footpath that connected with the carriage road, proving he hadn't forgotten his way around in his years of absence.

"Horses cost much too much: to buy, to feed, to care for. With Arthur leaving for school, we'll have no one to tend the stable. Rob can manage the pony before school, but no more than that. I have two good feet." Brydie tried not to shiver inside her cloak.

Just because Damien thought he ought to take care of her didn't mean she ought to allow him to do so. She'd seen what had happened when Kate had been left a widow with three young children. She'd been helpless to handle the farm. They both had been. They were only just now finding their feet.

"I've savings set aside." He wrapped his arm around her shoulders to pull her against his warmth. "I won't let you go hungry if the court can't return my mother's investments. We won't need much to live on since the property is free and clear."

"Good thing, since we won't earn much by living in Gravesyde," she replied with tired humor. "Once Jacques has his shoe business set up, do you think he might rent the house from you? Then we could live closer to where we work."

"You're thinking about Willa's bakery, aren't you? Do you really want to be a baker?"

He knew her too well. "I'd never given it a thought before, but I like baking. Only, buying her house is about as likely as Verity adopting those children. The real owners will come along sooner or later. I was thinking more of the inn and your office."

"Willa's family might not want a house where a member died so violently. And Willa's reputation. . . I'm expecting men to come knocking at her door any time now. Fletch says he wasn't her only. . . visitor." Damien spoke frankly.

Brydie tried to puzzle out what he was telling her, but her mind was on baking. "I cannot imagine Willa knew many men. She went to bed early to get up and bake bread, so she didn't spend time at the tavern. Or church, now that I think of it. I suppose the former soldiers up at the manor might hunt bread for some reason. You don't think one of them. . . ?"

Damien sighed. "Sorry, I shouldn't talk about such things with you."

"You should talk about *everything* with me," she cried. "We cannot have secrets."

"I don't know how," he complained. "We're not married. You're an innocent lady who should not have even known Willa. I would be far more comfortable if you baked bread at home or the inn. I don't know how Willa found her male customers, and I fear no woman is safe there."

Brydie stopped in the middle of the dark lane with bare tree branches scratching in the wind above their heads. She'd grown up in a small community, but she hadn't buried her head in the mud. She simply had to get past her shock to grasp what he wasn't telling her. She ought to punch him again. "Mrs. Essex told us someone offered a king's shilling for Saturday night. What does that mean to you?"

Damien tried to drag her on. She planted her feet and refused to move.

"To take the king's shilling generally means to join the army," he said. "It may have meant something else to Willa. She did not live on just selling bread. Must I say more?"

Brydie thought about it. "Most of the soldiers who camped on manor land are gone. Hunt hired the few remaining. Are you saying. . . ?" She couldn't quite bring herself to say it.

"I am saying nothing except Willa had male friends." Damien dragged her on.

Male friends—puzzle pieces clicked. Willa had been a *barque of frailty*? Here? In Gravesyde?

This time she followed—because he was talking.

"The captain and his friends are making discreet inquiries of manor employees and guests who may have visited Willa. But why would any of them kill her? She had next to nothing, and we can't see that anything has been stolen."

"If there were documents in that desk, they're gone," she reminded him. "That may be all the killer sought. In which case, I doubt it was one of the soldiers. Most of them are illiterate. Verity has been talking about an evening school to teach them, but there are only so many hours in the day." She was much more comfortable talking about schools.

"I won't rest easy until we find who did it." Damien stopped outside Brydie's home and held her close. "Which means we must be suspicious of every man in town. Don't go anywhere without me."

He was her reality now. Forgetting Willa, Brydie hugged his neck and kissed him boldly, then stepped away. "I might as well tell you not to go anywhere without *me*. Women can kill, too, and a jealous wife— Perhaps the Uptons or the mail will bring us news in the morning. I trust they'll be picking the post up before they return home."

He winced at mention of a jealous wife and stuck to a safer topic. "Fletch said he'd take our post in the morning, but it could be after Christmas before we hear anything. Go knit gloves for the children and stay home!"

Brydie hurried toward the warm kitchen but threw over her shoulder, "Shawl! I'm knitting you a shawl, old man!"

WEDNESDAY

DECEMBER 20, 1815

THIRTEEN

RAFE

RISING IN THE DARK, RAFE BRUSHED A KISS AGAINST HIS SLEEPING bride's cheek, a rush of affection warming him as it always did in Verity's presence. A lady who had suffered at the hands of a greedy relation for all her adult life, she could have found better than an innkeeper's son. But starting out together, she'd fit into his world as if she'd always been there. He might not be a religious man, but he never ceased to be amazed at the miracle.

He fretted about her recent sadness, fearing she thought she'd made a mistake by marrying him. But the orphans had lifted her spirits, which made him as protective of them as his wife.

He stopped in the adjoining bedchamber to check on them. They were a cause for more concern than he meant to express. Verity loved children. He knew that. She had tamed a schoolroom full of rambunctious brats of all ages and had them learning their numbers and letters without a single complaint. But these two well-bred, educated youngsters. . . didn't belong in an impoverished inn.

Someone would come looking for them—and he feared they might not be the ones who should have them. Sending young children out without their belongings, in that broken-down buggy, at night, with a drunken driver. . . He suspected foul play. He didn't grasp the reason, only the danger. If Verity lost them like that. . . There would be no consoling her.

He'd posted the dead woman's image in the lobby. At this point, she was the only clue he had.

The little girl had crawled into bed with her brother and slept clinging to her new rag doll. The kitten had abandoned his hearth bed, climbed in, and curled up with them.

Last night, Rafe had talked to Daniel a bit and learned Daphne used to talk. Daniel didn't know why she quit. He'd come home from school to be told his mother had died. His sister hadn't said a word since. Things like that simply did not happen in respectable households. Rafe hoped and prayed the Uptons found *Beanblossom* and that it held people who knew the children.

He dressed and traversed the back hall to the kitchen, where he stirred the fire and heated water. With years of experience, he had the yeast and tea ready at the same time. He gulped a cup, then mixed the ingredients. After he washed and shaved, he kneaded the dough. He had bread in the oven and rashers and eggs fried as the servants straggled in to help. He slapped his food on day-old toast and left the women to finish up. They were capable of watching the bread bake while preparing breakfast.

Finishing his egg-bacon sandwich, he shrugged on his great-coat, and stomped up the lane to Willa's cottage. He wished he'd had training in how to be a bailiff instead of making it all up on his own. He was grateful for friends who gave him suggestions, but they didn't know much more about the position than he. They'd searched Willa's stable and yard as well as her house, but not knowing what was out of place or missing, they didn't learn anything. Fletch had only noticed her slow clock.

The aroma of bread baking permeated the chilly morning air. Brydie must have come in early.

Rafe studied the flagstone path as he traipsed to the back door. Had the killer come in front or back? Had she known the villain?

Fletch had said she hid a key under a flagstone beside the kitchen door. Any of her visitors might have known about it. There had been no sign that anyone had battered in the door, so her killer must have known—or he'd followed Cooper inside. Cooper hadn't regained much memory of his arrival. It seemed likely that he'd been hit when he'd walked through the door.

Meera had said the knife had caused a lot of splatter. But Cooper hadn't had a speck of blood on him, other than a few spots on his linen and around the bump on his head. How did one go about searching for blood-splattered clothes? They'd found nothing in the cottage. Rafe supposed clothes could have been thrown in those great ovens—which Brydie and Cooper had set alight. Would they have noticed clothes? Not if they were already ashes.

Brydie was feeding the guard Captain Huntley had sent in the kitchen.

"Quiet night?" Rafe asked.

The man shrugged. "Except for Fletch's snoring. He slept on the couch, Mr. Cooper, upstairs. We took turns patrolling, checking doors and whatnot. They stayed locked. No one rattled them. No one tried the windows. Any villain is long gone."

That's what Rafe feared.

Fletch sprawled on the sofa in the front room. The mantel clock was back in place, chiming as Rafe walked in. Fletch unburied himself from his greatcoat cover and rubbed his unshaven jaw, grumbling. He must have spent at least part of the night fixing the clock. It chimed seven times. Rafe didn't have a watch but he'd surmise that was about right.

Apparently drawn by the smell of breakfast, Cooper staggered down the dark stairs, holding the rail instead of lighting a lamp. He scrubbed a hand over his rumpled hair and glared at Rafe. "This is senseless, you realize. One of Willa's customers took it on himself to rid the world of her, and you'll never find him."

Fletch growled, but he wasn't one to talk much in the morning

—or at all. He staggered into the kitchen. The backdoor slammed, so he was on his way to the privy.

"Someone searched her desk," Rafe reminded him. "They sought something. I'm going to take her trinkets down to Oswald. He buys, sells, and pawns bits and pieces. Maybe he'll recognize one of them." He'd come up with that idea while staring sleeplessly at the ceiling last night.

He hated the idea of a killer running free, but he'd be relieved if he knew the town wasn't under any threat.

Fletch returned while Rafe gathered the trinkets they'd collected so far. Holding out the box of rings and spoons and pins, he asked, "Any of these belong to you?"

His friend didn't even look. "Nah. I gave her coin. There's a silver spoon in there comes from up the manor, though. Recognized it yesterday."

"Quincy wouldn't steal spoons. He's in charge of them, isn't he?" Rafe suspected the portly ex-fighter butler was sweet on the housekeeper. It was doubtful if he'd jeopardize that relationship visiting Willa. Besides, an ex-boxer like Quincy would have been noticed anytime he stepped off the manor grounds.

"Footmen set the table. Kitchen help washes. Anyone could slip a spoon into a pocket. Quincy usually counts them. You might ask if any went missing and when. But even if one of the footmen stole it, it proves nothing." Fletch pulled a stone from the fireplace and reached in, producing another small bundle. "She hid these things all over, for her old age, she said."

So Willa had trusted Fletch with her secrets. Or he'd discovered them and questioned. Interesting.

Fletch hid his grief well, but it was there, in the angry rumble of his voice as he handed over the cloth-wrapped bundle.

"She showed you where she hid these?" Rafe opened the cloth, finding a tiny pearl stickpin, a gold watch fob, silver coins, and silver needles.

"Nah, I noticed the stone was loose when I was reaching for the clock. She'd stashed a few coins in the clock as well. I left them on the desk. Ought to be enough to pay for a decent burial, shouldn't there?" He looked uncomfortable asking.

"I'm pretty sure the curate intends to see her respectably buried. The woman from the buggy. . ." Rafe added the fob and stickpin to his collection for taking to Oswald. "Had coins enough for tolls, not coffins. Did Willa ever talk of family?"

"We didn't spend much time talking. I didn't even know about Cooper. I thought she was all alone." Looking uncomfortable, Fletch returned to the kitchen.

Rafe searched the rest of the house while he waited for Oswald's mercantile to open, turning up several more small hoards tucked away in fairly obvious hiding places. It would take a thief a while to gather them all. But if anything had been stolen, Rafe had no way of knowing.

He heard Brydie scolding the men in the kitchen just as the clock chimed eight. The market would be opening. Wrapping the small box of gewgaws in his handkerchief and shoving it into his pocket, he trotted back downstairs.

Brydie tucked bread and buns into baskets and scowled at Rafe's approach. "These oafs are eating up profits. We should charge them."

"I'll add it to the expense sheet I send to Hunt." Amused, Rafe helped her prepare her market basket. "Guarding a house against a killer ought to earn something."

She rolled her eyes. "So the captain ends up paying them double for guarding *and* eating, paying the curate for a funeral, and offering a free coffin and burial site on the manor grounds, plus your services. This does not sound like a reasonable means of running a village."

"Alternative is taxing everyone and having a village treasurer pay the bills." Rafe helped himself to one of the buns the others had left. It was pretty decent, if he did say so himself. He'd have added a spoon of sugar.

Humor restored at that ridiculous notion, Brydie laughed. "If we could collect taxes in the form of cabbages and carrots, that might almost work."

"Since the church hasn't even been able to collect that much in tithes, I'm guessing you'll need a tax collector with a big stick. Are you walking? I'm going that way and can help you carry the load." Rafe picked up several of her baskets. "You really need a cart to set up in."

"Arthur delivered Lyn and Rob to your place. He'll water the pony and leave the cart for me. What can we do for Verity to make up for all the time she's spending watching Kate's children?" Brydie hauled the rest of the bread baskets out after him.

"I'm not helping her much either." Rafe sighed at the pleasant image he'd once imagined of the two of them running the inn side-by-side. "I need to hire more staff."

"Well, we met a Mr. Ralph Parsons in one of the cottages up the lane, says it belonged to his granny. I'm thinking he's the chicken thief. He might be looking for work." Brydie sounded half-amused, half-worried.

"Just what we need, more scoundrels. You recognize him?" Rafe carried the baskets to the pony cart waiting in the inn yard. The mercantile wasn't that far away. She just needed a place to display the bread out of the dust of the road.

"I wouldn't want to testify in front of a judge, but I'm pretty sure he's the one who grabbed me. He was roasting chicken when we stopped by. Has a horse too. He could be another ex-soldier come home to roost. Check to see if his shins are bruised if you go out there." She climbed into the cart and grinned at him.

Rafe really didn't want this job.

Walking beside Brydie's cart, he studied the women selling their goods in front of Oswald's store. Gravesyde was inhabited by widows and a few young women who, like Brydie, never married because the men all left for war or employment in the city. Rafe knew there were farmers still around, but they didn't do the shopping. He'd be better off hunting killers at the tavern. Not a pleasant thought.

He waited until Oswald's customers had left before stepping up to the counter with his box. "These are from Willa's house. Do you recognize any of them?"

A gray-haired, wizened man of diminutive size, the post-master and mercantile owner also acted as a pawn shop. He poked through the boxes and held up the stickpin. "Willa some-times brought this in when she was short on blunt. Said it was her father's. She always bought it back."

"Nothing else look familiar?" Rafe hadn't expected much, but he had to do everything he could think of, which obviously wasn't enough.

"Spoon belongs to the manor." Oswald shrugged. "All the rest are pretty common. Nothing worth more than a few shillings."

"Thank you." Rafe tucked the box back in his pocket. "Did Willa have you read her correspondence?"

Oswald nodded. "She could barely write her name. She had me write her answers. She didn't really have no one to write though."

What a sad small life the poor woman had lived. The men who visited had probably been her only glimpse of the outside world. "Do you remember what letters she received recently? And her replies?"

The merchant puckered up his nose beneath his wire-rimmed spectacles. "Few months back, she had a note saying Margie was ill and asking if she'd come visit. Margie was about the only one ever wrote her. They grew up together."

"Did Willa reply?" Rafe remembered being told the baker's daughter was named Margery, so that was most likely the Margie. "Do you remember the address?"

Oswald wrinkled his brow trying to recall the replies. "I think it came from Stratford, but that's where most everything comes from, so I could be mistaken. Willa paid me by the word, so she was terse, just said she had no way of traveling, but she had room if they wanted to come to her."

"*They*? As in the ill woman?" Rafe tried to puzzle that out, but the minds of women escaped his understanding.

Oswald frowned more. "I think the exact wording was something like 'The place is yours. They can come any time.' Or maybe she said 'You can come.' It's been a few months. But far's I know, no one ever came."

Until the other night, when someone killed her. Rafe's gut churned, but his mind could make no sense of any of it. "No letter from Mr. Cooper?"

"Not that I recall, but I was down with the catarrh for a few days and my wife gave out the mail."

Rafe had seen the letter, so he knew it existed. He'd have to question the wife. And then the ugly thought occurred—was Willa's only correspondent the cousin whose funeral Cooper was to attend?

FOURTEEN

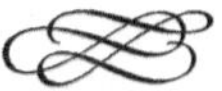

Minerva winced as the loose carriage wheel hit a rut and they nearly bounced into the ragged hood over their heads. "I can see why the post rider was eager to cut Gravesyde off his route. We need some wealthy landowners to pave the lane."

"And charge tolls no one can afford. I'm pretty sure toll keepers don't take apples or sheep in payment." Paul grinned even as he attempted to steer the old mare around a half-frozen rut.

"We're dreaming if we think we can lure customers here to buy Lavender's dresses and Sofia's perfumes." Minerva scowled at the smoke rising from the manor's chimneys. An earl's family simply did not have the proper mercantile connections.

"Or Jacques's shoes," Paul agreed. "We are not too far from the Birmingham road. Perhaps that stretch of Gravesyde's lane can be paved, once the bridge is rebuilt, but the paving would have to extend all the way through the village to reach the manor drive."

They were avoiding thinking of murder and kidnapping and the causes thereof. Minerva was convinced the children had been stolen for reasons unknown. She and Paul had spent a restless evening tossing ideas about in the luxurious chamber Bosworth had provided. The banker's hospitality did not include discussing possibilities for murder. He'd retired to his office shortly after dinner and hadn't been seen again.

Another jolt caused a rattle between the cushions. Minerva slid her gloved hand between them to be certain the springs weren't coming unattached. Her fingers closed around a tin. Twisting it back and forth until it loosened, she pulled it out, frowned, and pried off the lid. Inside were what appeared to be a few pink-coated candies. "Digestives?" she suggested, holding them up for Paul to see.

"Candies of some sort?" He shrugged, thought about it, and scowled. "Don't taste one. We are assuming the driver was drunk, but she could have ingested something that disagreed with her. Let's ask Meera what they contain."

"Looks like candy to entertain the children. They seem to be fine." She sniffed the small sugary pellet. "Ugh. Might be anise in the coating." She snapped the lid shut. She hated anise but it might be a flavor the children enjoyed. Someone had tried to make them happy with candy. It could be a clue to who had sent them away.

Her husband drove the buggy into the inn yard around noon. No one emerged to greet them. Paul helped Minerva down, handed her the mailbag, then led the horse around to the stable. She'd been dying to root through the post in hopes of finding anything useful, but her proper husband had insisted the bag should be delivered to the postmaster. This was one of those times when her pragmatism clashed with his propriety.

Brydie's eldest nephew hurried from the lobby to take the heavy bag and heave it onto the counter. "I'm to help Mrs. Russell," he said in explanation. "So I've been trying to watch the inn while Mr. Russell is questioning suspects."

"I take it that means Rafe hasn't found who killed Willa yet?" Miranda shuddered. It would be a gloomy Christmas if they all had to huddle indoors to stay safe from the attack of a knife-wielding madman.

Arthur shook his head. "Should I look in the mailbag for responses from Mrs. Willoughby's family?"

"Paul thinks we must deliver it to the postmaster. He'll be in shortly and we can watch the desk while you carry it to the mercantile. Then Mr. Oswald can collect Mr. Cooper's postage and officially hand the post to him." She hoped he had the coins to pay. "That is, if Mr. Cooper is still here?"

"Mr. Russell is making him stay at the bakery." Arthur cast a glance over his shoulder at the sound of footsteps down the hall. "I don't think he wants anyone around the babes."

Minerva didn't take long to ponder that. She smiled in delight as Verity rushed out holding the youngest orphan. The pig-tailed child was almost too big for Verity to carry, but the innkeeper looked happier than she'd been lately.

"Any news?" she asked anxiously, setting tear-stained Daphne down beside the hearth where Wolfie slept. The child petted the enormous hound without fear.

"We found Beanblossom. The trunk with all their possessions is in the carriage. There's something you might do, Arthur, while we're waiting for my husband. Carry it in?"

Verity didn't look relieved but watched anxiously as the boy loped out to fetch the trunk. "Did you find their family? Do we need to send them on?"

Arthur returned with the baggage. Minerva shook her head and said nothing while the child eyed the old box but remained where placed. So the trunk wasn't familiar? "Is Daniel around? He might like to see if we found all his books."

Given a task to make the children happy, Verity departed to find the boy.

Arthur eyed the battered trunk with curiosity. "Is it because nothing ever happens here that an old box seems exciting? Maybe it should be saved for Boxing Day."

"I promise, the only excitement in that trunk is for the children. The rest of our news is still as much a muddle as when we left." Minerva watched out the mullioned window as Paul checked the carriage for the trunk, then hurried into the lobby, swiping off his tall hat as he did so.

"May Arthur carry the mailbag down to the mercantile so he can see if any of Mr. Cooper's family has had time to respond? I can't think they have yet, but hope never dies." Minerva helped Paul untangle his scarf while he pulled off his gloves.

"We saw Fletch riding toward Stratford, one assumes to collect today's post?" Paul gathered his outer garments and hung them on the hooks by the door. "That's more likely to hold a reply."

Arthur nodded. "That's why I'm minding the inn and not the hardware."

"Then trot the bag down to Mr. Oswald for me, thank you. Have him tell you if there's anything for Mr. Cooper so you can let him know."

Minerva wished she knew more of Mr. Cooper, but he seemed exactly what he claimed to be, a traveling gentleman caught unawares. He must have traveled through Stratford to reach Gravesyde by evening. With the bridge out, he'd not have made it to any funeral in Birmingham, even if he'd been on time.

Finally overcoming her shyness, Daphne timidly kneeled beside the trunk, and Minerva's heart broke all over again at the sight of that beautiful, abandoned child. How could anyone lose such precious children?

By the time Verity arrived with Daniel, the little girl was tugging uselessly at the top. Once Daniel joined her, Paul unfastened the latch and opened the lid. Both squealed in excitement.

Verity closed her eyes in what appeared to be a brief prayer. "Thank you, thank you so much! I hate to see children unhappy. Sit down in the pub. I've sent for tea. You must be frozen through."

"Let us all gather by the hearth in there." Waiting until the children had filled their arms with belongings, Paul carried the trunk into the pub, where they could watch the excitement while they talked. It was a trifle like Christmas and Boxing Day combined.

Between them, Paul and Minerva explained what they'd discovered in Stratford while they sipped hot tea and nibbled on Rafe's scones. Minerva knew a good wife would ask for the recipe, but the chances of her ever trying it. . .

One of the kitchen maids carried out bowls of cabbage and sausage soup before Verity was done asking questions.

"I must say, I prefer the hospitality here to the stifling one we received at Bosworth's home," Minerva said in appreciation, warming her insides with the soup. "He is so ungraciously formal that I want to blame him for everything that goes wrong."

"I'm fairly certain he would have been recognized if he'd stolen the Beanblossom silver and the children," Paul replied in amusement.

"But he didn't recognize the children or the driver or know anything about them?" Verity asked in desperation. "I just cannot believe such well-cared-for children were brought up by a gentleman's consort. I supposed I am prejudiced."

"If he provided her with a generous allowance, it's not unheard of. But giving the children his name and not giving it to her as well, that's a trifle odd. And having her funds go through a London trust instead of the local bank, where she might find help in investing or disbursing. . . It's as if she'd been deliberately isolated." Minerva savored her soup. Rafe was a most excellent cook.

"And no one recognizes the driver who died? I hate to be such a fuss-pot, but I am terrified someone will show up to claim them, and I will have no way to prove if they are kidnappers or a relation." Watching the children anxiously, Verity left her soup half-eaten.

"No one in Stratford recognized the sketch of the driver. Let's see if anyone here does. Today is market day, so there will be more people in the village than usual. I trust Rafe is showing the sketch about?" Paul scraped his bowl clean. "It seems unlikely the nanny was driving this way unless she knew someone here."

Like Willa? *A mistress, a nanny, and a prostitute.* . . Minerva rubbed her temple to rid herself of ridiculous notions that a city mistress might know a rural prostitute and the nanny. . . Was a procurer? *It takes one to know one* might apply occasionally but was not a reliable adage for a courtroom.

The children had barely touched their luncheon and were blissfully engaged in emptying the trunk all over the floor. Daphne hugged her doll with one arm while happily pulling on a pair of nearly new slippers. Daniel had donned his school coat and now organized his books in an order known only to him.

"Rafe is more concerned about catching a killer." Verity fidgeted while she watched the children. "He and Brydie are interrogating anyone who visits the market. I simply don't want to believe a murderer would stay around after committing his dirty deed. He's probably long gone. But the nanny. . . That's different. Surely she knew someone here." She lowered her voice to almost a whisper. "Meera thinks the nanny may have had some kind of fit, but I keep thinking two deaths in one night must be related. Only, I cannot fathom how. Did the killer see the driver was dead and rode in to kill Willa? That's foolish."

Exactly where Minerva's errant thoughts circled, for no logical reason whatsoever. Maybe Willa and the nanny were sisters? There was some small resemblance in age and the black hair. But Cooper had said Willa was an orphan.

"Since the buggy went off the road, can we know for certain if it was driving away from Gravesyde or toward it?" Now that she was warm and full again, Minerva pondered the puzzle. "We might make a case that the mysterious driver killed Willa for some unknown reason and was racing to take the children back to Beanblossom."

"It makes about as much sense as anything else, except no one around here claims to have seen the driver." Paul rose to join the children at the hearth. "The lady driving the carriage that took you away from Beanblossom was your nanny? Did she say where she was taking you?"

At mention of the nanny, Daphne's terrified expression returned. Daniel frowned and shook his head. "Elton told Nanny to take us where. . . baterds. . . like us belong."

Minerva winced. The child didn't even know the word, must never have heard it before.

"I was scared, so we hid." His lower lip trembled. "Daphne cried and they found us and he hit her."

Verity raced to crush them both in her arms, and Minerva almost wept.

"This *Elton* may have been the thief who filled the cart with stolen goods," she said softly. "Surely no respectable solicitor or estate agent would have hit children."

"No respectable solicitor or agent would have left children with a powerless servant. Someone official was there to arrange the funeral. He must have given orders to the servants." Paul did not generally show anger, but his voice held it now.

"Unless the servants were in league with the official." Minerva sometimes hated her suspicious mind, but she'd grown up with men who plotted war. "The neighbor said she saw an elegant carriage."

Paul grimaced and spoke soothingly to the weeping children in Verity's arms. "Did your nanny say where she was taking you?"

Daniel frowned. "To mama's family, if we quit crying and went to sleep."

The tin in Minerva's pocket rattled, and she tried another tactic. She held them out to see. "Did she give you sweets like this?"

Both children wrinkled their noses and pulled away. Daniel was the one who answered. "They're nasty. She took them away when we spit them out, called us ungrateful. . . baterds."

"And then what happened?" Paul asked gently.

The boy shrugged again. "We fell asleep. Then the carriage broke and woke us. Nanny was still sleeping, so we ran away."

"That was very, very brave of you," Verity assured them. "Let's have Mr. Upton carry your trunk back to your room where you can put things away. I'll see if we can find better sweets while you rest."

Left alone, Minerva studied the nearly empty tin. The children hadn't eaten more than one of the candies each. The driver must have finished them off. The lid was sealed quite tightly. They hadn't fallen out. Who had provided the candies?

"I'm going up to see Meera," she told Paul. "I'll be right back."

The brilliant apothecary physician might tell her if they had a second murder on their hands. That just seemed to fit better into the tale of that night of tragedy. And *scarier*, if the orphans were in danger.

FIFTEEN

BRYDIE'S NEPHEW RETURNED FROM THE POSTMASTER TO SAY THERE had been no letter from Cooper's family. Verity hoped they might eventually find who owned the bakery, but the deceased nanny and the difficulties the Uptons had described in Beanblossom worried her more. As a precaution, she warned the staff not to talk about the children. No one needed to know their whereabouts until they learned more of their family.

Brydie sold out her bread by noon and returned to report that people knew *about* Willa, but they didn't *know* her, even though she'd spent most of her life here.

Verity thought that horribly sad but it didn't relieve her escalating anxiety. "Did anyone recognize the sketch of the nanny?"

Brydie shook her head and prepared to head back to Willa's, where the men were apparently scouring the house for clues and waiting for suspects to knock on the door. Or perhaps they were making suspect lists. Verity didn't pay attention.

"Other than one saying the sketch was 'right ugly,' no one recognized that poor woman," Brydie admitted.

"You didn't tell anyone about the children?" Verity had specifically asked that no one mention them.

"Not a word, although I think that would be the best way to identify her. Do you really think they were being kidnapped?" Brydie finished drawing on her gloves.

"Nothing else makes sense." Verity didn't know whether to be relieved or not that the nanny hadn't been identified, especially if she had been taking the children to an orphanage. But they'd said she was taking them to family. . . Lying to keep them quiet? As far as she was aware, no one in the village was expecting the arrival of children.

She wished Rafe would come home and tell her what he'd learned from the mercantile owner, but he was back at Willa's. He worked hard, and she needed to support him as best as her limited skills allowed.

As a welcome distraction, the ladies strolled down from the manor that afternoon for tea and to discuss holiday festivities. Verity greeted them with Rafe's scones and some sweet buns he'd been testing.

"Mrs. Upton tells us the village once had a Thomasing tradition on St. Thomas's Day, but her husband—our previous curate —persuaded the beggars to go to the manor and sing for their supper on Christmas Eve, instead," Clare Huntley announced, sipping her hot tea. "Since this is our first Christmas here, we wondered if we might establish a new tradition. We might direct the singers to the inn, rather than have them climbing the icy hill. We would, of course, provide the supper."

Verity enjoyed the late earl's great-granddaughter and her managing ways. The lady had never asked to be put in charge of Priory Manor. Clare had married the irascible American before he'd become magistrate and had more or less inherited her duties as family descended. She'd simply grown into the role. Verity prayed she might do the same as Rafe's wife, but she was so ignorant of inns, that she feared she was failing him badly.

"We could decorate the pub with evergreens and provide a

wassail bowl, as well," Lady Elsa suggested. "I'm preparing small bundles of fudge and biscuits for the children, and Jack thought we might hand out apples with a coin in them for the adults to take away."

Patience, the curate's statuesque stepsister, leaned forward eagerly. "I have been teaching a few old carols to the ladies at church and they are teaching their children. We hope the men will join in eventually. It will be such fun!"

"Will Rafe mind?" Descendant of the late earl, daughter of another, Lady Elsa had been raised in wealth, but she wrapped her plump figure in kitchen attire and riding habits more often than silks.

"I know nothing of the tradition," Verity admitted, hiding her anticipation with a shrug. She hadn't celebrated a Christmas since her mother died, and that had been ten years ago and a very meager one at that. To be part of restoring a beloved tradition. . . It made her feel as if she might belong. "Rafe loves entertaining. I'm sure he'd be delighted to contribute." She glanced at the enormous chimney that served pub and kitchen. "Might we decorate a Yule log?"

After agreeing to direct her gardeners to cut greenery and hunt a suitable log, Patience asked eagerly, "May we meet the children?" She was growing round with the child she carried, but she still enthusiastically shared her lovely voice in her husband's tavern as well as the church. Verity would like to know her better.

Of course news of the orphans had made its way to the manor. Rafe would have had to make inquiries. And the nanny's body was stored in the crypt until she could be buried. Verity mentally called up a few of Rafe's swear words. Telling the manor ladies to keep a secret when it was already out. . . Perhaps she was fretting too much. The ladies would help her keep the children if their family wasn't found.

"Lynly has the children helping sew her mother's Christmas gift," Verity acknowledged in amusement at the highhandedness of Brydie's niece. "I will just ask them in to give their courtesies. I don't want them to feel stared at." She didn't want them seen at all. . .

"Do you think it might help if we had Arnaud sketch their likeness and send it around to our families?" An heiress, Thea Talbott was slowly redecorating the crumbling manor as time and money allowed. She and the impoverished artist, Comte Arnaud, had not announced their banns yet, but they were almost always together. Her family moved in London society, which might be why the impoverished émigré was so slow in his courtship.

Verity panicked at the suggestion and explained all Minerva had told her about the children's home. Before she fetched them, she added to discourage the drawing, "Their mother seemed to be very isolated, with only neighbors visiting. I don't think she had a family or visited Town, so the children are unlikely to be recognized."

She couldn't help preening like a proud mother when she brought them out and the ladies exclaimed over how well the towheaded pair performed their courtesies. They admired Lynly's quilt as well. The girl beamed when Clare told her she had learned to sew almost as well as her mother, who was one of the best seamstresses in the sewing room.

Elsa produced a package of sweets, and Verity sent the beaming children back to their room.

"Mistress or not, their mother did a fine job of raising them," Clare Huntly declared as the others gathered hats and gloves and said their farewells. "Despite what Meera tells us, I cannot believe anyone meant to kill such lovely children," she whispered to Verity alone.

Verity slapped her hand over her mouth to smother an inappropriate exclamation. Perhaps she had misunderstood? "Meera thinks what?"

Clare lingered behind while the others clattered out. "I shouldn't have said that, but. . . if there's any possibility she might be right, you and Rafe need to know."

"What did Meera say?" Verity asked in terror. She had

complete confidence in the apothecary-physician's knowledge. Meera's advice had been invaluable too many times.

"She only had a few candies to test," Clare warned. "She needs to examine the. . . nanny. . . further. But she thinks those little pills contained opium."

Opium. Verity tried to remember what she knew of opium but it only had to do with laudanum and Chinese pirates. "For putting people to sleep?"

"One candy might have done that," Clare acknowledged. "But a whole tin? Opium overdoses kill. We have no way of knowing if the tin contained three candies or thirty or if all of them contained the drug. We might be scaring ourselves for nothing. They could simply be an apothecary's formula to put distraught children to sleep and meant to be taken only one at a time."

But in Gravesyde, they had learned to look for the worst of human nature. Trying not to shiver, Verity watched the ladies depart, then raced back to be certain the children were safe. If they hadn't already eaten their sweets, she might have taken them away, terrified they'd been poisoned—by *Lady Elsa!* She was losing her mind. How did mothers *do* this?

If the children had been the target of those pills. . . she *definitely* needed to keep strangers away from them. Her instincts had been right from the first.

But the news about the children must be all over the village by now.

In a panic, she sent Rob in search of Rafe and began securing the inn against intruders. Rafe had just strengthened the outside shutters. She'd grown up in a dangerous area of London. She knew how to lock shutters and prevent windows from opening.

Once she had done all she could, she stayed with the children, hiding her fear while helping the girls sew and cut quilt squares while Daniel read to them from his favorite book. In her waistband under her bodice, Verity tucked a knife from the kitchen. She'd brought in a poker from the pub hearth. She pulled her chair in front of the bedchamber door—until Rafe attempted to open it, and she had to move away.

Being the understanding man he was, he admired the quilt, congratulated Daniel on his reading abilities, and left Rob in charge of whittling pegs for clothes hooks, before steering Verity into the hall and closing the door.

"What?" he instantly demanded.

When Verity explained about the opium, he understood at once. Cursing, he pulled her into his embrace, hugging her close until they both calmed to some degree of sensibility.

"I will not believe anyone would deliberately poison young ones too innocent to harm a soul," he stated, as if reassuring himself as well as her.

Verity had had more time to think, and her own experience drove her thoughts down dark pathways. "Daphne has stopped talking for a reason," she reminded him. "Minerva says she was most likely frightened by someone or something, so she has already been harmed. It sounds as if the nanny was ordered to take them to an orphanage, where they'd be lost forever to any family they might have. No one has come looking for any of them. They were meant to disappear."

They were meant to *die*—by opium poisoning and a carriage accident in the dead of night, that no one would investigate.

Someone wanted those two precious children *dead*. Verity had tried and tried to think of any better outcome to all they'd been through, and she couldn't see it. She read a lot. She had a good imagination. She might just be conjuring bogeymen out of whole cloth. But even Clare had assumed the worst.

Rafe rocked her back and forth while he worked through her horrible conclusions. "If you are right, or if it's even one of many possibilities, we need to take them to the manor. We can't guard them here, with strangers going in and out at will."

"I can't abandon them!" she cried, tears crowding her eyes as she thought of sending them away. "They've lost their mother, their home. . . We're all they know."

"I can't take chances with you, either," he said firmly. "You'll go with them. Pack your trunk. Let's settle you at the manor, then I'll figure out how to keep the inn running without you. If scoundrels come looking, I want to be prepared. Where are our guests right now?"

She'd been with the ladies and the children and had no idea. Which was his point. She couldn't be everywhere at once. He waited for her to accept it. A whole host of men roamed the inn and grounds and any one of them could be a killer.

Verity wiped hastily at her tears, her mind racing over all the things she must leave behind and undone. This was to be her first Christmas in her new home, with her new husband. She didn't want to leave them.

She hadn't left her old home when she should have, she knew, but she hated being disrupted from the comfortable routine that made her feel safe in a world gone mad. Rafe shouldn't have to manage everything all on his own. She had staff who needed orders, Kate's children who needed care. . .

"Will anyone really come looking?" she asked in desperation.

Grimly, Rafe shook his head, destroying her hopes. "Minerva and Paul told everyone in Stratford that the children are alive. If we are right about the opium—if anyone wanted them dead— they will know their plans failed and come after them."

Verity wept into Rafe's broad shoulder.

SIXTEEN

BRYDIE

RATHER THAN MIXING MORE BREAD DOUGH, BRYDIE SCRUBBED Willa's kitchen, leaving it tidy for whoever owned the cottage now. She accepted that she couldn't shirk her other duties any longer—

Until Rafe stalked into the kitchen with a scowl as black as a thundercloud. "Is Cooper here?"

Brydie blinked at his harsh tone. "I have no notion. Ask Damien or Paul. They're in the parlor."

"Gather your niece and nephew and take them home, Brydie."

Gaping at the usually gentle giant's curtness, she didn't form a question before he stomped into the front room, slamming the door between them.

Something was very wrong.

And she wasn't leaving until she knew what, not after she'd worked her fingers to the bone, then gone out investigating all day, leaving all her own chores undone.

She wiped her hands on Willa's apron, hung it on a hook, slammed the parlor door open again, and marched into the front room. Startled, the three men glanced up expectantly. Still standing, Rafe glowered, but Paul and Damien rose in respect, acknowledging she was not a servant, especially since she was empty-handed, to their obvious disappointment.

Brydie propped her hands on her hips. "I am not meekly bringing you tea or supper. You can go home for that. If you are plotting, I want to be part of it. I have lived here all my life and know everyone in this village better than *any* of you."

Rafe and Paul seemed dubious. Damien frowned. She gave them a minute to think about it. She could tell when her beloved reached a conclusion he didn't like. His handsome visage wrinkled with displeasure and the sparkle left his eyes. She glared and waited. If he didn't accept her as his equal partner. . . She dared not consider it.

"As much as I detest admitting it, Brydie has a point." Damien glared back and continued unwillingly, "She will not only recognize anyone or anything out of place, she's also capable of defending herself better than most men. Plus, her mind is convoluted enough for two lawyers." He handed her a sheaf of yellowing papers.

Startled, Brydie accepted them. The elegant handwriting had faded with time and was barely legible. She ought to be angry at her fiancé's reluctance, but she understood to some extent. She might not appreciate his male protectiveness, but Damien was just learning to live with others. His family had been a pack of wolves.

"Letters from Willa's cousin, Margie," he explained. "The ones from nearly a decade ago talk about her visit to Bath. Later, she announces her betrothal to a fine young man of good family whom she calls *Mr. Turner*. The letters are brief, presumably because she knows Willa can't read and has to pay the postage. Some of them apparently contained bank notes, which may explain some of Willa's income."

"And?" Picking up a pillow to comfort her fears, Brydie settled in a low rocking chair none of the men would take. It was uncomfortable, but Willa was *dead*. She could suffer a little discomfort to find justice for the baker.

"Our fear may be far-fetched," the curate warned, sitting down again. "The children say their last name is *Turner*, but the woman living in Beanblossom was buried as Peggy Smith, not Margery Turner, Willa's correspondent. Only—Daniel recalls being called 'baterds,' excuse my language. It's a bit of a leap, admittedly. But if the Turner estate believed their mother wasn't married. . . An orphanage or workhouse is where they'd be sent, unless they had family."

Setting aside the pillow, Brydie looked at the letters in bewilderment. The letters said Margery had married a Turner. . . her children couldn't be baseborn, if this was the same family. Then who was Peggy Smith? "And this has what to do with Willa?"

Rafe practically growled. "Oswald tells us that Willa received a letter some months ago asking her to visit someone who was ill. Willa's reply merely indicated she couldn't travel, but someone could come to her, that the place was *theirs*. Oswald can't remember if that's plural or singular."

Damien added, indicating the letters she was holding. "The odd part is, even though Willa saved every letter she ever received—and few of them indicate where the writer resided—we couldn't find that one or any from this past year, except the most recent, from Cooper."

Returning the letters, Brydie vaguely grasped the connection, and her mind nearly boiled with horrible possibilities. She picked up the pillow again and hugged it against her.

Paul confirmed her worst fear. "The children said their mother had written to family, but no one came for them. While still calling them bastards, their nanny claimed to be taking them to their *mother's family.*"

On a road that only led to Gravesyde—where no one knew them, except—Willa? Brydie was glad she hadn't eaten yet. Her stomach churned while she ran all the likelihoods through her head. "So it is possible that the nanny may have been told to take the children to an orphanage, which would be in Birmingham, and given coins for the toll. Instead, she kept the coins and was bringing them to Willa instead?" That was beyond far-fetched. . . but the puzzle pieces almost fit.

"We can't know anyone's intentions," Paul admitted. "But the children say their name is Turner and the neighbors confirm it. Admittedly, their mother wasn't buried as Margery Turner, but the letters Willa received were from Margie. And the one Oswald remembers indicated Margie was ill. It is possible Peggy Smith and Margery Turner are different people. . ."

But unlikely. The children and Mr. Oswald had no reason to lie. There seemed to be only one horrifying conclusion. Brydie simply couldn't accept it easily. "You are saying all the *recent* letters from Margie are missing—presumably stolen from Willa's desk? I assume no thief perused the cellar, which is why you have the old letters. And we have only Oswald's word about the new ones?"

Damien nodded. "Willa's clutter is mostly organized. The boxes in the cellar had letters dated until December of last year. Someone who can't read must memorize what the letters say if they need to find them again, but after a year—Willa most likely carried the old ones down and started collecting the new ones with the new year."

But there would be no new year for her. Brydie bit back anguish at how abruptly life could end. Willa should have had more time. Would she have been a good mother for the orphans? Given her occupation, possibly not, but she never had the chance to find out.

Still angry, Rafe crudely stated their conclusion. "Meera is performing tests, but she's convinced the nanny died of an opium overdose from a tin of candies meant for the children."

In horror, Brydie hugged the pillow and tried not to rock the chair too hard. It was almost too much to comprehend. The monster who had killed Willa might have tried to kill *children*? She wasn't ready to accept that insanity, but safety first. . . "Verity knows this?"

"I've taken her and the orphans up to the manor. They are

setting up beds near the schoolroom with the tutor and the manor's heirs. It's safe, but Verity insists on staying with them. She still has nightmares, and this. . ." Rafe's usually open face mirrored his anger and concern. "I want this. . . brute. . . caught."

And there was the reason for Rafe's fury—fear for his family.

Brydie had little experience in pure evil. She sought logic. Children harmed no one. Willa might have had knowledge someone wanted hidden but children. . . "Surely, Willa's killer will be long gone. He killed Willa and—if I accept this wild theory— believes he's poisoned the children and maybe the nanny. He'd escape as fast as he could. The village is suspicious of strangers. Lingering would be foolhardy."

"Cooper is a stranger," Damien corrected. "Parsons, Willa's neighbor, just arrived. Jasper at the hardware. Even Cratchit, the assistant at Paul's woodshop, is new. We've been bringing in any number of strangers now that the manor is open. And even the manor has guests from London visiting for the holidays. For all we know, Fletch or any of the men who visited Willa could have stolen her letters or tried to poison her family."

Brydie had been comforting herself with believing the killer gone. Damien shattered her illusion. "But *why*, if he found what he wanted?" And even as she said it, she knew the answer.

"Any of them could have heard about the crashed cart and Verity finding the children," Damien said softly, forcing her to understand.

Brydie shut her eyes and shook her head. "It makes no sense. If Willa's killer lingers, it means he didn't find what he was after. But why, by all that is holy, would anyone want to kill two orphans, their nanny, and a recluse who probably never set eyes on them?"

"Two murders and an attempted two more just don't happen in one night without reason," Paul said gently. "And Willa wasn't exactly a recluse. She received and sent letters, entertained gentlemen who brought news of the outside world. Since it appears she may have known the *mother* of those two children—"

"Then Willa may have known their father." Brydie thought that solved part of the mystery, until she followed the thought further. "But he died years ago, if the children are out of blacks. I can understand a brother or greedy relation wanting to claim his estate, but why wait until now? Why not right after Mr. Turner died? And why *kill* children if they're born on the wrong side of the blanket? The heir has nothing to lose."

"We have no way of knowing until we learn who their family is." Damien pointed at the stack of paper she held. "We'll question Cooper some more. You need to sift through all that, see if you can find family names you recognize, other people we might question."

"I've already written our vicar for church records of marriages for a Margery Bartlett and a man named Turner at the approximate time of those letters, but if the marriage took place in Bath, as these letters indicate. . ." Paul sighed. "We need to write more letters."

Brydie frowned in dissatisfaction. "Perhaps what we ought to be doing is inventing new names for the orphans and telling everyone they're Verity's cousins. Do you really want to find who they are if their family is trying to kill them?"

That shut them up.

THURSDAY

DECEMBER 21, 1815

SEVENTEEN

GLANCING AT THE PARISHIONERS HUDDLED INSIDE THEIR COATS IN THE chilly chapel, Minerva decided Willa's funeral had a respectable showing. She didn't need to know how many of the men sitting beside their wives mourned Willa's loss as more than their baker.

Cooper, still looking haggard, at least managed to attend this funeral, if not the one he'd been sent to attend. Damien and Rafe had questioned him last night. He'd confirmed that his mother had written of the death of his cousin Margery Bartlett Turner and asked him to represent the family. He claimed ignorance of nannies or children or even the estate. The funeral had been over by the time he arrived in Stratford at noon. The gravediggers knew nothing. So he'd simply gone on to Willa's. Since the sun set early at this time of year, he'd arrived well after dark, expecting her to let him know if there was more to be done.

The killer must have arrived first.

As a baker, Willa quite likely retired when darkness fell, if she wasn't entertaining. . . clients.

Cooper hadn't seen the buggy, knew nothing of his cousin's children, and had been out of the country at the time of Margery's marriage. Minerva thought she and Brydie might dig a little deeper, but it would be good to have answers to their letters first. She continued studying the congregation.

The women who relied on Willa's baked goods lined a few of the benches. Brydie and Damien were there, along with Major Fletcher and Rafe. Patience and her husband attended, because Patience always brought flowers and sat in on her brother's services, and Henri drove the cart that would carry the coffin to the cemetery.

The poor, unnamed nanny would be buried, unmourned, in a pauper's grave at the same time. The manor couldn't keep a body in the crypt until someone identified it.

Minerva had hoped some of the single men who had knocked on Willa's back door might put in an appearance at the chapel so they might question them, but that was a little too much to ask. At least Fletch had the manners to pay his respects.

Paul spoke of Willa's contributions to the community and her life without close family and sermonized a bit about community being family, but he kept it short. Minerva's perceptive husband would note any strangers at the cemetery, as would Rafe.

As the men trudged up the manor hill from the chapel to tend to the business of burying the dead in the former priory's grave-yard, Minerva and Brydie detoured to the manor.

Instead of letting them slip up the servants' stairs for the attic schoolroom, the tall, barrel-chested butler marched them to the main marble stairway. Minerva had lived here for months and knew her way around. She wasn't arguing with Quincy about propriety. He and his staff were the guardians who kept the inhabitants safe.

A trio of laughing male guests emerged from the former ballroom as they passed. Wearing country tweeds and leather breeches worth more than most villagers earned in a year, they paid no attention to Brydie and Minerva in their unadorned church attire. Minerva preferred anonymity. Brydie charged up the stairs without even noticing.

They found Verity in the new schoolroom with Mr. Birdwhistle, the manor's handsome tutor. A former attic storeroom, the space wouldn't be opened for a schoolroom until after the first of the year. It didn't yet have much in the way of desks, but chairs and benches had been acquired. Lovely windows overlooking the drive below would let in air once the weather warmed. A teacher's desk had been positioned with a large chalkboard on the wall behind it—far better than the pub where Verity had been teaching. Books filled the shelves. The one advantage Gravesyde had was books, lots of them.

The four boys, Daniel, Brydie's nephew, and the two eight-year-old earl's heirs, were arranging furniture in proper rows.

Daphne and Brydie's niece had opted out of furniture pushing and were sitting on the floor by the bookcase, evidently hunting for books with pictures. They glanced up with interest when Minerva and Brydie entered, but noting they carried nothing exciting, returned to the books.

Verity led Minerva and Brydie away from the activity and into Mr. Birdwhistle's smaller schoolroom where they had privacy. "Any news?"

Minerva shook her head. "Other than Cooper, none of our newcomers attended the service. We'll have to find some other way of questioning them. We miss your ability to engage people who visit the inn."

Verity turned anxiously to Brydie, who made a wry face as she explained, "I've been reading through Margery's letters to Willa. The ones from this past year have disappeared. The most recent we can find occasionally reference Margery's parents in the Americas. The really old ones mention aunts in Bath. Margery calls them Bee and Boo, so one assumes Willa knew them. We have no notion of their family names or where they are now. Margery didn't reference them again after she married and left their home nearly ten years ago."

"Paul is writing the vicar in Bath to have him search the registry for the marriage, but we can't trace a *Bee* or *Boo*. If Willa knew them, then perhaps Mr. Cooper does. The men didn't ask." Minerva produced a notebook she kept her notes and tasks in. "What we need to do is start a list of questions we must ask the people who knew Willa, or might have known her, and the strangers who arrived about the time she died."

"You don't think Willa's killer has left?" Verity asked worriedly. "Surely, he would not stay to be caught."

Minerva examined the schoolroom tables, noting only slates scribbled with unfathomable sums. Her notebook would have to suffice. "The men fear the killer wants something and may not have achieved it. If Willa's death is related to the death of the nanny. . ."

Looking very pale but determined, Verity had apparently reached the same conclusions. She retrieved paper from a shelf and sat down at a student desk. "Did this Margery mention any names after she married? People who visited?"

"There were fewer letters once she married, mostly mentioning excitement at setting up her own household, at learning she was to have a child, and worry over her husband when he left for war." Brydie paced the room, examining the view from the windows. "If Margery had visitors, Willa probably didn't know them. She occasionally asked for recipes, although how Willa would have sent them, I don't know. We need to have the recipe book copied. Perhaps we could sell copies to raise funds for the chapel."

"Concentrate, Brydie." Minerva settled in the small chair across from Verity. "What questions do we need to be asking and to whom? And how?"

Minerva had a high respect for Verity's astuteness—or cynicism. The former sailor's daughter had spent a lifetime observing people. She might be quiet and ladylike, but she understood human nature better than most.

"We should probably give the list of questions to Rafe and not try to ask them ourselves," Verity suggested. "We really can't be talking to people like the hardware clerk or a chicken thief. And who wants to volunteer to question Fletch?"

Brydie laughed and continued exploring the schoolroom. "Fletch just walks away. Even Rafe can't question him. We ought to have my sister do it. No one can be impolite to Kate."

Verity cleared her throat to catch Brydie's wandering attention. The innkeeper's wife generally maintained a proper decorum, with her golden-brown hair brushed into a tight chignon and her good broadcloth gowns topped with fine linen and pinned with brooches. Since Verity had come into her inheritance, her wardrobe had been helping keep Lavender's sewing ladies employed.

But Minerva had seen the polite lady in full warrior mode. Long lashes concealed a militant gleam now.

"Kate and I have spoken," Verity admitted. "She agrees it might be unwise to have Lynly and Rob at the inn, but with Christmas and Boxing Day on Monday and Tuesday, school won't start for over a week."

What else had she and Brydie's older sister spoken of? Fletch? Minerva waited.

Brydie paced, wearing a worried frown. "Kate needs to work. She's helping Lavender sew new gowns for several of the ladies for the festivities. Thank you for taking her children while we attended the funeral, but I *told* her I'd look after them. Only, if I keep them home, there is no one to watch the inn while Rafe investigates."

Ah, now it became clear. Minerva enjoyed it when she didn't have to be the one manipulating. She watched Verity expectantly. The lady had obviously been plotting here in her lonely tower.

"Kate has suggested that she might do her sewing at the inn, if I will look after the children here. And as you say, few men dare ignore Kate. She might not be large, but she could intimidate a queen, if required."

Minerva wondered how a quiet, polite woman like Kate Morgan had developed that defiance, but she was a Calhoun, like

Brydie. There might be little physical resemblance, but upbringing would tell. They had been the daughters of a wealthy squire, raised to take a role in the community. Older than Brydie, Kate had quietly raised her children through turbulent times. Having recently cast off her widow's weeds, she was apparently ready to start taking her place in the village.

"For the children, for *any* children, my sister will cut off noses if necessary." Unable to settle into the schoolroom's small chairs, Brydie halted her pacing to think about it. "Kate needs to take the children home at night to feed the animals and fix meals. Arthur cannot be left to roam alone and should go with her. But I—"

"Don't say it until you talk with Damien," Minerva warned. "He will not like you staying in town at night, unchaperoned."

"I will have to be running the back of the inn all day. Kate can't be in the kitchen and sewing gowns at the same time," Brydie remonstrated. "She can greet people at the desk, tell the staff what to do, but if Rafe is out and about, someone needs to take charge of the kitchen and pub. And night is when working men need their meals, if Rafe is to have an operating pub."

"Let's take one thing at a time," Minerva suggested. "What questions do we need to ask and to whom? I can question the ladies helping decorate the chapel and plan Christmas services, but how much will they know?"

Verity turned a page in her papers. "I have started a list of questions. I want this villain caught and those poor orphans safe. I am not convinced finding their family will help in either case, but we need answers."

"First, we have to find out where everyone was the night Willa died, and find witnesses to confirm their claims." Minerva already knew what needed asking. She doubted they'd gather satisfactory answers. She'd been through this before. But collecting all the stray pieces eventually painted a picture.

"It would be good to know where they were in the days *before* the buggy crashed," Verity added. "The 'bad man' Danny mentions was in Beanblossom then."

"We must find the servants from Beanblossom. I have utterly no idea how we do that." Minerva jotted another note.

"Have the solicitor's clerk look into it," Brydie suggested. "I'll ask Damien to inform Mr. Browning's office that they should be more responsible for the estate and the children, now that we have some confirmation of their identities. Perhaps, as a lawyer, Damien can pry the name of the family or trust from him."

They had their battle lines drawn and their ammunition prepared by the time the men returned from the cemetery.

"If we're all up here, who's minding the inn?" Minerva asked, a little belatedly, as they all trudged down the manor drive back to the village.

"Staff," Rafe growled. "No one comes mid-morning unless they rode out before dawn. Not that we have guests arriving at noon, either. Takes time for word to spread that we're open."

"And word won't spread until the post runs regular." Fletch had gone to the funeral instead of Stratford this morning.

"Mr. Oswald can't be expected to provide post boys and horses." Carrying her large sewing basket, Kate had no difficulty keeping up, even if she was half a foot shorter than Brydie. They'd released her from the sewing room to help at the inn. "How long will it take to repair the bridge?"

Minerva nudged her husband to take the basket since the other men didn't offer. Kate thanked Paul politely but held onto it. Minerva resisted the urge to see what Kate kept in there.

"Too long, if we want answers to our questions." Impolitely, Fletch snatched the basket and strode down the drive with long lopes, leaving everyone behind.

"We need to find more clocks for him to repair," Rafe observed. "Riding for the post isn't helping."

"I don't suppose Brydie could be using your ovens to bake bread while she's watching over the inn and keeping Major Fletcher from offending guests?" Minerva knew she asked too much, but she couldn't keep frying bread in the mornings. "I do not seem to have found time to learn."

"Your skillet bread is excellent, my dear," Paul said generously. "I do not expect you to do everything, especially with the holidays."

"Rafe only has the hearth oven. It's practically medieval and not made for producing large quantities, especially if he means to cook anything else. We must catch a killer and find out who owns Willa's cottage so we can look for a new baker." Brydie restrained her impatient long strides to accommodate Minerva and Kate.

"If the Bartletts owned the cottage, and Margery Turner was their only daughter, then it's possible the orphans own it." Damien adjusted Brydie's cloak hood more warmly against the chilly December wind. "Unless Cooper has been named Bartlett's successor. Has anyone written to see if the Bartletts are still alive?"

"We have," Minerva said. "But it will be weeks, if not months, before we have any response. Cooper is family, he's an adult, so surely he can make decisions in the interim?"

Except Brydie was the only baker they knew, and she'd be watching over the inn. Minerva was almost desperate enough to offer to take her place, but a curate's wife had more important duties. Paul would not appreciate indulging their need for bread over his parishioners.

"I'll have a word with Cooper," Damien suggested. "He's not been doing anything useful that I can see."

Fletch's bellows from the inn sent them all racing down the drive.

EIGHTEEN

A SPEW OF UNINTELLIGIBLE CURSES EMERGED FROM THE INN, NOT IN just Fletch's baritone.

As Brydie raced into the muddy inn yard, Damien attempted to restrain her, but she dodged his protective embrace and strode for the open door, calling over her shoulder, "Have you never heard a tantrum before? We should send Kate in. It will be amusing."

Brydie checked to see her shorter sister lagging only slightly behind Rafe. Minerva and Paul had slowed down, though, presumably so as not to sully their ears.

"We need to enforce the cursing fines," Kate declared, not hesitating but marching ahead of the laggards, with Rafe on her heels. "If Arthur is anywhere within hearing, I'll have that lout's tonsils out."

Brydie snickered and let her older, exceedingly capable, sister proceed inside. "You see?" she whispered to her bewildered intended. "She is not a little girl any longer."

The three of them, along with Damien's brother, had grown up together. Only recently returned to Gravesyde, Damien hadn't spent much time with busy Kate. He was still adjusting to the fact that Brydie was no longer the naïve adolescent he'd once left behind.

"*Neither* of you are little girls," he agreed, which didn't stop him from following her. "That still doesn't mean you have to do your own fighting."

"Maybe we'll learn to send the pawns ahead," she laughed. "But right now, with a killer on the loose, we're too confused, angry, and terrified to be logical."

"I think we'll be on our way," Paul called from the yard. "We have a list of tasks waiting and the inn is in good hands." He turned Minerva around and steered her toward the parsonage. Staying out of a brawl was probably a wise decision on the curate's part.

Reluctantly, Damien took Brydie's elbow and followed Kate inside.

In the lobby, Fletch bunched his fists and glowered thunderously, but he snapped his mouth closed when Kate snatched up the basket he'd taken from her.

"The fine for cursing is a copper per word, gentlemen. You can put your coin on the counter where the bailiff can collect it. I think by now, both of you must owe a shilling. This isn't a sailing ship." Kate glared at both men.

From her observation, Brydie decided neither of them appeared to be gentlemen in any sense of the word. Fletch had at least cleaned up a bit for the funeral. His opponent, with his back to the door, appeared to be a ruffian in a worn coat, wilted linen, and overlong black hair.

In the sudden quiet, Rafe stalked to the desk, crossed his arms, and glared, waiting for the coins to be deposited on the counter. Brydie wished Verity were here. She'd know how to handle this brangle in a proper manner.

But when the stranger grumbled and turned to depart, she gasped at the familiar visage. "Parsons! The chicken thief!"

Pushing Brydie behind him, Damien swung, punching the thief in the jaw before Brydie had a chance to kick Parsons' shins. The thief staggered but didn't fall.

Kate swung her sewing basket at the back of his head. Parsons dropped to his knees. Fletch guffawed.

Which had everyone turning to him in amazement. He never laughed.

"They's my sister's chickens. I didn't steal nothin'!" Parsons shouted, staying on the floor rather than be hit again.

"You nearly strangled me," Brydie retorted, unable to kick his shins while he kneeled.

He'd shaved the worst of his heavy black stubble, but his dark hair still straggled over his graying linen. He'd apparently been sleeping in his wrinkled clothes. He didn't stink, at least, so he must have washed.

Brydie really hadn't needed to be defended or avenged, but having the rotter on his knees soothed her savage response to his appearance in public.

With his back to the counter, Rafe rested his elbows on the polished old wood and studied the newcomer. "I went looking for you the other day. Were you off stealing more chickens? Threatening another woman?"

Brydie tugged Damien's arm and whispered, "He was stealing *Willa's* chickens. Is he claiming to be *her* brother?"

And that's when she realized— In the bright light of day, Parsons looked almost exactly like Willa: broad, square chin, nearly black eyes with thick lashes, coarse black hair. Willa, of course, had been voluptuous, but she'd been of similar height, raw-boned, and broad-shouldered, just like the thief.

"You said you didn't know Willa!" Brydie cried before anyone else worked it out. They were all newcomers and hadn't known Willa well—except Fletch, of course, who was looking a bit smug.

"You didn't ask! Besides, my sister's name's Rose! I don't know no Willa." Parsons stood again, out of Damien's reach, and regarded them warily. "Ain't seen Rose since she started growin' her bubbies."

Brydie winced.

"But you knew they were her chickens?" Damien asked in his courtroom voice of disapproval.

Fair point. Brydie's mind raced through all the questions they'd been gathering, but this connection threw out everything they'd assumed about Willa.

Parsons twisted his hat nervously, presumably seeking the right words. "She always raised them cackling pullets. Old Bartlett said he'd let her take them with her after Ma died and she'd come to live here. Reckoned if that were still his place, they's hers. But with all the fancy folk over there, I stayed out of the way."

"Fancy folk?" Brydie laughed, shaking out her dull wool skirt. "Where have you been that we look *fancy*?"

"New South Wales." He backed warily toward the door. "I only stole what Ma needed, but I was young and stupid and got caught."

Brydie wanted to believe him. The penalty for first offenders was transportation if they stole even a shilling. But she disliked his showing up now.

"Willa said she had a thief for a brother." Fletch removed the basket from Kate again, this time hiding it behind the counter. "He might be telling the truth. I caught him harassing Miss Butler, demanding to see whoever's in charge."

Kate sent Brydie a meaningful look. "We should check on the staff, reassure them we're not being invaded by barbarians."

Brydie smiled and took Damien's arm, resisting her sister's order. "Tell them I shall be there shortly, as soon as I settle everyone in the pub with a mug of ale. They should start luncheon. I have a few questions first."

"Brydie. . ." Damien said warningly.

"It was *my* neck he throttled. I understand now that he may have learned to live rough, but I will not be left out. We need information." She dropped his arm and strode for the pub when he did not immediately follow her lead. Two strong characters. . . She and Damien had to learn how to act together, if they meant to marry.

"I'll mind the counter." Fletch returned to his usual surly self. "Convicts also learn to lie, and I'll not be hearing his tall tales. Willa deserved better."

Fletch actually talking— Brydie liked him better when he was silent. In the pub, she slid behind the bar and brought down mugs so Rafe could draw ale. He was experimenting with making his own and she didn't know one barrel from another.

"You said you were living in your granny's house. Is that true?" Waiting until Parsons took a seat, Damien took the mug Rafe handed him and sipped.

"Oncet was hers, long time ago. Didn't look like no one there. Didn't see no reason not to use it. Thought maybe old man Bartlett bought it for Rose when granny passed." Parsons warily accepted the drink handed him.

"When did you get here?" Rafe didn't offer Brydie a drink but glanced toward the kitchen door. He'd be wanting to oversee dinner preparations.

"Only day a'fore you brought me food." Parsons bowed awkwardly at Brydie. "Mighty appreciative. I hoped Rose would feed me, help me find work."

"But you didn't visit her." Brydie wasn't ready to forgive him for his shocking assault on her person. He may have learned to survive by attacking first, but he shouldn't have been stealing chickens.

"Like I said, there was gentry all about. I thought I'd catch Rose at the henhouse of a morning." He glared at her. "Then you showed up."

"Decent folk knock on doors, not lurk in henhouses. You're back in civilization now. You have to behave civilly." Brydie opened the kitchen door and noted with relief that Kate had the ladies assembling a cold collation. Expecting hot food out of the new staff was asking too much. They might learn to take initiative in time but not yet.

"You haven't seen Willa since she was a young girl? Twenty, thirty years?" Damien asked, taking his mug to a table. "Did you write to her, let her know you were coming?"

"I don't write. She don't read. What's the point? Either she takes me in or she don't." He took a defiant drag on his ale.

Parsons passed that little test, Brydie thought. But she didn't doubt he was related to Willa. In a closely-knit rural village of blue-eyed blonds and red-haired Irish, the Willoughby's square faces, black eyes, and coarse hair stood out. "What brings you here now?"

He shrugged uncomfortably in his ill-fitting coat. "Earned enough to take sail home from that hellhole, but oncet I got here, couldn't find a place to hire me." He flashed the branded hand exposing his conviction. "I thought maybe I could help Rose, if the old man weren't still around."

"Bartlett?" Rafe asked. "He's your uncle?"

"Rose's uncle. We share a ma, not a pa. He hates my guts, says I'm a scoundrel. But if nobody gives me a job, how'm I supposed to eat? Not all of us was born well equipt." Parsons didn't even look up. Defeated, he sipped his ale.

"You know we just buried Miss Willoughby?" Brydie was tired of skirting around the subject. She was hungry and wanted to be in the kitchen.

"I worked that out when that fine fellow in t'other room tried to punch me for not attendin' her funeral. Unless you want to throw me in a cell for bein' ignorant, I guess I'll just be movin' on."

"Not if we arrest you for killing her." Rafe swigged his ale.

Terrified, Parsons heaved up from the table.

Damien shoved him back down. "Or you can stay here and help us find out who did. Do you know a Geoffrey Cooper?"

This was one of those times when Brydie knew she and Damien were meant to be together. Her cautious heart filled with love, and knowing the interrogation was in good hands, she sailed off to help Kate direct the kitchen ladies in preparing luncheon.

NINETEEN

AT THE END OF A LONG, MISERABLE DAY, RAFE DRAGGED A CHAIR
from the pub to set before the dying embers of the lobby fire. He
needed a few good leather chairs here, like the ones in the manor.
He didn't know if he'd ever be able to afford even third-hand
ones. Dreaming of a fancy posting-inn wasn't the same as
building one from the bottom up.

He desperately missed Verity's wise assurances.

They'd allowed Parsons to stay at the inn with the promise of
finding him work in the morning—if only to keep him around for
questioning. Rafe had no idea if that was the right thing to do, but
Brydie hadn't pressed charges.

Fletch had left to pick up the post in Stratford. Kate had taken
her children and Brydie home. Damien was still dragging shelves
and tables into a room down the east hall, setting up his office on
the ground-floor. With more rooms than guests, the inn didn't
need ladies' parlors or private dining or whatever the damned
room had once been. The bloody inn was a village all on its own.

He'd been mad to invest all his earnings in a sprawling,
ramshackle, medieval barn. With Verity at his side, it had made

sense. He'd wanted Verity. She'd wanted a home. She'd been raised in a huge mansion and deserved better than a cottage. So he'd given her a barn. And she'd quite rightfully taken the first opportunity offered to move into the manor.

All those years on his own and now he longed for the company of a banty hen of a *lady*. He wanted to hear her clucking about this and that. Worse, he wanted to know what the little imps were equal to. In his years of fighting across the Continent, he'd never given children any thought, but now she'd put the notion in his head, he could imagine the inn full of little gingers raising a ruckus. And a pair of towheads, too, he supposed, if no one claimed them. They'd have a heritage to be proud of one day, if he made the inn work.

But this bailiff business. . . He wasn't cut out for it. He wanted to be up at the manor, protecting his wife and the children. He didn't want to be suspecting men of being monsters. He was a soldier. He was aware that, given good reason, *all* men were monsters, including himself. He resented the reminder.

Carrying his heavy greatcoat, his new tenant emerged from the east hall, looking as weary as Rafe felt. "You could lock up for the night," Damien suggested. "It's unlikely you'll have anyone arriving after dark."

"Can't leave the maids alone. Can't go up to my wife. What else can I do? I'd hire a night clerk, but who can I trust? Parsons is a filching cove. I can't believe a word he says."

They'd interviewed Cooper again, introduced him to Parsons, but they'd learned almost nothing. Neither of the men claimed to know each other, which made sense, Rafe supposed. Cooper was related to Bartlett, not Willa. She'd just been an orphan Bartlett had taken in for his wife's sake. Neither man claimed to know much of Margery Bartlett. They needed to question every damned man in the village.

Fletch had not been helpful either. Rafe suspected his lonely partner had hoped to persuade Willa to make him exclusive. She evidently wasn't the type. From what Rafe had learned from

Parsons, Willa had learned the oldest trade from her mother. Baking, she must have learned from the Bartletts. A tart baking tarts made utter sense for Gravesyde, where everyone had multiple employments.

Rafe sighed and sprawled deeper in his chair. "Cooper is a deuced slippery fellow. How can he not know anything of his family?"

"A gentleman generally does not use names like Bee and Boo to address ladies, so we can't expect him to understand the reference in Margery's letters. And they may be on the mother's side of the family, if they're related at all." Damien shrugged into his caped coat. The wind was freezing at this hour.

"We can hope Fletch will return with a few answers in the morning post. If he doesn't, I'll ride to Stratford, see if I can bully information out of Browning." Damien donned his hat. "He knows the Turner estate. He can tell us who might benefit from the children disappearing."

"Except he claimed to know nothing of the children, and even if he did, I can't arrest some toff in London." Rafe swung his feet down from the fender. He'd have to add expensive coal if he meant to keep the fire burning.

"But now that the Uptons have announced to the world that the children are still alive, anyone interested will know. Word has reached London and possibly even Bath. Perhaps Bee or Boo will show up," Damien suggested.

Rafe grimaced and took a shovel to the coal bucket. "What are the chances a killer will proclaim his arrival by stopping here when we have an entire village of empty cottages to hide in?"

"If the culprit isn't local, it will depend on who they send—a criminal or a respectable sort." Damien glanced out the mullioned window. "Speak of the devil, that might be them now. There's a proper *carriage* coming down the road—lanterns and driver."

"Respectable company or killers?" Rafe stirred the fire, doffed the greatcoat he'd been huddling inside to keep warm, and straightened his neckcloth. "This is Gravesyde. I know the answer to that."

"Killers in a barouche? Unlikely. The manor has guests for the holidays. . ." Damien grimaced as he watched the window. "Any weapons on you?"

Rafe sighed. And here he'd thought life would be easy once he left the army. "Shotgun under the counter. Sturdy fire irons." He wielded the poker to stir the coal. "An innkeeper carrying a sword is not a welcoming sight."

"I'll linger in the pub. I have a pistol, sword, *and* knife." Damien lit a lantern from the counter and carried it into the empty pub.

An illusion of company might deter a villain from storming the lobby, but Rafe had the notion that guests arriving in a fancy carriage didn't intend an armed raid. Still, he was glad the children weren't here.

One of the lads ran out to the horses. Priory Manor's stalls often overflowed, so they usually kept a well-trained man or two at the inn's nearly-empty stable. It had room for both horses and servants. The fellows worked for tips and food and a roof over their heads.

Rafe carried a lantern to the door. A barouche ought to have a footman, but it was the driver who climbed down to let out two gentlemen passengers.

For once, Rafe thought he might be ahead of the game. "Damien, would you mind hauling Parsons out and smartening him up a bit? He can fetch and carry. Let's throw some oil on the fire and see if any of them know each other."

He could hear Damien snort before he strode off to dig out Parsons. Rafe liked keeping an eye on troublemakers. In the army, they sometimes straightened out. And if they didn't. . . well, he knew how to squash them.

Watching his fancy new guests, Rafe decided the damned inn needed a name. He and Verity had discussed it but never made a decision. Still, he'd grown up with an excellent example and knew how a good innkeeper behaved. He stepped out with his lantern. "Welcome to Wycliffe Inn, gentlemen." That name didn't quite suit now that the earl's title was retired, but it would work for now.

"I hope we have not arrived too late for a room and a bit of supper." The younger, more slender man spoke first. He wore a decent but inexpensive cloak and hat—not the barouche's owner.

"Cold night for travel. Not many on the road, so we have room. Visiting for the holiday?" Rafe gestured for the ostler to unhitch the animals and let the driver unload the baggage. Only two valises—his guests weren't here for long.

"Business." The second passenger was older, bulkier but not better dressed. Odd. When he removed his hat, he revealed a balding head with a few greasy strands of blond hair combed over it.

Parsons stumbled out, his thick black hair pulled back in a string, his linen hastily tied. Rafe gestured at the bags. "If you'll carry those up to the first rooms at the top of the stairs, I'll see about mustering up some supper."

Wearing his usual disgruntled expression, Parsons did as told. A convict knew how to take orders. Rafe prayed the filching cove didn't open the bags and search the contents. He'd meant to run a respectable inn. The likelihood grew slimmer every day. He should hire lazy Cooper as clerk and give up the dream.

The passengers followed Rafe inside and warmed themselves at the hearth. Decent-looking fellows, Rafe concluded, but not gentry.

"If you'll sign yourselves in here, I'll give you the keys. It's a shilling a room per night, breakfast included. If you want ale, that's extra. We carry only the best." Rafe pushed the guest log toward them.

The younger man signed them in and set a small purse on the counter. "Mr. Browning says you run a respectable house. I'll trust you to take what you need and return the rest when we leave."

Interesting. The man couldn't count coins? Or thought Rafe

might keep the purse from his companion? Rafe took what he needed, put the coins in his pocket, then locked the purse in a box nailed under the counter.

Browning most likely owned the barouche. "The solicitor in Stratford? He sent you?" Rafe checked the register—Dryden and Elton. *Elton.* Hadn't the curate mentioned an Elton? He tried to recall while listening to his guests.

"He did. I'm Dryden, his clerk. A Mr. and Mrs. Upton brought a sketch to our office of a woman who died in a carriage mishap?" Dryden shed his cloak, revealing a decent coat and trousers, although not tailored or good quality.

"We buried her today. Very sad. Do you have a name for her?" Rafe heard Damien stirring the hearth in the pub. The man might be a wealthy landowner, but he'd earned his living on the road. He knew what needed doing.

"The sketch looked like my sister, Mary Elton," the larger, older man said.

Fat jowls sporting a grizzled beard, Elton didn't remove his cloak to reveal his attire, but his neckcloth was properly tied and clean. The "nanny" hadn't been exactly gentry, either, from the looks of what remained of her—although she'd had black hair, not blond. For Verity's sake, Rafe wanted to prove he lied, but looks alone wouldn't do it.

"I'm sorry," Rafe said honestly. "We had no way of identifying her." He couldn't say she died of opium poisoning. He was basically an honest man but he didn't have to flap his tongue. No sense in letting a killer know that they suspected murder.

"The children are too young to know their nanny's name?" Dryden asked sympathetically.

And now Rafe remembered. . . the children had said their father had sent *Elton.* Elton had called them *bastards.*

Shaken now that he faced the first danger to those beautiful children, Rafe was relieved when Damien stepped out of the pub as if he were a departing customer. A smooth-talking lawyer knew how to finesse this conversation.

"The children?" Damien asked, distracting the pair. He swept off his hat and bowed. "Damien Sutter, at your service."

The clerk bowed. "George Dryden, sir. Mr. Browning has mentioned your name. I have a letter for you." He produced a missive from his coat pocket. "He says you've made inquiries about Miss Smith's estate?"

"Mrs. Turner's estate," Damien corrected with authority as he hastily scanned the letter in the dim light. "Her parents, unfortunately, are in Virginia, and cannot be easily reached to verify her marital status." He tucked the letter into his coat and turned to the second man.

Rafe had to admire how Damien smoothly directed, distracted, and twisted what little they knew into plausibility.

"And you are? A trifle late for traveling. Have you come from Stratford?" Damien shoved his greatcoat back by putting his fists on his hips in an intimidating stance that revealed his tailored frockcoat, silk waistcoat, and buff trousers, every inch a London gentleman.

"James Elton, sir," the older man said gruffly, shying backward into the shadows. "I come too late for my sister, but I'll be takin' her children with me. She would have wanted that."

"She had children with her?" Somehow, Damien arranged to look shocked. "Upon my word, I did not know that. Do you think they're lying dead in the ditch like your sister? It wasn't a pretty sight. Animals are hungry this time of year."

That was mean, and disgusting, but if it protected the babes. . . Rafe didn't know whether to laugh or gag at the unhappy faces his guests pulled.

But instead of expressing concern for his sister or her children, Elton regained his composure and glowered. "We was told there was two lost childern. That'd be my sister's babbies."

Rafe wanted to hide in the kitchen, prepare food as he was brought up to do. But he had to witness whatever Damien told them, so he could give an honest reply if asked.

"Well, no," Damien said, returning the tall hat to his golden-brown locks, tilting it stylishly. "The physician said the driver of the carriage was well past child-bearing age. You may have come all this way for nothing. Sorry, gentlemen." He bowed and glanced at the clerk. "I'll see you in the morning?"

"Certainly, sir." Dryden spoke politely, as if his companion weren't turning purple with rage.

"Them babbies were hers!" Elton shouted as Damien stepped into the night.

Taking Damien's indifference as example, Rafe gestured toward the pub. "If you'll have a seat, gentlemen, I'll bring you a cold collation and ale shortly." Pretending to be completely ignorant of the conversation or children, Rafe strode toward the kitchen.

Leaving Elton howling his outrage.

The man had claimed his sister's name was Elton, like his own. She hadn't been married then, and she'd been too old to have children that age. The man was a liar. So who was that poor woman?

Rafe feared this was the Elton who had worked at Beanblossom and terrorized the children.

How the hell did he interrogate him when he couldn't arrest him for lying?

TWENTY

IN THE ROCKING CHAIR THE KIND LADIES OF THE MANOR HAD provided, Verity held a weepy, tired Daphne. Daniel sat propped against pillows on his cot, a lamp shining on the book he struggled to read.

The pair had been happy enough playing with the other children in the attic, but now that night had arrived—they lived with monsters in their heads.

Verity knew monsters. They looked like normal people. Sometimes, they even pretended to be kind. And then they tore apart your home and tried to kill you. She never wanted these two to understand that.

But, at some point, they might have to ask the children to identify suspects. Right now, Rafe didn't know enough to risk exposing them to killers.

"You read very well, Daniel. Your teacher must be proud of you." Verity lifted the sleepy little girl to her cot, snuggling her rabbit and doll on the pillow beside her.

"He said I could do better if I practice more." Even the boy sounded tired and discouraged. "Will I go back to school?"

He asked this at least once a day. School was obviously important to him.

"You will, I promise, although I may be your teacher until Mr. Birdwhistle says you're ready to study with Oliver and Davy. Do you like him?" The tutor was younger than Verity, fresh out of university, but he had blended his exceptionally brilliant students with the rambunctious Morgan children and the quiet orphans with easy assurance.

"He's nicer than Mr. Clapper. He said I didn't have to learn Latin if I don't want to." Daniel put down his book and snuggled under his covers when Verity kissed him good night.

"I like him too. We'll decide what you should study after Christmas. I'll be in the front room, if you need anything. If Daphne wakes up crying, you can tell me, all right?"

He nodded, and she turned off the lamp and slipped out.

They'd chosen the divided baggage room across the corridor from the schoolroom for their bedchambers. The interior room had no windows and only the one entrance. Servants had been redirected to haul guest trunks to the other attic at the back of the manor. Verity had set up a cot for herself in front of the only entrance to the chambers. It wasn't luxury by any means. The attics were freezing. But without exterior walls, no drafts reached them.

It was too early for her to sleep. She missed Rafe fiercely. After spending so much of her life alone, she craved company. She could talk to Rafe, and he'd understand her fears. He'd suffered a hard life as well.

The young university man had led a pampered, protected life, she could tell. But he was smart and understood the old earl's odd, mostly silent heirs better than most would. Should she try to talk with him?

Deciding to take another look at her new schoolroom, perhaps find a book to read from the selection they'd carried up here from her library and the earl's, she carried a candle into the main attic corridor. The manor's original nursery and schoolroom were across the hall—spacious, with windows overlooking the drive. Mr. Birdwhistle would teach the more educated students there.

As a woman, Verity wasn't formally trained as a teacher. She'd only had a governess. But she knew how to introduce the younger ones to letters and numbers. The village had plenty of need for that. It was very forward-thinking of the manor gentry to encourage literacy. And the sewing ladies knew their children had a place to go while they worked.

Deciding not to disturb the tutor in his quarters, she turned toward the new schoolroom. It had once stored furniture too good to throw away. The inn had benefitted from that frugality. An earl's castoffs were far finer than anything Rafe and Fletch could afford. And removing the furniture had opened up the lovely area for the village children. She couldn't wait to teach here.

The scraping of wood on wood startled her. The doors along this corridor were closed. She had only her bed candle with her. The flickering light didn't reach the front hall. They had closed the schoolroom door, hadn't they? The day had been so hectic. . .

It was ridiculous to be so afraid. The manor was full of gentry and their servants. No monster would look for the children here. They were perfectly safe. Where was her courage?

Hiding in an alley watching her home explode.

That monster was dead. She needn't fear him any longer.

A light appeared at the far end of the corridor, to the left of the new schoolroom. Service stairs, she remembered. Until they'd been redirected, the footmen had carried luggage up from the portico entrance using that staircase. Would they do so at this hour, even if they'd forgotten the baggage room had been moved?

Perhaps it was just Mr. Birdwhistle returning from supper? Would he be so secretive? The intruder appeared to be casting his light about, as if unfamiliar with the attics. One of the manor guests?

At which point, she panicked and scratched at the tutor's door. He appeared at once, his linen untied and his coat off but otherwise respectable in waistcoat, trousers, and slippers. He glanced at her and reading her fear, questioned wordlessly.

Verity nodded in the direction of the flickering shadows. His eyes widened, understanding at once. He had two young heirs to protect.

Holding a darkened lantern, he followed her out, securing the door and the heirs with a key. Verity needed a key for her treasures as well. She'd ask in the morning.

The tutor gestured for her to block this passage, where the children slept, while he slipped down to the servant's hall and cut off the staircase exit.

She'd done far worse than confronting intruders in the not-so-distant past. Waiting until he was position to reach the exit, she lifted her candle and strode briskly down the main passage, practically shoving the flame in the prowler's face so he wouldn't notice Mr. Birdwhistle.

In the dim light, she didn't recognize the intruder. She smothered panic by accepting that she couldn't possibly know all the manor servants. He wasn't wearing a footman's livery, but those weren't the tailored clothes of a gentleman.

"And you are?" she demanded haughtily, as if she were the lady of the manor she no longer owned.

He stumbled and lowered his flame so she couldn't see more of his face than shadows. "Just a valet, ma'am, looking for my master's trunk."

"Then you should have taken the stairs in the servants' wing," Mr. Birdwhistle said from behind, opening his lantern, causing the man to swing around. "These are private quarters."

In the tutor's brighter light, Verity caught a glimpse of a haughty Roman nose, fleshy lips, the hint of sideburns. A former soldier? The accent hinted at Irish but had enough polish not to stand out. He just might be a valet who had refined his speech to earn his position.

"Sorry, sir. I lost my way." He eased past the tutor in the direction of the staircase.

Lovely that he ignored *her* existence.

"Ask directions next time," Mr. Birdwhistle advised in a stern tone of authority unlike his usual calm voice. "Quincy will send someone with you. Servants travel in pairs in this house, or you're likely to become lost and never be found again."

Was that a warning? Verity liked the sound of secret places where intruders might vanish and never be found again.

She'd grown bloodthirsty with age.

When the man clattered back down the stairs, far noisier than he'd come up, Mr. Birdwhistle shut the staircase door and examined the lock. "I've never had need to ask for a key. I suppose we should ask for one now."

She breathed a sigh of relief that he understood and didn't dismiss her fear. That intruder might just have been a thief, but they needed to take every precaution. "And the door from the tower into the schoolroom?"

"That leads to an outside door. I have a key for that. Arnaud insisted when we opened the attic into the tower. Apparently Miss Talbot believes the tower is haunted because pirates hid jewels in there."

"And the good comte assumed thieves will go looking for ghosts?" she asked, seeking amusement that she didn't feel. How did one hunt for a servant in a house full of them?

Mr. Birdwhistle shrugged. "The manor has seen worse. I haven't locked it because I don't wish to lock out the village students. I had foolish notions of this being a safe retreat. Balancing compassion with caution is fraught with complications."

Verity understood too well. Bullies took advantage of weakness. So the compassionate had to be smarter than bullies and work with others to protect the weak. Nothing worth doing was easy.

"Will you be going home for Christmas?" she asked, not knowing how much protection she could rely on.

He shrugged worriedly. "I'd thought to do so, but I dislike leaving if there is any danger."

She wanted to hug the poor forlorn boy. "If we don't solve this problem soon, Rafe can close up the inn and move in here for the duration. You should visit your family."

He didn't seem reassured but nodded.

Leaving the tutor to lock up, she rushed back to the children, verified they slept soundly, then pushed her cot in front of her door before she undressed for bed.

She wanted Rafe here with her.

Because if someone related to the children's father had killed for his small estate, that someone could very well be gentry with connection to the people in the manor.

FRIDAY

DECEMBER 22, 1815

TWENTY-ONE

MINERVA

THE NEXT MORNING, WILLA'S KITCHEN SMELLED AS IT SHOULD AGAIN. Minerva gratefully accepted the still-warm bread Brydie offered. "Bless you, Brydie."

"For you have sinned?" she teased. She nodded at the front room. "Since Mr. Cooper is sleeping upstairs, Damien has set up an office in the parlor to keep an eye on us both. Rafe ordered me to stay out of the inn until the strangers leave. Poor man is torn between his desire to be the best host in the best inn in all England or grilling his guests until they admit guilt. So I might as well bake."

"If his guests came here lying about the orphans. . . We don't even know he's the real Elton." Minerva had pried the story out of her friend earlier. "How does one prove a liar is a killer? We need the children to identify him—except we can't let a killer know we have them." She slipped the bread into her basket and felt militant enough to lead armies—if she only knew the direction.

"You've met Mr. Dryden, so we must assume he legitimately works for Mr. Browning. The letter he brought from the solicitor's office says there may be irregularities with the estate trust. And that this Mr. Elton is one of those irregularities. He was warning us." Brydie took off her apron and reached for her cloak. "I think I should talk to Elton. Women are better at devious questioning."

Minerva wrinkled her nose and shook her head. "Not yet. It's much too early for anyone to be up and about. Put some more loaves in the oven, let me feed Paul, and then we should visit Mr. Jasper at the new hardware. He arrives early. After that, we can interrogate Rafe's guests."

"Jasper? Why?" Alarmed, Brydie stood with her cloak still in hand. "Arthur has been working with him! What has he done?"

"Arrived the morning we found Willa, and the nanny, who did, presumably, work for Mrs. Turner since the children called her *nanny*." Although, now that Minerva thought about it, the neighbor hadn't mentioned a nanny, just two servants. "Jasper was there when Verity found the children. He may have been the one who spread the word."

Or the Stratford curate or the nosy neighbor. . . But they hadn't known about the inn. Minerva had been making lists and connecting dots. None of them connected. Yet. She needed more information.

Brydie still didn't abandon her cloak. "Now I'm even more worried. Should I send Arthur up to the manor with Verity?"

Minerva hadn't wanted to say anything that would alarm Brydie, but the more information they all had— "Verity and Mr. Birdwhistle have called for more locks on the schoolroom and attic doors. Paul is to run up after breakfast because Verity doesn't trust anyone else to do it. They had an intruder. Harmless, apparently, but he frightened her into realizing one of the manor guests could be the person claiming Beanblossom."

That was a far leap of imagination, but Minerva knew better than to ignore Verity, who had saved the inn with her fears not long ago.

She couldn't tell if hotheaded Brydie was praying or cursing under her breath at the news. "Don't do anything yet, please? It's very early. Let me feed Paul, then he'll go up to the manor. I'm sure they're all fine."

"I'm carrying a hatchet from now on," Brydie warned, finally hanging up the cloak. "It's Christmas. I want to work on Lynly's quilt and make rag dolls for the orphans and learn to bake hot cross buns. I don't want to interview killers."

"*Potential* killers. Rafe and Damien are watching and questioning the more obvious suspects, although there seem to be an awful lot of them. You and I will simply poke around the edge, clear a few people from the list, so they might concentrate on the more likely."

She left Brydie grumbling and looking for a way to store a knife under her bodice. Brydie wore breeches under her old-fashioned skirts.

Paul was in his study going over his accounts. Minerva knew he was hoping to find a way to expand the chapel—or at least buy decent pews or even cushions for the benches. He earned almost nothing as a curate since the village was too poor to tithe wheat or eggs, much less sheep. Most of everything the manor contributed went to the rector, whose parish this was. The pinch-penny occasionally sent a small sum as salary, enough for Paul to buy new shoes every few years, and linen to have made into shirts and neckcloths.

Minerva didn't sew well enough to do more than hems and buttons. She felt guilty about not being the helpmeet who could save him pennies, so she contributed most of her pin money toward household expenses, leaving Paul to save his carpentry income for the chapel repairs. Her salary for keeping up the manor library almost paid enough to keep them both dressed suitably to go visiting—if she didn't spend it on bread. They were scraping by. The free parsonage and eating regularly with his mother at the manor helped—but this was Christmas. They needed extra.

She prepared eggs and toast and kissed Paul when the aromas

drew him from his study. "Is the captain looking for the valet who frightened Verity?"

"I'll ask when I'm up there. They're taking every precaution. The children should be fine." He held out a chair so she could sit.

"But what about Verity? She'll go after bad men with a fiery torch. You've seen her in action. I'm trained to use weapons. She is not. Should I be there with her?" Daughter of a colonel, she'd grown up surrounded by soldiers. And even when her father had retired, she'd learned from a duke's sons.

Paul considered this as he chewed but shook his head. "There are more than enough people up there, including trained soldiers. You need to be our warrior down here. Asking questions is what you do best."

"Damien is doing that," she said crossly. "A man claiming to be the nanny's brother, and calling himself Mr. Elton, showed up last night. He could provide no proof of his claim. He could be the killer and no one is doing anything!" She sounded hysterical even to herself. That wasn't like her. It was pure frustration at not being able to undertake the problem on her own.

"The captain and Rafe are the law," Paul said mildly, digging into his eggs. "If he's dangerous, you do not need to be making yourself known to him. Elton, you say? I wonder if I should add that to the poor woman's grave."

Minerva thought she might scream, but it wouldn't do any good. Her husband was imperturbable. "You should probably try to have us and Brydie and Damien invited to dinner at the manor so we may meet their guests. We need to know what *other* strangers are around."

She had spent far too much time hunting pieces of this puzzle. It needed to be finished *now*. Then she could apply her mind to the more joyous occasion of Christmas. They had only three days left to plan their celebrations!

"Perhaps an invitation for Rafe as well, if Fletch returns from Stratford in time." Paul cleaned his plate and carried it to their sink. "With Verity away, I imagine he's pawing the ground like an angry bull."

He'd succeeded in distracting her. Minerva had to smile at the image. "You are most likely right. Put the poor man out of his misery. He works hard."

Minerva had enjoyed more freedom than most, following the drum with her parents and managing her widowed father's household. She appreciated that her new husband didn't curtail her independence—too much.

At the same time, however, she was aware she was no longer an invisible librarian. For Paul's sake, she had responsibilities as a curate's wife. Unfortunately, those duties often involved activities of which she knew nothing, like sewing and the various projects the ladies of the church took on. Embroidery wasn't a skill she'd ever needed. Arranging flowers. . . She was grateful for her sister-in-law. Patience had been raised as a curate's daughter and knew the tasks far better than Minerva ever cared to.

So when the deacon's wife knocked at the parsonage door after Paul left for the manor, Minerva had to stop and listen.

"A Christmas Faire? When is that scheduled?" Minerva had already tied on her bonnet. She pulled on her redingote while she spoke.

"I explained it to Mr. Upton earlier. We hold the faire the day before Christmas Eve. We sell simple gifts," the deacon's wife explained. "Things the children can make themselves. The better off bring cakes or biscuits so everyone has a little something to look forward to."

If Paul had mentioned this. . . she didn't remember.

"But if they have the coin to bake a cake and others don't have the coin to buy them, wouldn't it be simpler to just donate the funds to a poor box?" Minerva finished struggling into her coat and led Mrs. Jones out, locking the door behind her. Curates probably shouldn't lock the parsonage, but she didn't appreciate surprises if someone chose to help themselves. She truly didn't trust as she ought.

"That's just it." Mrs. Jones followed Minerva down the walk. "No one likes asking for help. Those of us who have sufficient funds will donate our baked goods to the church to sell for pennies. Others will have a table of homemade gifts to sell so they'll earn the coin to buy the goods. And we'll all come away with a few pretties to unwrap for Christmas or to give on Boxing Day. Mr. Jones says we may raffle off one of our geese. He thinks maybe a ticket for every penny spent but we're still debating that."

"I am sure you and Deacon Jones have it all arranged, thank you. Perhaps the manor may be equally generous." Minerva hoped it was all arranged because she had no notion of fairs.

Mrs. Jones hesitated. "We've always held it in the chapel before. We thought, maybe, now that the inn has opened again. . . ?"

Ah, there was her purpose. "Shall I ask Mr. Russell for use of his pub to hold the market? If we hold it during the morning, he should be agreeable. He has guests in the evening now."

They'd reached the lane where they must part ways. She should have told Brydie to meet her here. The hardware was in the opposite direction of the bakery.

The inn was right next door to the parsonage. A carriage had pulled into the yard to pick up passengers. They seldom saw carriages in the village, so they both stopped to watch. Was the suspect escaping already?

Alarmed, Minerva decided she needn't wait for Brydie. She could interrogate as a curate's wife! She took Mrs. Jones's arm. "A gentleman arrived last night claiming the poor woman in the accident was his sister. We should offer him our respects and condolences."

Mrs. Jones was always agreeable to gain a bit of gossip. They found Mr. Dryden handing his valise to the driver but no sign of his companion.

"Good day to you, sir." Minerva bobbed a slight curtsy, giving the clerk a chance to remember that they'd been introduced.

"Mrs. Upton, well met!" the young man cried. "Mr. Browning says to tell you that we have safely stored the Turner valuables until we're completely clear on ownership. A few smaller pieces are missing, I fear."

"That was almost to be expected. It is good to know the bulk is intact. We are still attempting to locate the orphans' family." Recalling what Brydie had told her about the suspicious Mr. Elton, she added, "Should the silver belong to the children, it would go a long way toward supporting them, would it not?"

The twinkle in his eye indicated Dryden received her message. "Very astute, Mrs. Upton. We must be careful to avoid the sorts more interested in their wealth than welfare, if it becomes apparent the silver is theirs."

"Is there any chance that Mr. Turner might have had a new will drawn up when he married? And that it may be with a solicitor in Bath or elsewhere?" Without knowing for certain when or where the marriage had taken place, Paul had written the bishop about parish records, but they'd heard nothing yet.

"Now that you've brought the children to our attention, Mr. Browning is making inquiries about marriage documents with the bishop for Somerset. He should have the parish records for Bath. If they married more locally. . . We'll have to write Staffordshire and Worcestershire and maybe more. We will find them, eventually, if the legalities were followed."

That was a tremendous amount of writing and waiting. Minerva tried not to be discouraged but it didn't look as if they'd know much before Christmas. "Since you are solicitors for the estate, are you retrieving any post that comes for Beanblossom?"

Mr. Dryden wrinkled his brow. "I don't believe we have thought of that. I will arrange to do so as soon as I return. Family would surely write, would they not?"

They parted on that happy possibility. Minerva led Mrs. Jones into the inn as the carriage rumbled off—without its other passenger. She heard Kate ordering the maids about upstairs in Verity's place. No one minded the lobby. Which probably meant. . .

She found Rafe scowling irritably, clearing a breakfast table in the pub. He glanced up at their entrance. "Parsons might make a good footman someday, but he's rotten as a night watchman. Elton broke into my cash box, stole Mr. Dryden's purse, and vanished last night."

Alarmed, Minerva considered what that might mean. "Escaping after you exposed him as a liar? Where could he go? The bridge to Birmingham is still closed. Did he steal a horse too?"

"Had to have taken shank's mare. That sort don't ride and nothing else is missing. He'll have the coin to buy a ride though—if he crosses the river to the highway somehow." Rafe glowered as if harboring murderous thoughts. "He could be in Birmingham by now."

"Or he can hole up in an empty cottage and wait for a chance to kidnap the orphans," Minerva said in dismay. She had learned to consider all options at her father's knee. This one was frightening. She needed to warn Brydie.

Mrs. Jones gasped. "A thief roams the street? Is it possible he's the murderer?"

Minerva hadn't wanted to look past stealing the children.

But yes, killing them might possibly have been the ultimate intent.

And now that the church's primary prattle box knew about the children, the entire shire would know before day's end.

TWENTY-TWO

BRYDIE

FURIOUS OVER LEARNING THE BEST SUSPECT TO COME ALONG HAD escaped, Brydie stalked down the village's main street to the hardware, accompanied by a silent Minerva. A silent Minerva meant she was plotting. And that was always dangerous.

But Brydie understood the need. The thief and possible killer could be anywhere! How would they sleep nights unless he was caught? Christmas would be exceedingly grim if everyone cowered at home in fear. Verity was likely to flee to the Outer Hebrides to protect the children. Rafe would follow, the inn could close. . .

Reaching the new hardware, Minerva stopped to study the collection of cooking pots in the mullioned display window. Brydie examined the traditional Tudor exterior. The stucco had recently been whitewashed and the door and timbers had been painted a shiny black. Having a hardware next to the mercantile was convenient for folk bringing their goods to market, even if the stack of baking pans currently displayed left much to be desired. Well, the store wasn't yet open for business. Perhaps the display would be rearranged.

She wasn't letting any more suspects escape without inter-rogation.

The door was open, so Brydie boldly strode in, with Minerva trailing behind her. The gray winter day reduced any light to dim. Brydie concentrated on verifying that her nephew was alive and well. Arthur nodded at her and continued prying open a crate.

A sturdy counter held a few household items that might interest her once she had a kitchen of her own. Behind the counter, the walls held shelves and hooks with mysterious inven-tory she assumed of more interest to men. She recognized garden implements in the crate Arthur unpacked.

Realizing her librarian companion was cataloging the interior and not socializing as a good parson's wife should, Brydie led the charge. "Does your family live here, Mr. Jasper?" she asked while admiring a large mixing bowl. "We would not wish you to be alone at Christmas."

Mr. Cratchit, one of Paul's carpenters, was straightening a poorly attached wall shelf. Arthur had told them that Mr. Jasper might be good at selling hardware, but not at using it.

"No, ma'am, it's just me and my uncle, and he's back in town. He heard there was business to be had here and came down and bought this place. Said I needed to stand on my own feet." The skinny young man ran a broad hand through his disheveled brown hair and glanced around. "I know how to sell but I don't know nothing of setting up, so it's taking a bit of time."

That much was obvious when he carried the shiny new gardening tools to a dark corner where they'd never be seen again.

"It must be difficult not having family with you. Have you met anyone here yet? Your uncle should have introduced you about." Brydie thought the gangly clerk to be an unlikely killer, so now she had to wonder about the uncle.

"Oh, he gave me a letter of introduction to Captain Huntley and I've met a few of the manor gentry, right enough." He studied the empty shelves Cratchit was straightening. "And I met some nice fellows at Monk's."

Well, a tavern was the place to meet his customers. He did know a little something.

Minerva carried over a baking pan. "Will you list prices when you're open or will we need to inquire?"

"I'll post a list of popular items," the young man said, eager to be distracted from shelving. "Maybe make a list for window displays like that one. I'm hoping that window will bring in the ladies."

Brydie hid a snort. *Ladies* did not bake. The poor wives of the village made do with what they had. Besides, women had no money. Perhaps some day, there would be a surge of newly married couples building their households. . . If all these murders didn't scare everyone away.

"I don't suppose your uncle gave you an introduction to Mrs. Willoughby, the baker who just died?" Minerva examined the heavy baking pan as if planning on buying it.

Brydie took the pan away and returned it to the window. Every kitchen hereabouts had more than one baking pan. The curate's wife shouldn't have to waste coins on what she didn't use.

The clerk seemed a little twitchy at the question. "He mentioned her, ma'am."

Ah, helpful uncle, that. Brydie eyed him carefully as he picked nervously around the subject.

"He didn't introduce me. He said I'm to make myself known to the right people who will buy our goods." Mr. Jasper brightened, finding another tack. "But I'm that sorry about the baker. I'll be setting up housekeeping above, and I like a bit of toast of a morning." He turned his attention to Arthur opening a crate of hammers.

Remembering her odd exchange with Willa's neighbor, Brydie asked, "Did he mention the king's shilling to you?"

Mr. Jasper turned a bright red and stuttered, "May have, in

passing." He bent quickly to take an armload of hammers and looked around to find a place to shelve them.

Mr. Cratchit began to whistle loudly and beat a nail with his hammer. Ah, so he knew of Willa too. And the king's shilling was some kind of. . . code?

Fine. One must assume they both knew *of* Willa, but she had no means of knowing if they *visited* her. Interrogation wasn't easy when one had to be discreet. Brydie wondered what Mr. Jasper had been up to back in town that his uncle thought it necessary to tell him of the village prostitute, then send him off on his own.

But opium? How did one question if he knew of its existence? And stabbing a baker. . . The notion was ludicrous. Mr. Jasper could barely wield a hammer. He might have killed Willa by accident had they been playing with knives—an unlikely situation.

Minerva evidently came to the same conclusion. She offered invitations to church to Mr. Jasper and Mr. Cratchit, then praised Arthur for his hard work before they took their leave.

"Should we have questioned Mr. Cratchit as well?" Brydie asked, unsatisfied with their visit.

"Paul has done that. Willa entertained a number of single men, including the former soldiers working at the manor. Cratchit is one. None of them have coin to spare, so visits were rare. They have no jealous wives, so she couldn't extort them. Fletch was her only regular, it appears. I don't believe the good major is capable of faking his grief. So let us learn more about chicken-stealing Mr. Parsons and the vanishing Mr. Elton." Minerva marched toward the inn.

"I wish to talk more to Mr. Cooper." Brydie slowed her stride to match her petite companion's. "He seems to do as little as possible but has lost interest in leaving. I appreciate that he's waiting for letters from his family, except a man who spends his life gambling and drinking but does not appear to starve is very suspicious."

"Or owner of a significant annuity," Minerva said dryly. "London is quite full of wastrels like that. If we are to believe him, he is only a second cousin to the orphans' mother, so I cannot see how he would inherit her husband's estate, or even the bakery, for all that matters. He has shown as little interest in that as the children. Besides, he didn't knock himself over the head."

"Parsons is equally unlikely as a killer," Brydie had to admit. "He does not stand to inherit the Bartletts' cottage since he isn't related to them. I just don't like that he attacked me, and violence is quite likely the only way he knows to survive. Do you think Willa might have known something about him that he didn't wish known? Perhaps she threatened him?"

Now that she'd said it, that possibility seemed far more likely than most.

"Parsons is a convict and *looks* like a killer, so he's easy to suspect. You may be right and he had an argument with Willa, then hit Cooper when he walked in. It's just hard to believe the nanny's death isn't related. How might we connect Parsons to a *nanny*?" Minerva halted outside the inn gate to see who was about.

"The nanny. . . do we call her Mrs. Elton now?" Brydie shoved her gloved hands under her arms while they lingered in the wind. "I think I just want this to be simple and believe the nanny is linked to Willa's death. If she'd been *leaving* Gravesyde, the connection might even make sense. But the children and the position of the carriage rather prove they hadn't arrived yet. So anyone giving her those pills had to have been in Stratford, not here. We may have to accept that we are wrong about coincidences. How could the killer be in two places at once? Who else is on our list?"

Two killers. It barely bore consideration. Brydie shivered.

"There is the mysteriously vanishing Elton, who probably was just in it for what he could steal? I haven't seen him, so I cannot be prejudiced by his looks or lack thereof, as we are with Parsons." Minerva scanned the yard again before opening the gate. "Elton has proven himself a thief and a liar. That does seem to make him the most likely suspect to have provided the candies—if he thought the children had something worth stealing."

But they'd arrived with nothing. Studying the sprawling inn, Brydie wanted to grab her family and run home. So very many places a killer could hide. . .

"I fear it is out of our hands," Minerva admitted unhappily. "We must wait for letters from the Americas, from bishops, from Cooper's unknown family. . . It is not quite the same as being useful. I may as well help the ladies plan a Christmas market. Am I expected to bring something to sell?"

"Do you have any wedding gifts you can't use? Anything new or remotely fancy will be pounced upon. Christmas encourages generosity." Brydie picked up her old woolen skirt and proceeded into the inn yard. It hadn't rained recently, so the mud wasn't too bad. And one of the stable boys was cleaning up after the horses.

She needed to return to her baking, but she'd like to see Damien first. Once she'd left Willa's, he'd left for his new law office. Not that anyone in Gravesyde could afford a lawyer, but he was trying to settle down for her sake. At the grand old age of thirty, she didn't have the same giddy illusions of romantic love she'd had when they were younger, but she still loved him for many excellent reasons, despite his trying to make her into the fragile lady she was not.

Apparently tired of his own company, Cooper sprawled in a leather armchair that hadn't been in the lobby yesterday, while Damien, Paul, and the blacksmith examined Rafe's damaged counter. A middling sort of man in expensive attire, Cooper folded his hands over his waistcoat and watched.

Damien's worried frown disappeared at sight of Brydie. "More bread baking?"

"I've sold the first loaves. The others are rising. This isn't market day, so I needn't do much. How did the thief break into Rafe's cash box? And where did the chair come from?" Brydie cast a glare at Cooper, who belatedly dragged himself upright to bow a greeting. His fashionably cut hair fell in a neat curl over his unmarred brow.

"I'll have to start locking up my shed," the carpenter-curate admitted ruefully.

Damien came around the counter to press a discreet kiss to her temple. "Our thief slammed the lock open with an awl and hammer from the workshop. Cash box is still here but the lock is worthless now. And the chair is an ugly castoff from my father's unused study. Whoever guards the lobby ought to have a place to rest."

"I thought you meant to use that chair in your office." Brydie squeezed his hand, then skirted around the counter to see what the blacksmith was doing.

"I cannot bear using a chair he may have sat in even occasion-ally," Damien admitted, unapologetically. "Thea said she'd find a good chair for me next time she goes hunting for the manor. It's a shame we can't ask her about safes."

The ethereal heiress knew about ghosts, art, and old furniture. Safes were definitely not her expertise. If fairies disliked iron. . . Brydie shook off that silly thought.

"Has there been any sighting of Mr. Elton?" Minerva perched on the now unoccupied chair, giving it a bounce, leaving Cooper standing about awkwardly.

"Now that I am here, Rafe is gathering men to search vacant cottages. He assigned Parsons to go through the inn's empty rooms and search the stables. One wouldn't think Elton could go far at night, on foot. Even the soldiers have quit sleeping rough in this cold." Damien offered the young blacksmith a coin but he waved it off and wandered off to return to his own work.

Rafe could be heard from the stable yard, barking orders like a good sergeant should.

"If Elton came here to claim the orphans, then wouldn't he be looking for them?" Cooper suggested. "Have they been taken somewhere safe?"

Brydie frowned, trying to remember when or if Cooper had

heard about the children, but she supposed everyone knew by now. Verity had chosen a good hiding place if even he didn't know where they were. Of course, he was a stranger and ignorant of the manor inhabitants and their generosity.

"They have." Kate came down the stairs with her sewing basket and addressed Damien. "Will Mr. Cooper be watching the front desk? I'd like to set the staff to preparing tonight's meal."

Her sister was losing much needed income by helping Rafe at the inn instead of finishing her piecework. They needed to resolve this mystery soon.

Assured that they could do naught else, Brydie accepted Damien's escort to the bakery, leaving Kate bossing everyone at the inn, including the lazy Mr. Cooper. She'd straighten him out soon enough.

With a list of her own tasks to accomplish, Minerva waved them off and hurried down the path to the parsonage.

Brydie and Damien hadn't gone out of earshot before they heard Minerva scream.

TWENTY-THREE

RAFE

"Stop pacing. You'll turn me into a complete bedlamite if you don't sit down and tell me exactly what is wrong." Rafe hated looming over the curate's petite, blond—exceptionally educated—wife. He hated worse that the lady seemed volatile enough to explode like gunpowder.

Minerva's screams had brought him and her husband running, as well as Brydie and Damien, but her person seemed in its usual immaculate state. Except she wouldn't sit down.

Furiously biting her lip, Minerva pointed at the open drawers in the study and the contents of the ladies' writing desk dumped and smashed on the worn carpet. Rafe had seen those. Unless she told him the desks contained gold or jewels, he couldn't grasp her rage. He wanted to ask if the thief had insulted her person but couldn't find the right words.

Paul Upton cradled his ball of fire in his arms, preventing her from turning into the wrath of God. Rafe knew anger when he saw it. The lady wasn't frightened. She meant to murder. He briefly wondered if a curate's wife might kill the village tart for

Biblical reasons, but Minerva didn't appear to be the fire and brimstone sort.

Rafe had ordered Brydie away to stand guard with Kate at the inn. Damien had gone out to search the parsonage grounds, with Rafe's wolfhound at his heels.

Returning, Damien's grim expression indicated what Rafe had expected. He'd found nothing. Too many people trampled the grounds for a dog to follow a scent.

"We don't own any valuables," Paul said tightly. "Thieves know better than to rob parsonages. Whoever did this was after something else. When we made our inquiries in Stratford, we tried to hide our location from people who don't know us. But a parsonage isn't hard to find. I assume this is related."

Which might explain Minerva's fury, if it was about the children.

"You think Elton is looking for the orphans?" Rafe asked. It was the only thing that made sense, but Upton was an educated man. His opinion mattered.

"Yes," Damien spoke first, confirming what they all feared. "We need to remove the women to the manor. If he's this desperate, he'll resort to hostages next."

"The intruder was looking for papers," Minerva reminded them sharply, pushing from Paul's arms and gesturing at her desk. "Did Elton seem the sort to read?"

"Dryden signed the register for them. He might simply be searching for the parish ledger. It's unlikely he can read any documents he might find, but we can't take chances." Rafe glanced around the cottage for anything he might have missed. The contents were modest but well-kept and tasteful. It helped to have wealthy friends with excess furniture, as Rafe well knew. And Paul was a carpenter who could repair anything. "Verity will be glad of your company."

That Minerva did not argue as she stomped off to pack clothes proved how shaken she was at this invasion of her new home.

Rafe turned to the other two men. "Are we certain this is about the children?"

"Not completely," Damien admitted. "But I'm seeing no other motive for a document search. Elton is a thief. He's after coin, one way or another. If we accept that he might read, is it possible he thought the orphans might be sold and was searching for clues to their whereabouts?"

Paul's mouth flattened angrily. "It's possible. The world is full of despicable people who buy children for virtual slaves. I fear there is more to the matter, though. He wouldn't need documents to sell children. My concern is that if we take the women to the manor, that we may be taking them straight into the villain's arms."

That silenced them briefly. Rafe pondered what he was saying, then shook his head. "Easier to secure the perimeter if we're all at the manor. Then we set up another perimeter upstairs, guarding the women and children. The attic has far fewer accesses than the inn or the entire village."

Paul didn't argue, but Damien scowled as he paced. "I don't know if I can persuade Brydie and Kate to stay at the manor. Women have odd notions about propriety. They're very independent."

"Tell them Kate's children will be safer remaining at the manor, and that I need you to be my eyes and ears with the gentry, but you refuse to abandon them. They won't shirk their duty. They'll have to come with you. I want Paul and Minerva there too, but they are better equipped to keep an eye below stairs." Where Paul's mother insisted on living, even if she was great-granddaughter of an earl.

"I'll tell Brydie my Christmas gifts to the children rely on her and Kate consulting with Lavender," Damien decided. "Lavender needs the business. That should tilt the scales, I hope. And if I say I'll see that their chickens and pony are fed, they'll have no other excuse."

"I am glad I'll never meet you in a courtroom, and should I

ever have an estate requiring a trust, I'll be glad to have you write it up." Rafe pounded Damien's shoulder and sent him off to round up the Calhoun sisters. His inn would suffer without them, but Fletch, Parsons, and Cooper could manage. Maybe.

"If you're certain nothing has been taken, I'll go back to searching cottages." Rafe knew the futility but he was incapable of doing nothing. He snapped his fingers for Wolfie to heel. Wrapping his broad paw in the dog's fur helped soothe his confusion.

"I've lost my sense of security." Paul rubbed his jaw unhappily. "I'll install new locks here and on my workshop. If Elton jammed your cash box open with my hammer and awl, then chances are good he did the same here. He may have been hunting for the registry, but I learned early on to hide it. If he thought it contained information on the orphans, we don't have it, but he doesn't know that."

"We'll keep the new hardware busy at this rate." Rafe donned his cap and strode out, pondering whether Jasper had wits enough to drum up business for his hardware by breaking old locks.

Parsons had been a convict. The conditions in the Antipodes were cruel. Over all those years of deprivation, he would no doubt have learned a few villainous tricks. Where had his new employee been this morning? Supposedly, sleeping, since he'd been assigned to guard the inn last night. Except he'd been sleeping instead of guarding. Damnation. Maybe *Parsons* had robbed the cash box? But then, what had happened to Elton?

Rafe stopped at the inn to secure all his own locks. He informed the staff they wouldn't be accepting new guests until after the holiday and that they had the day off. Not that the old women had families to go to, but they seemed content with each other's company. Warning them to keep the doors locked, he left them deciding what kind of pudding they'd like to fix for themselves. He'd have to buy them a fat goose for Christmas dinner.

In his absence, Brydie and Kate had taken over his kitchen to prepare a noon meal and bake the dough Brydie brought over from the bakery. Waste not, want not had been their motto for too long. At least they'd agreed to stay where he could keep an eye on them—until Damien persuaded them otherwise.

Rafe sent Wolfie patrolling the inn halls. The dog was better at hunting rabbits, but just his size might terrify intruders. Disregarding his new employee's privacy, he checked on the room he'd assigned to Parsons, finding him sawing logs as if he hadn't slept in a week. As a soldier, Rafe knew the exhaustion of stress. He still couldn't trust that the man hadn't robbed him—except it was Elton who was missing.

At noon, Fletch finally rode in with the post. After handing his horse over to the stable, he stalked in with only a few letters in his hand. If he'd had a mailbag, he'd left it with Oswald at the mercantile.

"I didn't see the reason to pay Oswald's postage for personal mail I spent a day retrieving and for which he'd only reward me a few measly pennies for delivering." Fletch tossed the letters on the counter.

Rafe would work out that excuse another time. Besides a letter from his own parents, the post contained a letter to Willa—and none for Cooper. Rafe had been hoping Cooper's family would have responded by now.

"Do we ask Cooper to open Willa's correspondence?" Rafe asked, poking the folded paper with his thick finger.

He didn't know where Cooper had got to. He wasn't an employee, so Rafe couldn't expect him to linger if he had better things to do. He couldn't even ask that Cooper stay until Willa's murder was solved. A judge would have to demand his appearance as witness should the killer ever be identified. That wasn't Rafe's responsibility.

Disregarding propriety and probably the law, Fletch slit the seal and unfolded the letter. He examined it front and back, frowned, and handed it to Rafe. "This person in Bath appears to be asking Willa if the children have arrived yet, and if Willa could keep them a while longer. There appears to be some delay in transport."

Rafe skimmed the feminine handwriting and noted the signature: *B.* Bee or Boo? Probably Bee. He was starting to imagine the Turners' mysterious relations as fraternal twins with freckles and unruly blond curls. He was out of his friggin' mind.

"Or they didn't wish to disturb anyone's holidays with two grief-stricken tykes," Rafe said cynically. "But this does mean someone out there knows about them." The return address was only B and B, Clement Circle, Bath.

Verity would be destroyed if she had to give up those children —especially to people who hadn't come running to take them.

"How the devil do I protect the children, my wife, the inn, the village, while riding all the way to Bath to look for a Bee and Boo?" he cried in frustration, flinging the letter back to Fletch.

"You don't." Unwilling to do more, Fletch stalked back to the kitchen looking for food.

Rafe winced as someone, most likely Kate, flung a pot at his partner, who didn't know how to ask politely.

The army had been simpler.

TWENTY-FOUR

"Rafe believes Mr. Elton broke into the parsonage, since the thief used the same method to steal from his cash box. Mr. Parsons says he slept through the robbery, but he has no witnesses until Rafe checked on him at noon. We can't *know* Elton is the killer, but the men. . ." Trying to explain to Verity, Brydie shrugged. "They're behaving as if this is war and have turned all medieval on us. They'll be building drawbridges next."

"I am glad of the company, for whatever reason," Verity admitted. "I love children but I miss adult conversation. Mr. Birdwhistle is pleasant, but he has two excessively active boys to mind, plus Rob and Daniel. That's more than a handful and doesn't leave him time to converse."

"Rob hasn't been naughty, has he?" Brydie sounded appalled, as if little boys never misbehaved. Sitting at one of the school desks, she was showing her niece how to embroider a stitch for her quilt edging.

"They're building forts." Lynly spoke up cheerfully. Despite the difference in ages, she was nearly as small as her fairy-blond companion. "They put me and Daphne in the dungeon."

The solemn five-year-old, her hair in beribboned pigtails, looked up at the sound of her name and nodded with a cherubic smile, indicating she enjoyed the game. That small smile nearly broke Verity's soft heart. The children were adapting.

"The Reid heirs have created a maze of the furniture," Verity murmured. "I suspect the attic may now contain as many snares and pitfalls as any medieval castle. They do not trust locks and have taken it into their heads that it is their duty to protect the weak."

"Meaning you and Daphne?" Brydie asked in amusement. "That's thoughtful. Did they learn that from the men? They start young, if so. Although if I remember correctly, as heirs to a few fortunes, the boys are in more danger than us."

Verity wrinkled her nose. "I would disabuse them of their beliefs that women are weak, but it keeps them occupied. I am beginning to understand that males need goals and targets to direct all their energy."

Brydie appeared to digest that observation. Having spent half her life quietly watching, Verity thought her friend needed to apply that understanding to Damien so she did not stand—or gallop into—his path.

"Will you and Damien be eating dinner downstairs tonight?" she asked, changing the subject.

Brydie glanced down at her woolen gown. "Lavender has promised that she can make over the bodice of one of Patience's dinner gowns to fit me, but I lack finery and finesse. I would be more comfortable here with you."

"You cannot uncover evildoers while lurking up here. Do you know what color the gown is? Rafe packed a trunk for me, but I can't leave the children unattended. Paul and the blacksmith are still working on the locks." Verity rose from the desk where she'd been scribbling lesson plans.

Wearing a dubious expression, Brydie pushed out of her too-small chair. "Lynly, will you be all right here for a little bit?"

"Oliver and Davey are hiding in the wardrobes." Lynly

nodded at two massive cabinets guarding the tower entrance. "We are princesses in the tower."

"And where are Rob and Daniel?" Verity asked, knowing she'd left all four boys with Mr. Birdwhistle.

"They are planning an attack on the castle. We are to be rescued before dinner." Lynly shook out her almost-finished quilt.

Smothering a grin, Verity steered her reluctant friend from the chilly schoolroom toward the warmer interior. "Come along. You'll turn blue if we don't get you somewhere warm. Lynly is wearing mittens and coat. You aren't."

"Who thought to cut the ends off her mittens so she could sew? You?" Brydie stopped to study the layout of the narrow hall between the stairs and the new schoolroom, before taking the wide corridor down the middle of the attic. Through the open door of the old schoolroom, they could see Mr. Birdwhistle drawing at an easel, from which position he supposedly kept track of his charges.

"They are old mittens we found in one of the trunks, already moth-eaten. I know the two of you have thin skin and need extra warmth. I will watch over Lynly, Brydie, I promise. You need to help Rafe catch a killer so those poor orphans can be safe and happy again." Verity led her into the small cubicle she'd claimed as her own.

She hoped Rafe might join her here tonight, but he was busy wearing himself ragged setting up protection for the entire manor.

Seeing Rafe's wolfhound emerging from the maze of trunks and furniture the boys had created of the storage area, Verity snapped her fingers and set Wolfie to guard the new schoolroom. The patient dog allowed a head scratch before settling in front of the door.

"I heard the captain's hounds earlier. Did Rafe set them loose?" Brydie peered into the miniature nursery Verity had set up for the orphans.

"They're not as well trained as Wolfie, but he's taught several of the former soldiers how to walk them around the grounds.

Hunt says he can justify paying the soldiers from the trust if he calls them grounds men. The earl apparently left a very large trust for maintaining the manor, if not its inhabitants."

"Has the family questioned the servants about your intruder yet?" Brydie rubbed her hands and studied her surroundings nervously. She seldom visited the manor.

Verity could appreciate her friend's discomfort, but Brydie was a squire's daughter and about to marry—someday—a respected solicitor. She needed to learn she was not just a farm girl.

"The ladies are making lists of all the servants and checking it twice. The manor has any number of guests for the holiday, and their servants are all strangers to Rafe. That's why we're locked up here." Verity opened her trunk and rummaged. "Color?"

"Green. Rafe is quite confident the soldiers aren't dangerous?" Brydie peered over her shoulder.

"They drink too much. They aren't always reliable. But they're loyal to the captain, Rafe says. Patrolling, they know how to do, but it won't help if the killer is among the guests or their servants. For them, we have Mrs. Upton, Paul, and Minerva snooping." Verity understood that, knew she was the last line of defense, and prayed her friends would root out the villain before he tried again.

Once upon a time, she would have found it impossible to believe that fashionably dressed society contained killers. She had since been disabused of such innocence.

Brydie offered a sigh of awe at the jewel-toned Kashmir shawl Verity produced from her trunk. "My mother once wore gorgeous pieces like this, when I was very young. Kate and I did not appreciate them until too late, after the moths and old age destroyed them. It's not as if we wear silk to feed the chickens."

"Meera gave me that one. You should see her collection! But the colors are much too vivid for me and lovely with your auburn hair." Verity handed over the shawl and rummaged for her jewelry box. "I lived in a cellar and had no chickens to feed, so I wore my mother's gowns. I spent years adapting her wardrobe to suit me and fashion. In a way, it allowed me to feel closer to her. I lost most of it in the fire, but I'd hidden some of her jewelry and finery with my books thinking I'd one day run away."

"You're the lady and should be the one going to dinner." Brydie swung the shawl around her shoulders and admired the fringe. "Kate and I tried to keep a formal table after mother died, but father wasn't interested. We were young and gave it up."

"He was the local squire, wasn't he?" Opening her jewel box, Verity found a choker of seed pearls and showed them to Brydie. "You have every right to sit with gentry. My father was merely a sea captain. My mother was gentry and aspired for me, but she died, and I was never presented to society. These days, I'd far rather be with the children and Rafe."

"There may be dukes and earls at the table," Brydie whispered in horror, admiring the pearls but not touching them. "Look at my hands." She held out fingers red and roughened from hard work. "I won't be able to take off my gloves."

"Then leave them on, if you wish. Tell everyone you're subject to chilblains, which is the honest truth. Arm yourself and *catch a killer.*" She shoved the pearls at Brydie. "I'm relying on you."

"My suit of armor." Reluctantly, Brydie accepted the necklace. "I need to go down for a fitting. Kate's doing most of the sewing. I'll send her up here to keep you company when she's done. She says she's still in mourning and has no escort and would rather be with Rob and Lynly. You have time to change your mind. If Kate's here, you could go down with Rafe."

Verity shook her head vehemently. "I am an innkeeper's wife now. But there might be interesting single men down there for Kate. How long has it been since her husband died?"

"Just before last Christmas. It's been over a year, but she's. . . shy of men. Just having her here at the manor where she can watch gentlemen come and go, while she's surrounded by Lavender's sewing ladies, is helping. She's spent far too long alone on the farm, with only me and the children for company. Once I'm wed, I'll work on her."

Brydie left, holding her treasures as if they were real jewels.

Rafe arrived a little later and hugged Verity, offering her the strength she needed. He'd brought Arthur with him. "The boy says he'd rather eat in the schoolroom than downstairs. And he can take Wolfie outside and feed him," he murmured while the younger boys crowded around Kate's eldest son, sweeping him away to excitedly point out their castle's traps.

Verity showed Rafe the newly installed locks. "Arthur is good with the boys. But if he's off to school in a few weeks, he ought to be downstairs, gaining a little polish."

Following the boys, Rafe peered into the dark storage area next to her closet room. "Kate did a good job with him. And he's a fast learner. Damien's teaching him how to use a sword and fists. It can't hurt to have one more layer of protection up here."

"You really believe Daniel's *bad man* is in the manor?" Verity whispered, keeping an eye on the boys as they balanced an ugly marble bust in the seat of a rocking chair on top of a three-legged washstand.

"Elton may have come to Gravesyde with kidnapping in mind, but whoever broke into the parsonage was most likely after the birth records Upton asked the Stratford curate to send. Fortunately, they haven't arrived yet. Whether Elton knew about those remains to be seen, but it does appear the parsonage thief would need to read." Rafe hugged her reassuringly.

Which did limit them to mostly gentry.

Verity buried her face in his shoulder and drank in his masculine scent, before straightening her spine and pushing away. "Catch the scoundrels so we may have the merriest Christmas anyone has ever known."

"That's my ferocious Verity." He kissed her again and strode off, every bit the confident soldier she loved and adored.

Rafe would go after killers and thieves with fists and swords.

Verity suspected the boys had a better notion—defeat the sneaky snakes with deviousness.

TWENTY-FIVE

MINERVA

"Verity said the attic intruder claimed to be a valet." Still unnerved by having her cozy new home invaded by an evil miscreant, Minerva settled into one of her mother-in-law's comfortable armchairs and scowled. As head housekeeper, Mrs. Upton had created a compact apartment for herself off the manor's kitchen. "It would be so much simpler if she described a man who looked like Mr. Elton, or even Mr. Parsons, but her description simply isn't enough for comparison."

Mrs. Upton filled her teacup and settled into her own chair. She watched fondly as her son repaired the leg of a wooden table chair in her small dining area. "As I recall, Mrs. Russell said the valet had a Roman nose, fleshy lips, and possibly a hint of sideburns, but it was quite dark and she only had a glimpse. And if she was frightened, she might not remember rightly. Does Mr. Parsons fit this picture? Did you actually meet Mr. Elton or are you relying on description?"

Paul stood and tested the chair to see if it still wobbled. "Parsons has no sideburns and his features are rather distinctively angular and square. Elton. . . Rafe's fairly accurate in his reports, but he only saw the man in lantern light. He said Elton is an older, balding blond man, larger than the clerk he arrived with but smaller than himself. Unrefined features, which reminds me of Parsons, but probably means weathered or tending toward jowls. Parsons has a full head of black hair. A Roman nose is rather distinctive and doesn't sound as if it fits either."

The logical exercise of describing potential thieves and killers soothed Minerva's rattled nerves somewhat. "If Mr. Elton arrived by carriage at the same approximate time as Verity's intruder was in the attic, we must assume they are two people. And Rafe says Parsons helped unload their luggage, so he couldn't be at the manor either."

"Which probably means that the intrusive valet was not one of your suspects and is quite innocent." Mrs. Upton rose to set the table. "You are all just overwrought."

Or there was a third villain, which unsettled Minerva all over again. She tried to let the more experienced woman reassure her, but she couldn't. "Two women *died* and the children almost did. We need to reassure Verity that the orphans are safe. She's under a terrible strain."

Even worse so because soft-hearted Verity wished to keep the children and feared whoever had a right to them did not really want them. The letter from Bath, that Verity had told her about, had not been reassuring in the least.

Minerva gathered the pieces of her shattered self-esteem and went out to the kitchen to ask if she might help with the food Lady Elsa always prepared for them.

The kitchen was its usual chaos. Dinner wouldn't be served soon.

Wrapped in a gravy-spattered apron and carrying a large wooden spoon, Lady Elsa stopped to offer Minerva a taste of her. . . Minerva wasn't entirely certain what it was but it had carrots and wine and bits of beef and was temptingly delicious.

"Like it?" The blond, buxom, beautiful earl's daughter had once made Minerva feel like an ugly bug, but she had learned Elsa was as beautiful inside as out. She beamed proudly at Minerva's hum of pleasure. "It's French. Let us see if the company turns up their elegant noses at something that isn't bloody rare beef."

"Will you be going up to dine with them so you may enjoy their reactions?"

"I think I shall. Anne is quite good at overseeing the staff, and my pastry cook has the puddings in hand. I'd like to hear more of what everyone expects from our Christmas feast." Elsa wiped her hands on her apron. "I heard you had an intruder today? Who in their right mind robs a parsonage?"

"Possibly someone after the registry or the orphans' birth documents. Rafe has stationed men there in case he tries again. We are staying out of their way. Did Verity ask you about the valets?" Mrs. Upton may have dismissed Verity's fear, but Minerva simply could not. She had learned from experience that even children were capable of throwing grenades.

"Hunt asked me to watch for a servant with a big nose and a fat mouth and maybe a soldier's sideburns. I don't think I've seen anyone like that taking their meals down here."

"That would have been too easy." Minerva wrinkled her nose unhappily. "I'll help serve Mrs. Upton when you're ready. She and Paul need a little alone time. I might just come eat with the staff. Will they mind?"

"The visiting staff doesn't know who you are and the others think of you as the curate's wife and love having you to their selves." Elsa chuckled. "You'll hear more than you like."

"That's what I'm hoping. I'll let you know what they're expecting from Boxing Day." Minerva let the cook go back to work and returned to inform Paul of her plan.

"They want coins and new uniforms for Boxing Day." Mrs. Upton said comfortably from her chair. "Lavender and her ladies have been working all hours on the maids' dresses. Henri has scavenged secondhand coats and waistcoats for the footmen that will have to be fitted. They'll have new knee breeches and stockings this year."

"Hunt says he can employ a large number of poorly dressed servants or a small number of smartly dressed ones." Paul sat in the chair he'd just repaired, testing it with his weight. "He chose people over clothes."

"Given how the rest of us dress, that was an excellent choice." Minerva didn't want to sit still. She paced. "And I believe the dowagers intend to contribute coins for all the work everyone does serving them in their lair. If enough people contribute, the ones who want new clothes can buy them. Should I run up and check on Verity?"

She wanted this mystery over and done so she could celebrate her first Christmas with her new husband as the first curate the village had seen in years. It should be a time of joy and festivity. After all the years of war, she hadn't had much of that.

She despised her helplessness now.

"I'd check on Brydie first, if I were you," Paul warned. "She's in a stew over dining with gentry in fancy dress. She hasn't quite accepted that she's more than a farmer's daughter."

"I think it's partially her size making her feel awkward among strangers." Glad of a task, Minerva grabbed a shawl for the drafty walk upstairs. "The locals accept her as she is, but she has this foolish image of gentry being refined and elegant. We simply need to disabuse her of that fustian."

"I never realized that." Paul frowned, considering it. "She's always amazingly self-confident."

"You don't understand women well. Yet." She kissed his auburn hair and fled up the stairs, determined to solve some part of their plaguesome problem tonight.

Upstairs, a maid told her she'd find Lavender still in the sewing room. Minerva had lived in the manor and knew it was late. Most of the sewing ladies should have gone home. Entering the darkened ballroom, she noted the tables of uniforms neatly laid out to be sewed on in the morning.

But someone was working late. Minerva could hear Brydie fretting and Lavender soothing her, so they were about somewhere. Now that the tower had been opened to the ballroom, Lavender had moved her own workspace and dressing rooms in there.

The door between ballroom and tower was open, although Minerva needed a lantern to traverse the vast expanse of floor cluttered with wardrobes and boxes of old clothes. Safely reaching the tower entrance, she peered in.

Tall, not-quite-statuesque Brydie practically shimmered in the dim light, wearing an emerald gown Minerva almost didn't recognize as one of her sister-in-law's. On golden-haired Patience, the gown had been drab—probably because her bounteous bosom drew the eye. Brydie's rich auburn brought the color to life. Lavender had concealed Brydie's less voluptuous bosom with ruffles, but whatever corset she'd been given gave her cleavage Brydie hadn't previously displayed.

Kate finished knotting a thread on the hem and gestured for her sister to turn around to face the mirror.

At the sight in the tilted cheval glass that was Lavender's pride and joy, Brydie hastily covered herself with a jewel-toned shawl.

Minerva laughed and entered to tug the shawl down Brydie's arms. "This is how you wear it."

Brydie tugged it over her shoulders again and glared. "I shall freeze."

Noting the gloves her friend often wore, Minerva dropped that argument and preceded to the next. Nothing stirred Brydie like a good argument. "You should have Meera prepare some of her hand cream for you. You will want to take off your gloves when Damien places his ring on your finger."

Brydie hastily hid her hands behind her back. The shawl drooped down her arms again. Even solemn Kate laughed at that.

Eighteen and confident in her blond beauty, Lavender held up a seed pearl necklace. "You should wear emeralds with that gown, but these will suffice."

"I am a thirty-year-old spinster," Brydie grumbled, allowing

Lavender to fasten the necklace. Minerva was almost too short to reach. "I should be wearing black and caps and sitting upstairs with the dowagers."

Both Minerva and Lavender laughed. Kate shrugged. She worked in the sewing room and had probably never met the haughty dowagers.

"They'd eat you alive," Minerva assured her. "You need another thirty years before you could survive that lion's den. Besides, we need you at the table to make note of all the visitors. I will be eating with the staff downstairs to make a list of any valets with big noses and fat lips." She almost giggled at the captain's translation of Verity's more circumspect description.

"Spies on every floor," Lavender crowed in delight. "Everyone knows me, so I shall run up and downstairs, carrying messages, and no one will notice."

"The men will," Kate said, speaking up for a change. "You could wear a sack, and they'd notice."

Lavender grinned wickedly. "But all they see is a silly chit to be seduced. My loving grandmother has made that very clear."

"Lady Marlow is one of the lions," Minerva explained to a wide-eyed Brydie. "I can't say she's wrong, though."

Lavender shrugged. "I am not my mother. I don't need men. If anyone is to do the seducing, it will be me." She tugged a fold of Brydie's gown, stepped back to admire her handiwork, and nodded approval. "You are a goddess. Go slay the dragon."

"Will you be at the table?" Brydie asked Lavender anxiously.

"I suppose I shall, for a while, if only to watch Mr. Sutter's eyes fall from his head when he sees you. You are not to allow all the flattery to go to yours. Gentlemen are trained to charm. You must see past the surface to find the evil that lurks within." Lavender rummaged in a dresser and produced long, white silk gloves. "You should have bracelets, but these will suffice."

Leaving Lavender and Kate to argue about finishing hems, Minerva steered her terrified friend from the sewing room. "Do not think of yourself. Think of Daphne and Daniel and poor

Verity. If you see or hear anything unusual, summon one of the footmen and send word to me. Paul and I will be only a staircase away."

Brydie took a deep breath, shivered, and tugged her shawl around her, only remembering the gloves she clutched when she nearly dropped them. "I do not even know what is unusual."

Minerva considered that. "Neither do I. And if Verity's intruder is actually a valet, you won't see him. But his employer is bound to be part of the company. Perhaps listen for anyone talking about Beanblossom or the children or asking odd questions?"

Brydie nodded. "I can do that, although with so many people. . ."

"Clare will see you placed near the most likely visitors. Rely on her. And when the ladies leave the men at the table, follow her lead. She'll introduce you to anyone she wants to know more about. You're in good hands."

"Clare Huntley barely knows me as more than one of Rafe's staff," Brydie whispered as they reached the gaslit marble stairs in the central corridor.

Minerva chuckled. "Watch her. I always thought proper ladies were a useless lot. Clare is the perfect portrait of all the smiling, empty-headed, beautiful debutantes you may have imagined gracing London's ballrooms. Then remember she survived being almost blown up in Egypt, rescued her nephew from avaricious relations, and someday, take a look at the books on the shelves in her study. She may be quiet as a mouse, but she's stealthy as a cat. She knows you, all right."

Brydie looked puzzled at the mention of books but they weren't Minerva's story to tell. She had only discovered it because she was a snoop who liked putting puzzles together. Clare would let people know of her secret occupation when she was ready.

Sending Brydie off to her room to wait for the dinner bell, Minerva took the servants' stairs up to visit Verity in the attic, and to check on the children's safety. She had Mrs. Upton's keys and hoped to find all the doors locked.

The lock on the one at the top of the staircase, going into the attic, had been loosened, and a piece of leather jammed into it to prevent it being locked again.

Someone intended to return tonight.

TWENTY-SIX

Brydie heard the massive case clock on the landing chime twelve and shivered. She knew the clock didn't work properly, but the midnight toll still seemed portentous. A draft blew around her ankles despite the brazier in the small guest room she'd been assigned.

She understood that the manor wasn't wealthy and hadn't been kept up for decades, so she was grateful that she at least had a room with heat and a down-filled cover. The maid had even carried in warm water, and amazingly, a jar of hand cream with a note from Lavender. The young seamstress was every definition of a true lady, even if she'd been born on the wrong side of the blanket.

The cream wouldn't be of any use tonight, but the new gloves were so thin and silky that they were better than her own skin. She didn't mind being deemed an eccentric.

She simply didn't think she'd be of any use spying on the nobility. It simply wasn't her place or, to be honest, in her character to be secretive.

Telling herself that she'd never see most of the guests again, she smothered her doubts and gathered her courage to open the door at a knock.

Damien stood outside, terrifyingly handsome and sophisticated in his tailored blue frockcoat, starched linen, and elegantly embroidered waistcoat. She'd never grow accustomed to believing this worldly man wanted a rural nobody like *her*.

"Did you bring Jacques with you?" she asked in awe. Someone had trimmed his thick hair to a fashionable London style.

"I did." He held out his elbow for her to take. "He makes a useful spy. Besides, I didn't wish to appear slovenly while escorting a princess. You will notice I am politely not letting my tongue hang out or look lower than your haunting eyes."

His nonsense relaxed some of her tension, and she couldn't help a thrill at his words. He almost made her feel warm, despite the drafty hall. She adjusted her shawl so his eyes didn't fall out as well as his tongue. "You could not appear slovenly even if I pushed you into a pigsty."

He squeezed her gloved hand circling his elbow and chuckled. "As you have done when I became insufferable. I am quite certain, though, that pig slop is not fashionable."

"You pulled my braid and made me fall from a tree! Really, insufferable is only half of it. It's a wonder I even speak to you." Jesting with the man she'd known from childhood eased her nerves a trifle more. Under the Town attire, he was still the country boy she'd once known.

Descending the marble stairs with half the elegant company gathering below. . . She tried not to tense again. She did her best imitation of a lady by discreetly lifting her skirt so she didn't tumble head over heels on her hem. Without her breeches underneath, it was beastly chilly, and she felt exposed.

"One of those salivating gentlemen watching you could very well be a killer," Damien reminded her, sounding as if he might be clenching his teeth. "You are not to go anywhere alone with them."

Concentrating on not falling down the stairs, she hadn't

noticed their audience. Brydie pinched his arm for reminding her. "Lavender has already warned me not to believe flattery. Is there anyone down there taller than I am?"

"Height has nothing to do with it! Do not be fooled by their elegant clothes. The marquess may be slender, but he fights regularly in a boxing salon and has been known to shoot two men in a duel. These are not all idle fellows."

"The marquess is Lady Spalding's stepson? He is married. I am fairly certain he will not attack me or even notice my existence." Reaching the bottom stair, she gave a curtsy to Captain Huntley and his lady.

"Married men are the worst," he whispered before he made his bow.

"We are gathering in the formal drawing room for sherry while we wait for dinner to be served." Clare Huntley gestured down the hall to a well-lit chamber. "Mr. Sutter, do you know everyone? Will you be able to introduce Miss Calhoun to the company?"

Brydie had sat with Clare in the inn's kitchen, conspiring to lure neglected women away from a preacher's camp, planning the new schoolroom, and other charitable discussions. This elegant lady wasn't the commonly dressed housewife who had sat at the inn's kitchen table. This one sparkled with gems, wore her gold hair in a complicated coiffeur adorned with pearls and delicate side curls. She had even darkened her pale lashes and rouged her cheeks. Brydie didn't know her at all.

Captain Huntley, however, despite his valet's attempts to squeeze his muscular frame into fashionable clothes, still resembled a pirate with his scarred features and abrupt manners. He jerked his head in the direction of a trio of laughing young men just entering the drawing room. "I'd start with watching that lot. They came down with Villiers. One is some relation to the duke and the others are friends. They have done nothing but drink my brandy."

"I thought they'd come down to hunt and fish." Damien watched the trio. "Why did Villiers bring them?"

Brydie did a mental tabulation of the manor folk and recalled the Earl Villiers was brother of Lady Elsa, the cook. The duke. . . was most probably the Duke of Castlefield, a bibliophile and frequent visitor of the manor library. He had half a dozen sons and numerous nephews roaming around. His title was in no danger of dying out as the Wycliffe one had. Just trying to remember all the names and relationships had her tense.

"The relation is feuding with his father and didn't wish to attend the duke's family gathering. Another is some distant rela-tion of Lady Marlowe, Lavender's grandmother. Lady Marlowe believes he's here to visit her and is quite pleased. The third. . . I have no notion. Younger sons tend to have empty pockets at the end of the year, before their allowances arrive. They'll go anywhere anyone feeds them." The captain abruptly turned to greet another guest who demanded his attention.

The drawing room's décor dated back a century, with plaster floral ribbons and cherubs on the ceiling, peeling gilding on the frames of ugly, dark portraits, worn silk upholstery, and faded carpets. But in the lamplight, glittering jewels, rustling silks, and blindingly white linen filled Brydie's vision. There was a marquess and an earl among the company. Verity ought to be here, not her. Or Minerva, who had worked in a duke's palace and probably knew the visiting relation.

A maid with a tray of glasses offered her a sherry. Brydie was quite certain she could not manage to drink while clutching Damien's arm.

Damien steered her toward the safe harbor of Henri Lavigne, the owner of Monk's Tavern, and his wife, Patience, who was forming a church choir. They were descendants of nobility but had lived hard lives and never owned land. She was comfortable with them.

"I will leave you in good company so I may circulate," Damien murmured. "I will return to lead you into dinner."

Abandoned, Brydie accepted the sherry this time, just to occupy her—gloved—hands. "May I spill this and go back to my room now?" she asked the welcoming couple.

They laughed, which helped settle her a little more.

"That gown looks far better on you than it ever did me," Patience said admiringly. "Now that I'm expecting, my top has grown beyond enormous. I feel as if I should wear a tent."

"You are radiant, as always," her husband assured her. "You could make a tent beautiful, but I must admit to a fondness for the gown you're wearing." He wasn't shy about glancing at his wife's ample bosom.

Patience rolled her eyes. Brydie's uneasiness transferred to thinking about Damien and his reaction to her bosom and the bed they'd someday share. Lust only muddied her thinking.

"Am I supposed to *circulate* as Damien is doing?" Brydie sipped her sherry and grimaced—not a taste she meant to acquire.

"Only if you wish to," Patience said with a shrug that drew more eyes than just her husband's. "But in emerald green, with all your dramatic auburn hair, you have been noticed. People will wish to be introduced. I believe all the men here are married except for Arnaud and those three young colts looking for fences to jump. Clare will have set you in the middle of them at the table to keep them from Lavender."

Brydie knew she wasn't beautiful. Her riotous hair had been tugged and crimped and pinned into momentarily behaving, so it looked respectable for a change. And she had a full, if not voluptuous, figure. But she was plain of face and knew it. As long as Damien accepted her as she was, she didn't mind her short lashes and freckles.

"And here comes Viscount Chatham now," Henri said with an ominous growl. "The title is newly acquired and he looks to burnish it with conquests."

"Am I to be pleased to meet him or punch him in the nose?" Brydie tried not to watch the arrogant lord approaching. She gauged him to be about her age, her height, and not given to activity that led to muscle. Henri's comment did lead her to hope he was a bibliophile, as were many of the manor's guests. He had an excellent tailor. The tails of his coat were longer than any here, and his gold buttons gleamed against a waistcoat so exquisite, it might be made of gold thread to match his golden hair.

"I never recommend punching at first introduction," Henri said solemnly. "But I have already met him."

Brydie was uncertain if he meant that as a threat and didn't have time to question. The young viscount was upon them.

Apparently having rejected sherry, he lifted his brandy snifter in salute. "You cannot occupy all the lovely ladies in the room, sir. I demand equal time." He made a polished bow that allowed him to ogle thoroughly without spilling a drop.

Nose punching might be required, but Brydie had learned simpler tactics over the years. A young viscount wasn't any more impressive than any other man who lacked respect for her person. And she was here to investigate, which gave her largess to act as needed.

After Henri performed the introductions, she smiled at the room past the viscount's shoulder. "And who are your companions, my lord? Shouldn't I be allowed introductions to all the interesting gentlemen?"

"I am far more interesting than they are. Shall we stroll around the room so I may prove my worth?"

He really was as shallow as Lavender had warned. A viscount, imagine that. Perhaps there was more to him than he wished the world to see, but she could find that out right here. "Decidedly not," she told him. "I am a mere farmer's daughter with no interest in titled gentlemen. Who are your companions? Are you all related to the late earl?"

Ignored by the suave gentleman, Henri and Patience stood guard in amusement.

"Both younger sons," Chatham said dismissively. "You may forget them. We are here for the hunting and fishing. His Grace recommended us, said we might learn something. So far, we have learned the brandy is excellent and the unattached ladies are few."

"Village life tends to be boring," Henri said with false sympathy. "Everyone working to put food on the table. . ."

Displeased, the viscount dismissed the taunt. "Servants put food on the table."

Apparently bored of each other's company, the other two Town gentlemen approached. The viscount was forced to make introductions. They ogled too. Brydie considered going fishing. The river was swift this time of year. Did gentlemen swim?

"Lord Chatham was telling us *servants* put food on the table," she told the thin-faced, rather mean-looking one called Watson. He had a sharp nose. Could that be described as Roman? "Our local baker died recently, so the rest of us are having difficulty putting bread on the table. Do you like toast with your morning tea?"

Patience uttered a muffled choke that might be laughter or a warning. Brydie didn't care.

"Find a new baker," Mr. Watson said callously. "The city is full of them."

"But this is not a city. Villages have only one bakery and the locals rely on it for their bread. Can you imagine going off to work with no breakfast? And no sandwich to tide one over at noon?" Brydie hid her spite with a smile. "Or can you even imagine going off to work?"

The one introduced as Shaw sputtered. Shorter and sturdier than his companions, his russet hair less fashionably styled, he appeared on the verge of apoplexy. "I cannot think this a proper discussion. I understand the poor woman murdered in her bed was not the sort a lady should even acknowledge."

"And *that* should not be mentioned now," Henri cut him off curtly. "If any of you are from around here, you should appreciate that every village has a bakery. Most people do not have ovens. We are all in mourning."

"Are you from around here?" Patience asked sweetly, redirecting the topic.

Having taken a dislike to the privileged trio, Brydie would have preferred to hammer toes and knuckles.

"London, Stratford, and all parts in between." Watson bowed. "Can you not send to Birmingham for a baker?"

"The bakery belongs to a family in the Americas. We're not likely to hear from them for weeks. Or even if we did, Birmingham is currently inaccessible, and it would be impossible to find a baker there." Brydie could tell she was making no progress on the investigation, but these simpletons increased her confidence. "The bridge is out."

The viscount blinked in surprise and looked concerned. "The bridge is out? We cannot go up with Villiers to his estate when we leave here?"

"You'll have to return to Stratford and take the toll road," Patience explained.

But that's when Brydie realized— Hadn't Rafe said the dead nanny had enough coins to take the toll road to the city? He'd assumed she'd taken the cut through between the toll road and the highway to save the coins for herself. Was this, perhaps, not all about Willa, but about greed and ignorance? Should they be searching Birmingham for the children's family?

But the highway also went south and Gravesyde would have been a less expensive route. . . *to Bath.*

The butler announced dinner was served. As Damien arrived to escort her, Brydie leaned past him to the young gentlemen. "Do any of you come from Bath?"

The shorter, russet-haired gentleman shrugged while eyeing Damien warily. "Chatham's family has a place in Bath, but they generally reside in London."

Chatham, the suave viscount. Viscounts had money and estates and wouldn't lower themselves to stealing from a parsonage or killing nannies. But perhaps he had a servant. . .

"What was that about?" Damien murmured as the young men fled his glower.

"The Birmingham highway also runs south to Bath, does it not?" she asked, fretting her bottom lip. She was better at action than puzzle piecing.

"Eventually, not directly, why?"

"What if. . ." She closed her eyes but couldn't work it out in her head. She needed to talk it through. "What if the nanny, or Mr. Elton's sister, or whoever the cart driver was. . . meant only to spend the night with Willa. What if she knew about family in Bath and meant to take them there?"

"And someone killed her to prevent that? And killed Willa for the same reason? It doesn't change much, does it?"

"I suppose not," she said slowly, still thinking. "Only, whoever may have sent her down this road must not have known the bridge was closed."

"And given that letter Willa received, whoever waits on the other end evidently has no idea why the children have been delayed. Even the post must go the long way around, so that letter she received could have been written before we found the children. And if anyone is actually looking for them, it will take a while before they come searching. That does not put us any closer to discovering a villain."

Brydie sighed. "I suppose, it's just nice to believe they have decent family somewhere. It would relieve Verity's mind."

In the enormous dining room, with places set for a veritable army, Damien hesitated at the place holder for Brydie, then checked the names of her companions.

"Does the killer know that the children did not arrive?" She glanced at the cards too. Mean-faced Mr. Watson and smarmy Viscount Chatham, ugh. "Our trio of young guests came from London, but they are familiar with Stratford *and* Bath and did not know the bridge was closed."

Damien appeared puzzled. "You do not think our London fellows are killers?"

Brydie glanced down the glittering, candlelit table at the fashionably elegant guests milling about, conversing civilly. "If we assume Willa's death wasn't a crime of passion, that her killer was a rough criminal sort like Parsons or Elton, doesn't it seem sensible that they did it for money? Except she had little and none seemed to be missing. And if we believe the opium was intended to kill, the nanny and children had nothing any more valuable than a few coins, which the killer did not take. In which case, isn't it more likely their killer was *paid* to remove them?"

Damien stared at her, considering the implications with obvious dismay.

Which was when Brydie murmured the fear that had bothered her all evening. "What if the person who hired the killer wasn't local and has just learned that the children are still alive?"

Damien had already deduced the answer. "Then if that killer is still here, he might be rather desperate to finish his task if he wishes to be paid."

TWENTY-SEVEN

RAFE

Having just reassured Verity that the attic was well secured and helped her tuck the orphans and Lynly into bed, Rafe swore vociferously when Minerva arrived to tell him the stair lock had been jammed.

Accustomed to rough soldiers, Minerva did not flinch at his profanities but Verity did. His wife was already round-eyed with fear. He didn't mean to upset her more—especially if the intruder had been up here *in the past hour* since he'd checked the deuced door.

He rubbed reassuringly at the delicate fingers clutching his big arm. "Now we know which door to watch."

"Or there is more than one intruder," Minerva warned. "They must know by now that the children aren't alone."

"We are leaping to conclusions. It may only be a thief intending to steal. Or worse, they could be after the heirs. There is no good reason to believe anyone wishes to harm either." Verity picked uncertainly at a thread in Rafe's coat. "Will it be safer if we have all the children in one room or will that unnecessarily endanger one set for the others?"

Even Minerva frowned at that conundrum.

Rafe knew all about divide and conquer, but he didn't think it applied here. "There is only the one corridor to reach both rooms and two entrances into it. Unless an army marches in, they cannot take us all at once. Are there any musical instruments or bells or other noisemakers in this maze of clutter?"

Both women brightened. With troops as intelligent as this, Wellington might have beaten Napoleon much sooner.

"Mr. Birdwhistle or the boys will know. I'll check with them." Minerva slipped across the corridor to the schoolroom. The tutor answered her knock immediately, threw an anxious glance to Rafe and Verity, and let her in.

"Once you're armed with noisemakers, I want to check the door on the other end leading to the new wings where the servants sleep." Rafe hugged Verity. "We are not a helpless baker or nanny."

"Be careful," she warned. "You cannot reach that door without going through all the mazes the boys have created in the storage areas."

"Then I won't need Wolfie to guard the storage area door. He can mind the stairway with the broken lock. I'll tie a trip wire across the opening. If an intruder stumbles, you and Wolfie will hear them."

"Kate is working late on the maids' uniforms," Verity warned him. "She is likely to take those stairs to check on the children when she's done. I don't know where she means to sleep."

"We'll send Minerva down to warn her. Those back stairs go to the bachelor's wing or I'd station Kate on the next floor. Damien is not likely to return to his room until late." Rafe paced the corridor. He'd been a mess sergeant, not an officer who plotted traps for enemy troops. The enemy had already killed two women. He couldn't let him take more.

He just prayed he didn't have two killers on his hands.

The gentlemen and ladies of the manor were all at dinner. The only troops he trusted were Verity and Minerva. He knew they would fight. He'd seen them in action. Mr. Birdwhistle, he didn't know. He had to strategize.

Minerva returned with a grin and a toy trumpet. "The boys are thrilled to be included. They had a drum and are fashioning more. I believe sleigh bells were mentioned."

"Even better! If they can fasten any sort of bell on doors, they might frighten an intruder away before he even reaches us." Rafe tested the trumpet with a soft toot, then handed it to Verity. "If necessary, blow really hard. I'll be patrolling up here and will come running. Don't worry about waking the children."

He turned to Minerva. "Could you see where Kate means to sleep and warn her that our doors shouldn't be breached? And if there is any way to warn the others. . ."

"I'll be dining with the servants after dinner. In the meantime, I'll talk to Kate and anyone else I find. We'll pass the word. I don't know if they can hear bells or toy horns from the ground floor, but you'll most likely terrify anyone before it matters." She slipped away.

"I need you to be brave and guard this room while I check doors." Rafe handed Verity one of the knives he kept about his person.

He didn't think she'd ever used a weapon, but she had certainly *intended* to in the past. She tucked this one in her waistband without a murmur.

"Don't attempt to dodge into any doorways if you need to conceal yourself," she warned. "I have no idea what traps the boys have set."

"I'll just flatten my slim form against a wall like a shadow," he said in amusement. "Or kick the manure out of anyone approaching, depending on my mood."

"If they have a pistol. . ." She finally look terrified.

"I have a bigger one. And I'm a fair aim with a few years experience. Besides, I know better than to dodge into doorways. I think I shall open them all in invitation."

She didn't laugh but hugged his waist. "You've been shot before. I do not ever want to see you hurt again."

Rafe caressed the caramel silk of her hair. "I really don't think anyone is stupid enough to attempt to steal young ones from an attic without an army. If your intruder meant anything at all, it was a reconnaissance mission, and you bravely thwarted him. I don't expect to be lucky enough to catch a killer tonight."

She nodded, accepting that theory.

Rafe thought if the killer could, he'd run a knife through the orphans the same way he had Willa, or feed them poison, but he kept that fear to himself.

He checked with the boys in the nursery, and as Minerva had said, they were eagerly fashioning noisemakers out of every toy in the room. He located Arthur showing his younger brother how to fashion a whip out of jumping ropes and beckoned him over.

"Yes, sir?" The fourteen-year-old would be a big man when he finished growing, and he showed every sign of possessing the Calhoun intelligence.

"I need you to slip out to the stable and see if they have bells I can fasten to doors. And while you're down there, see if anyone has a wire I can tie across the stairs."

The boy's eyes widened. "I can do that, sir. They have wire at the hardware. Should I go there if the manor doesn't have it?"

The new hardware had all sorts of tools a villain could employ. Rafe prayed Jasper wasn't a villain. "No, I'd rather have you up here with the youngers by the time dinner is done. If we're still here on the morrow, we'll do it then."

Arthur nodded and trotted off. After pulling the tutor into the corridor to explain what he planned, Rafe closed his lantern to a mere sliver of light and eased into the black recesses of the eternal attic.

TWENTY-EIGHT

MINERVA

Enveloped neck to toe in Lady Elsa's enormous apron, Minerva gingerly pushed her floured hands into the sticky bowl of bread dough. She'd delivered all her messages. Now, they waited.

While the rest of the staff ran about, tossing pots to the scullery maid, dashing in and out with drink trays, and attempting to create towers of pastries, Minerva claimed a dark corner by the pantry. Her mother-in-law instructed her on how to knead the doughy goo.

"Anyone can read a recipe," Mrs. Upton said dismissively. "But one has to actually experience mixing and kneading and timing the rising and baking."

Working with her hands had never been her life's dream. Now that she knew what baking was about, Minerva wasn't certain she wanted the experience. Still, knowledge was power. She'd learn. It was too late to save pennies for Paul's shirt, but perhaps she could surprise him and bake his bread. At least, for now, she was helping Elsa prepare for the morning while the kitchen staff apparently readied for battle.

Bracing a pantry shelf that had come loose—her husband never resisted a carpentry task—Paul emerged just as Minerva and Mrs. Upton had the dough kneaded and returned to rise by the hearth. Elsa had a fancy new stove but it was currently under siege and laden with bubbling cauldrons of what could be witch's brew for all Minerva knew. It smelled heavenly, though. She was starving.

"The ladies have retired to the drawing room," a footman announced. "The gentlemen do not wish to be disturbed. Captain says we should rest and eat."

Not once had Minerva ever heard those words uttered in the duke's castle. She seriously doubted if the duke or his sons recognized that servants needed to eat. They were fixtures, like clocks and pumps.

But all the clattering, shouting, and bustling immediately calmed into an orderly procession of chattering, happy staff carrying dishes and flatware to the kitchen's long trestle table. Washing her hands of flour, Minerva studied the people who poured into the room, jostling for position at the table.

She thought she knew roughly half the gathering servants. In the past year, the manor had grown from two ancient caretakers to a dozen maids and footmen. The men in the stable apparently ate outside, at least on busy occasions like this when the kitchen filled with the valets and ladies' maids of guests. These were the people Minerva didn't know.

"Take your meal with your mother," she whispered to Paul. "Let them think I'm invisible kitchen staff."

He eyed the puffy cap nearly falling over her eyes and the immense apron. "Even I wouldn't look at you twice in that costume. You have flour on your nose."

She poked him with a wooden spoon to prevent him from kissing her nose. "Pretend you are merely greeting me and go fill your plate."

"Aye, aye, general." He winked, sending her stupid pulse fluttering. They needed to find the killer and kidnapper soon so they could go home to their own cozy bed.

"Do not leave the kitchen without me," he warned, before picking up a plate to fill it.

Minerva took a seat between one of the women who chopped vegetables and the lady's maid who assisted the grand dames in the late viscountess's suite. The maid knew Minerva but scarcely cast her a second glance. She was too busy watching the stylish servants from London.

Minerva did the same. Verity really ought to be here to see if she recognized a Roman nose, but she would never leave those orphans if they were in danger.

At first glance, she counted no Roman noses, whatever they might be. Italian? Long? The London valet at the far end of the table had a distinctively aquiline beak and a surly attitude. Or perhaps he was too arrogant to speak with his rural counterparts.

She was familiar with Spaldings' and Villiers' valets. They were fairly high in the instep and talked among themselves, not acknowledging Surly Beak. Surly didn't acknowledge the footmen. Definite pecking order.

"Who is the man with the big nose?" she asked Clare's maid.

"He is employed by Viscount Chatham only recently, I believe," the maid replied in a low tone. "The others have ignored him all week. I don't know what he's done to annoy them."

"He's not insulted any of the maids?" Minerva knew Mrs. Upton ran a tight household, making certain the maids worked in pairs, but visitors didn't always obey.

"He does not speak to us unless forced. And without the aid of his fellow valets, he's forced to lower himself to speaking more than he likes. The others have been here before and know where to find the wash basin and soaps and brushes. He did not bring his own."

"Enlightening, thank you." Noticing Damien's suave French valet—and hopefully, the village's new shoemaker— enter,

Minerva picked up her plate and intercepted Jacques between stove and table. "Have you met the viscount's man yet?"

Slim, of average height, wearing clothes more elegant than some gentlemen, worldly Jacques knew exactly to whom she referred. He cast Surly a glance. "Calls himself John, more likely a Sean. He's not trained. Mostly, he runs errands. He asked me which of the maids might be interested in earning a few shillings." He added the last with a very Gallic shrug.

Jacques was probably the last man in the manor to ask about loose women.

"So, he does not stay in his rooms but wanders about, quite of his own accord?"

"I have only been here on this day," he warned. "But I speak with the others. Villiers' man fears Sean-John is. . . *scouting*, is that the word?. . . the manor, planning theft. Spalding's man calls him a blot upon the landscape, sticking his long nose where it does not belong. Me, I derive my conclusion from them."

Jacques had been spending too much time with Damien. In his attempt to bury his accent and become a proper English shopkeeper, he was learning to talk like a lawyer. Minerva hid her smile.

"Then we may have identified Verity's intruder. Lost as he is, our Irish John could very well have been looking for a trunk. What of the valets for the viscount's companions? I do not see any other new male faces."

"They are not *tres* elegant," Jacques said with a very French sniff. "They do for each other or borrow the manor's staff. They are not awash in coin, but they admired my boots." He glanced at his elegant footwear, exceeding anything any servant wore—or most gentlemen.

"You are a walking display of your most excellent work," Minerva agreed in admiration. "Keep your eyes and ears open. We have no idea of who or what we're looking for."

"Killers ought to wear cloaked hoods," he said dryly. "Velvet and silk are wasted on them."

She repeated that to Paul later and he laughed. "We will post a sign in the road—no killers allowed unless appropriately garbed in hooded cloak. Have you learned anything at all?"

"Not from staff, no. I gather from Jacques that Chatham's valet is most likely the bumbling man who disturbed Verity last night. I left Kate upstairs, helping gather bells and noise makers to set traps." Minerva removed her apron and cap and smoothed her serviceable twill with her palms. It had been a very long day. "If Snoop John tries to return, he will regret it, but I suspect he's simply incompetent."

"I cannot think that anyone here would harm children or cold-bloodedly stab a woman no one really knew." Paul offered his arm to lead her upstairs.

"Jacques says the viscount's valet was looking for willing maids, perhaps for his employer?" Minerva wrinkled her nose in distaste. "I hate thinking that way, but what if Chatham had used Willa in the past. . . ?"

"Unlikely. From the gossip I've heard so far, he's young and has never been outside London, until he came into his title and inheritance. I talked to a few of the stablemen and the marquess's valet. Chatham rode in on a recently purchased mare and barely knows how to ride. He doesn't belong to any of the gentlemen's clubs. So he does not originally come from money."

"Out of extreme curiosity, do we know if *Chatham* is a territorial or family title?" Minerva had spent a great deal of time in the duke's library reading up on the peerage for the duke's secretary. But she had not memorized Debrett's.

"No notion." Paul glanced at her in puzzlement. "Viscounts come with different titles, like earls?"

"Not many and I have not researched the history, but I assume, as in the rest of the peerage, the title was attached to either land or family at some distant date." There was her cynical mind at work, looking for evil under every rock.

Paul's more godly mind tracked her thoughts however. "So

Laurence, Lord Chatham could be a mere Laurence Turner and *Chatham* is the family estate?"

She grimaced. "It's possible. Not likely but possible. Laurence is his first name?"

"So I have heard. He did not ask me to call him Larry but I overheard his friends do so. How do we find out?"

"I sneak off to the library when none of the gentlemen are in there." Not easily done. The library was immense and always an attraction to visitors. Even though she was the librarian, she could not lock the doors and keep out family. "Who invited him?"

"He arrived on the coattails of the duke's grand-nephew by marriage."

"That would be Watson or Shaw? I heard nothing particularly untoward about either of them. I know most of the duke's close family but I recognize neither." Tired of fretting, Minerva lifted her hem higher than she ought as she preceded her husband up the servants' stairs. She was eager to reach their bedchamber.

"Shaw, the short, rumpled one. No income of his own. No army to join. Duke told him he'd offer a benefice in one of his parishes if he'd finish Oxford. Apparently, he's not a student either." He didn't sound offended by life's unfairness.

If Paul had a duke's patronage, he could do so much good with wealth and a larger parish. . . And here was a lazy aristocrat rejecting the largesse Paul deserved. Minerva was offended for him.

Paul practically pushed her up the last flight of servants' stairs to the wing where Minerva—as part of the earl's family—owned a room. *Owned*, according to the earl's eccentric will. They would never be homeless. But it had never been about the roof over their heads. They both wished to make the world a better place. Some days, Minerva wasn't entirely certain why.

"Idle young man, looking for trouble. Nothing new there." At the top, she leaned into Paul's embrace. "We should get them all bosky and ask if they know Willa."

Paul froze. "They're all still drinking in the dining room."

"Me and my big mouth," Minerva muttered, following his thoughts. "Can't we leave them to Damien and the captain?"

"The lawyer and the magistrate? Can they act as witness if anything incriminating is said?"

"What are they going to say?" she argued. *"I like killing helpless women?"*

"I shall moralize on opium and prostitutes and set Hunt's cousins to arguing." Paul dropped her arm and furrowed his brow.

"Which accomplishes what?" she asked peevishly. She was supposed to be the one with the devious mind. He was supposed to write sermons and save souls.

Except his devious mind had helped solve more than one murder.

"With luck, I shall establish who knows about opium and has knowledge of the local house of ill repute. We have to start somewhere." He kissed her brow and abandoned her to the drafty corridor to find her own way back to her room.

Devil take it, if he could go a-spying, so could she. She dashed for her room to clean up and change our of her flour-spattered attire.

TWENTY-NINE

BRYDIE

RUBBING HER GLOVED HANDS—SHE HADN'T SPLATTERED A SINGLE
drop on the lovely silk—Brydie glanced around the simply but
elegantly furnished withdrawing room. It was smaller than the
grandiose formal parlor. She had seen it under less formal circum-
stances and would have loved to drift aimlessly about, admiring
the artwork. But she didn't belong here with the fashionably
garbed ladies.

Now that Minerva had arrived, dressed as the lady she was,
Brydie gathered her courage to admit to Clare, "I fear I have been
of very little use in determining if any of your guests are villains."
She had been an utter failure, in fact.

"Ah, but blotting Lord Chatham's sartorial magnificence was a
moment of great enlightenment and entertainment," her hostess
said with amusement. "I don't believe I knew some of the words
he uttered. I mean to consult Hunt on their definitions."

The lech had deserved the dousing. His comments belonged in
a brothel, not a dinner table, no matter how foxed he was. And
once he touched her thigh. . . Brydie did not regret her *accident*.

"We really need to start enforcing the cursing fines. Had I been present, I might have collected enough to replace one of the chapel's bench pillows." Arriving in time to hear this last, Minerva didn't smile, which meant she hadn't learned much either.

Brydie was too overwrought to be amused. What if her failure meant harm might come to the orphans? "I am not sorry for dumping wine on his fine linen. He was insulting and deserved it. But it made him disinclined to speak to me again, especially with Damien glowering from across the table. I lack finesse." It had certainly not been one of her finer moments.

"I daresay once Damien has his hands on him, your fiancé will lack finesse as well—one of the many reasons ladies withdraw after dinner." Clare gestured at her guests whispering in groups about the room. "And did you see my charming husband seize Mr. Watson by the neckcloth and physically haul him back to the table when he attempted to follow Lavender? Some people simply must learn the hard way. Did Chatham have a particular target for his licentious tongue?"

"Among other insults, he thought Lavender should be grateful for his attentions since she is baseborn and probably no better than her mother." Brydie had been more furious about that than his groping. Spilling the wine had allowed her to continue eating without punching the lecherous beast.

"He appeared to be quite pickled," Clare suggested. "Perhaps he didn't realize what he was saying?"

Brydie's fault as well. "I spurned his dissolute attentions and questioned his lack of intelligence, which had him calling for more wine. Eventually, he talked to Watson around me and perhaps thought I was deaf and dumb. I cannot say that dining with gentlemen was much more educational than drinking at the tavern."

Minerva shrugged her elegantly-clad shoulders. "I could have told you that. Men aren't always polite at the kitchen table, either, but there is less to drink. Clare, do you know if Chatham's title is territorial or family?"

"I have no idea. I steer away from the unattached louts. Why?"

The subjects of titles was not one Brydie had cared to learn. "It's been a long day. Unless you suspect any of your lady guests, I think I should like to see how Verity and the children fare."

"Wise choice," Clare agreed. "I will linger to help Hunt sort out the drunken gentlemen should they dare to join us. I cannot believe any of them intelligent enough to plot murder, but it's best if you are upstairs, just in case you're next on their list." Casting a glance to the room's occupants, she drifted off to consult with Patience, plotting social warfare.

"I will join you shortly," Minerva said. "I have a few more questions I'd like to ask before giving up for the evening."

Brydie would very much have liked to see Damien first, but the men might spend hours at the table. He was bent on acquiring clients as well as questioning possible criminals and wouldn't leave until the last drop was drunk. She wouldn't wait for him. She knew her own way.

She said her good-nights, and with the idea of showing off her new gown and returning Verity's belongings, Brydie climbed the marble stairs to the family floor. She met Kate sitting under a sconce in the corridor, hemming a uniform. "What on earth? Do you wish to ruin your eyes? Is there no room for you to sleep in this maze of space?"

Kate's lips tightened. "Someone jammed the attic door. Rafe has set traps but I'm to warn you and Minerva or anyone else who might have a right to take those stairs so you don't set off alarms. Verity is likely to come after you with a knife."

"This is no way to live." In disgust, Brydie gazed around the late earl's echoing, dark corridors of ancient paintings and gilded sconces. "The single gentlemen are housed in that wing. They are all foxed. You can't sit here, blocking their way, in hopes of catching a criminal. Where is your room?"

"Next to yours, just down the other side of the guest hall, too far from the attic stairs to hear anything." Kate stood and led the way to the intersection of the main corridor and the guest hall. "The loft over the ballroom is through that door. I thought about sitting there, out of sight, but there is no light."

Brydie peered in at the loft railing. "Good for heaving drunken men over, but that's just more work to clean up."

Kate snickered. "I thought the same. You look lovely in that gown. We need to make you a wedding gown in that pattern."

"First, we need to cry banns," Brydie said dryly. "Go to bed, get some sleep. I'll go upstairs, check on everyone, then wait down here to warn Minerva. Do we give three knocks and a whistle to be allowed in?"

Kate laughed at mention of their old signal. "Avoid the trip wire, hold the bells hanging on the latch, and whistle at Wolfie."

"Nice. Go to bed. You need to save your eyes for better uses than uniforms." Brydie waited until her older sister traipsed down the hall. Kate would be old before her time if they did not find a better way to earn a living. They couldn't expect Damien to support her and the children.

Taking the stairs and following instructions, she patted the wolfhound on his big head and called softly, "It's just me. Are you awake, Verity?"

In shirtsleeves, Mr. Birdwhistle peered out one door. Across the hall, Verity, in her nightgown and wrapper, peered from the other. "Any news?" she asked when Brydie stepped over the wire and the guard dog.

"Nothing. The manor has some obnoxious London guests. Minerva is still downstairs questioning the ladies. I sent Kate to bed. All quiet here?" Brydie handed the necklace to Verity and tried to return the beautiful shawl, but Verity waved it away.

"Knit me a sturdy wool one sometime, in a quiet blue or brown, if you will. Rafe is patrolling, but it's been quiet. I assume everyone is at dinner, and it's later that we must worry?"

"I suspect the gentlemen will need to be carried to their beds by the servants who are currently enjoying their own repast," Brydie said. "How long does it take to sleep off drink?"

"They'll be abed until noon," the tutor surmised. "It's the wee hours of dawn when we must be wary of intruders from among the servants. We should get our sleep while we can."

After verifying the children slept, Brydie returned to the guest hall below just as Minerva approached.

"They're all fine," Brydie told her. "The door is guarded by a wire, a wolfhound, and bombs, for all I know. Mr. Birdwhistle believes they won't be invaded until the early hours, if at all. I learned nothing tonight except I don't like idle gentlemen. You?"

"I learned Lord Chatham has an incompetent valet with a long nose who might have been the intruder. The kitchen is poorly lighted and crowded, but it's possible that he had slight side whiskers. I'd love to set a guard at this door but who would we trust?"

"I don't know if we can even trust Mr. Birdwhistle." After this evening, Brydie wasn't prepared to trust anyone.

Minerva made an inelegant noise. "I'm quite certain he has no interest in poisoning children for money or fame. Whether we can trust his feather-headed idiocy is another matter."

Brydie raised her eyebrows at her friend's scorn for the friendly tutor, but she did not question. Minerva kept secrets. Perhaps Mr. Birdwhistle had worked for the duke at some point.

"Paul will be looking for me, so if there is nothing else to be done, I'll be off." Minerva stopped to add, "Oh, I also learned that our three visiting bachelors have no funds of their own and regularly sponge off friends when they can't pay their landlords. Apparently, Chatham has only recently come into his title after the death of an elderly uncle."

"Given his sartorial splendor, as Clare calls it, I'd say the title came accompanied with a degree of funds." Brydie tried to work out how that might matter but couldn't.

"A title buys him larger credit limits with the shopkeepers.

Since he's still sponging, I assume any inherited wealth is negligible."

New clothes could be purchased with a title? Interesting. Brydie followed Minerva down the hall until Wolfie began howling and an unearthly din rattled the attic.

THIRTY

Having just taken everyone's advice to go to bed, Verity had removed her wrapper when the unholy clatter startled Wolfie into howling.

Her first instinct was to shove the bed across the door as she'd planned, but anyone of size could shove that meager cot. The bed's placement had only ever been meant to wake her up if someone tried.

Hastily donning her robe, she lit her lamp again. She found Rafe's knife on the trunk she used as table, and clutching the key given to her earlier, slipped into the hall. She fastened the lock and placed the key into the pocket of her robe.

Mr. Birdwhistle popped out of his door, tugging on a rather rich-looking velvet banyan while trying to hold his lamp. Obedient Wolfie remained where placed, howling, probably in frustration.

The jangling had halted. No one lurked in the corridor. Verity whistled, calling the dog to her. "Guard, Wolf," she ordered, posting the animal between the two bedrooms.

At Rafe's shout, she hurried toward the storage area, heart

thumping. And then she remembered—she was leaving the children protected by a *dog*.

Torn, she stopped abruptly. Nearly crashing into her, Mr. Birdwhistle staggered and grabbed a wall to prevent collision. Alarmed at a new rattle of bells, she glanced behind them. Relief flooded her as Brydie and Minerva raced down the hall in their evening attire. Mr. Birdwhistle lingered, as well, torn between his charges and whatever was happening deeper in the enormous storage area.

"Give us the knife," Brydie demanded, holding out her hand. "We'll stand guard."

Minerva seized the stick the tutor held and gestured with it. "Find Rafe. We won't let anyone near the children without raising the dead."

"You'll have more difficulty keeping the boys in," Birdwhistle said dryly, but he stood guard at the attic entrance with Verity. "They're armed and creative."

Verity didn't linger for pleasantries while hearing Rafe's shouts and what sounded like an almighty battle. In her slippers, she opened the door into the storage attics. She held up her hand to the tutor and pointed at the marble bust in the rocking chair on top of the three-legged washstand. One jostle and they'd be beaned.

He lifted his lamp high and she held hers low so they could find all the traps the boys had set. She triggered one by pushing aside what appeared to be a drapery with her foot. She should have known better. She jumped backwards as a broken dress form toppled in their path.

The noise at the far end disintegrated into shouting and cursing with the occasional thud and crash. Rafe sounded more angry than hurt but that meant little.

Swallowing huge lumps of fear, she stuck to the torturous path the boys had carved through centuries of detritus. Most of the good furniture had been removed. The rest of this jumble probably ought to be tossed. Except, for all anyone knew, the eccentric earl had hidden more treasure maps in three centuries of rubbish. An excess of caution prevented wholesale burning.

Opening a door into a second attic that might once have been servants' quarters, Mr. Birdwhistle caught an oar swinging at their heads. Their lamps cast shadows on the interior and it took a moment to make out figures.

"Thank goodness," Rafe said in disgust. "I thought I'd kill myself trying to drag this scoundrel into the light. He kicked my lamp and I had to stomp out flames. We need someone to clean up the oil."

Verity nearly wept in relief at her innkeeper husband's pragmatism. He hadn't been getting killed. He'd been cleaning up, in the dark, in a maze of boyish snares.

Mr. Birdwhistle set his lamp on a wall shelf that might once have held a candle. The light shone on a large man bound and trussed in unraveling drapery roping. Her husband could capture intruders and truss them in the dark—a man of many talents.

Rafe crossed the room in two strides, sweeping Verity up and pressing kisses on her head. "I'm fine. The children?"

Clinging to his neck, she hadn't realized she was weeping. She sniffed and tried to wipe her eyes. "Probably not sleeping anymore but Minerva and Brydie are with them."

She wiggled so he'd put her down, then ran her hands over his face and arms, checking for blood. She still had a clear memory of the time he'd come home with his arm running red. Only after verifying that he was whole did she let him hold her again. She'd spent half a lifetime without hugs and couldn't ever have enough of his now.

"I've seen this chap in the kitchen," Mr. Birdwhistle declared. "Valet, I believe?"

Verity glanced down at the angry man twisting against his ties. "Long nose, fat lips, that's the one claimed he was hunting for a trunk."

Rafe set her aside to haul his captive to his feet. The servant wasn't small but Rafe had no difficulty shoving him toward the maze leading to the schoolroom attic. "I'll haul him down to Hunt. He's been warned to stay out of here."

"I didn't do nothing," the culprit claimed. "You can't arrest me for being lost."

"Sure we can," Rafe said with assurance. "We can arrest you for anything that makes us happy. You can plead your case before a judge."

Apparently understanding the truth of that, he shut up.

Minerva and Brydie looked relieved when they approached, not because the intruder had been caught, but because Arthur could only hold two of the three boys at once. Brydie had her younger nephew by the back of his nightshirt, which he was trying to wriggle out of. Thank goodness Arthur had offered to stay tonight to help the tutor.

"We want to see how the traps worked," Rob cried at sight of them. "Did we catch him?"

Verity noted the tutor's students mostly stayed quiet but, imitating their older companion, they were also attempting to wriggle their arms out of their shirts. She almost managed a grin, but she needed to see the orphans. Unlocking the door and hurrying to the back room, she found them sound asleep, with the kitten prowling restlessly. The events of this last week had overwhelmed the poor tykes.

Gently closing the door so as not to disturb them, she returned to the hall where everyone argued at once. Verity rapped her knuckles on Rob's head to shut up the most vocal and gestured for silence from the adults. "Who is he?" she demanded. "Stand up, sir, give us your name."

Hiding a smirk, Brydie lowered her nephew to his feet but kept her hold on him.

Minerva raised an icy eyebrow when the man refused to reply, even after Rafe shook him by his coat collar. "I was told his name is John, although the others call him Sean. He's Lord Chatham's valet."

"Manservant, he calls me," John muttered. "I ain't. . . I'm not trained."

"Evidently. I suggest you tell us the real reason you are in the attic, where you have been expressly forbidden to go." Verity crossed her arms and used her best schoolteacher voice.

The manservant shifted uneasily beneath Rafe's rough hold. "It'd cost me my position," he complained. "I was promised I'd be raised up to a proper valet if I did as told."

"And what were you told?" Minerva asked, looking sweetly innocent in her simple dinner gown, with her pale hair pinned up. In this light, with her petite size, the curate's wife barely looked old enough to be out of the schoolroom.

John glanced uneasily at her, then at the angry crowd, and shook his head in defeat.

Instead of rattling his prisoner's bones, Rafe released the prisoner to Verity and friends. "If you were only doing as your employer told you, you can't be arrested."

Verity thought that might be a lie, but it produced a result.

"Not Lord Chatham." John shook his head vehemently. "His solicitor."

SATURDAY

DECEMBER 23, 1815

THIRTY-ONE

UNWILLING TO DISTURB THEIR HOSTS SO LATE IN THE EVENING—
especially when everyone was foxed— wanting to remove the
ladies from the cold attic, Rafe simply locked up *John* in one of the
unused guest rooms for the night.

Spending the night in Verity's arms eased his inner turmoil so
he could think logically again.

If he didn't have to be a one-man army, he might almost
manage this bailiff business. Having women as his troop was
more than a trifle odd. Except, Gravesyde wasn't a war zone but a
domestic situation where women outnumbered men and had
ruled through years of a war that had taken their menfolk. Rafe
was under no illusion that he was smarter than they, just stronger
and more experienced in warfare. The women understood society,
a different type of battlefield.

He simply had to adjust his thinking, with Verity's aid.

After seeing Verity and the children fed, Rafe wound his way
downstairs. Not having drunk to excess as the younger guests
had, Damien and Hunt were already at the breakfast buffet.

"Understand there was some contretemps in the attic?" Hunt

asked. "Our lordly viscount raised the devil when he couldn't find his valet last night."

"Chatham passed out before Jacques could do more than remove his boots. Very fine boots, he reports," Damien said with a straight face.

Knowing Damien's peevish valet, Rafe assumed Jacques had more than that to say about a cup-shot lordling who'd probably cast up his accounts over said boots.

"Our attic intruder is a Sean who calls himself John and says he's a manservant aspiring to be a valet. Which I take to mean he earns half what a valet ought to be paid for the same duties." Rafe scooped up half the eggs on the platter and topped them with ham. He'd worked up an appetite and had missed dinner. He was also just annoyed enough to not care what the gentry thought of him. "He also claims a *solicitor* hired him to search the attic. I locked him up until we can question him at a more decent hour."

"Ah, thoughtful of you." Hunt gulped his coffee. "Last night, I might have throttled him. This morning, I'm brimming with Christmas joy and cheer and receptive to prattle."

Rafe tried not to choke on his ham. The one-eyed captain looked as dour and piratical as ever.

"I understand the women are holding their Christmas market at the inn today? Do you need to be there to prevent Fletcher from terrorizing them?" Damien politely cut his ham into bite-size bits.

More interested in food than etiquette, Rafe rolled his ham up in cold toast. "If I think my family is safe, I'll be there to supervise."

He bit off a hunk of his half-sandwich. *His family.* If they kept the orphans, he'd have an instant family. The idea was growing on him. He needed to quit thinking like that until the matter was resolved. The letter to Willa had indicated *someone* was expecting them.

"Well then, gentlemen, let's finish breaking our fast and interview our culprit. I, for one, would like to resolve this wretched business so the ladies will quit fretting and return to singing." Hunt concentrated on his food after that pronouncement.

Rafe heartily approved the sentiment, but he doubted that a viscount's manservant would provide sufficient insight to solve two murders.

The curate disabused him of that notion later, as he made his way to question the prisoner, accompanied by Hunt and Damien. "Minerva says the servant mentioned a solicitor sent him?"

"So he claims." Rafe unlocked the guest room. "But he fears for his position and is likely to say anything to keep it."

"It was someone from an estate solicitor's office responsible for calling the orphans' mother a *mistress* and burying her under the name of Smith," Paul reminded them. "It may be good to know the name of the one who hired this person."

"Excellent idea." Hunt stormed into the open room, catching the servant hastily yanking on his coat. "What's your full name, John?"

"Gillespie, sir," he said nervously. "From County Cork."

"I'm Captain Huntley, the magistrate. Rafe Russell, bailiff, Upton, curate, Sutter, a lawyer to make certain we stay legal. Lord Chatham is your employer?"

"Yes, milord. . . sir." Gillespie hastily wrapped his neckcloth. "Is he very angry?"

"He is irrelevant." The American army captain callously dismissed the viscount.

The room was almost too small for all of them. Rafe was happy to stand in the doorway as guard and hand off the questioning to Hunt. After the servant had terrorized Verity and the children, he'd not be so polite.

"And last night you said a solicitor ordered you to search the attic? What solicitor?" Hunt leaned against a wall and toyed with the cane he no longer needed but used for effect.

"Lord Chatham's solicitor, sir. He hired me when his lordship came into the title."

Rafe bit his tongue on his opinion of a man who couldn't hire his own servants. His foul humor was not helpful.

"And the solicitor's name?" Damien jotted in a notebook he produced from his pocket.

"Turner, I believe, sir," Gillespie said nervously. "That's what his lordship calls him."

Turner, the name of the orphans. Rafe stirred uneasily.

"You don't know the firm he works for?" Damien asked.

"No, sir. He hired me when my former employer couldn't pay my wages, said his lordship would be coming into his funds once they settled matters with the estate."

"Sounds like we need to question Chatham," Hunt decided. "Sutter, can your valet dry him out and prop him up? Or should I send mine?"

"Depends on whether you want your newly-minted viscount tormented," Damien said. "Jacques is insistent that he's a boot-maker and only acting as my valet as a favor to me. He took a dislike to his lordship."

"My man was once a sergeant, not a peacock like yours. I'll send him. While I'm gone, find out why this one thinks he's hunting through attics." Hunt strode off to set the fox among the pigeons.

Gillespie looked even more nervous. "He'll blame me. I'll lose my place. I've told you everything I know. His lordship doesn't know anything."

"His lordship needs to grow up and accept responsibility," the curate corrected. "He should know why his solicitor is telling you to trespass."

"I was just to see if there was any way in," the manservant protested. "I heard talk of pirate treasure and jewels. I thought it was some game among the gentry."

"Did you break one lock and jam the new one?" Rafe wanted a crime to prosecute. He felt sorry for this chap but he was still outraged that his orders had been ignored.

Gillespie twitched nervously. "It was what I was told to do."

"When?" Rafe demanded.

"Ummm." Gillespie fumbled with his buttons. "Day you told me not to use those stairs?"

"The solicitor is *here*, in the manor?" Damien asked with incredulity.

Gillespie shook his head. "No, sir. Elton told me. He works for Mr. Turner."

Rafe thought he might go through the roof. "*Elton*? Where is that miscreant? He's in the *manor*? I've been hunting all over for him."

"Don't know, sir. Thought he was at the inn, sir."

Rafe and Wolfie had scoured the inn, inside and out, but he'd be the first to admit the sprawling monstrosity could hide an army for a week. "Elton is a thief, a liar, and a potential kidnapper. Your lordship and his solicitor keep bad company."

The servant grew even more pale. "But I know he works for Mr. Turner. I've seen them speak."

Rafe straightened. "You can identify Turner?"

"Yes, of course, sir. He hired me."

Damien consulted his notes. "Let me see if I have this correct. Mr. Turner, presumably an estate solicitor, hired you to act as manservant for Lord Chatham after his lordship came into his title? Was this in London? How long ago?"

"Yes, sir, in London, sir, about a fortnight ago, after his lordship's uncle died."

Before the Widow Turner died. Rafe needed to connect all the nefarious events in some manner. When exactly had the widow been buried? This was Saturday. The orphans had arrived last Monday, nearly a week ago. They presumably left Stratford Sunday evening, which meant their mother had died less than a week after Chatham's uncle? Rafe wanted Verity here to prevent him from leaping to terrible conclusions.

He turned to the curate, who merely acted as witness, and

murmured, "Did you not say the servants were seen leaving Beanblossom? Do you know what day that was?"

"No, the neighbor simply indicated she saw a carriage shortly after the widow's death. I didn't ask for a death certificate," Upton whispered. He wrinkled his brow in thought. "I believe the Stratford curate said they'd buried her a few days before we arrived, which was on Tuesday. That would make the funeral most likely on Saturday or Sunday?" Now he, too, looked alarmed.

Good to know the Oxford-educated curate was having the same horrible thoughts.

"And where did you see Elton and Turner together?" Damien continued jotting in his notebook, a lawyer to the bone.

Gillespie wrinkled his large beak in distaste. "In Stratford, sir. Mr. Turner was at the inn there when we arrived on the Friday evening. I believe he brought bank notes for his lordship, because I was paid the wages I was owed from my former employer, as promised."

Money, always an excellent way to buy loyalty. "And that's when you saw Elton?"

"No, sir. That was the next day, noonish. Saturday morning, Mr. Turner borrowed his lordship's carriage to see to estate business. When he returned, he had Mr. Elton with him, to buy a carriage, I believe. The delay forced us to finish our journey on the Lord's day. Lord Chatham and his friends were displeased as the inn wasn't to their liking." Gillespie tugged at his neckcloth.

Rafe interrupted. "Was there anyone else in his lordship's carriage with Mr. Elton and Mr. Turner?"

"No, sir, just the two of them. Mr. Turner had his own horse on back. I helped him untie it so he might leave on errands, while Mr. Elton left on foot. I didn't see Elton again until the other night, when he brought me the message from Mr. Turner about leaving the back stairs open."

"Would you recognize Turner's handwriting?" Rafe asked, trying to hold his temper.

Gillespie frowned. "No, sir. The message wasn't written. I don't read so well."

Which meant the message was most likely not from the solicitor at all. Elton was still trying to steal the children.

THIRTY-TWO

MINERVA

"WE ARE HOLDING THE CHRISTMAS FAIRE," MINERVA INSISTED Saturday morning over the vociferous objections of the manor gentlemen. "Our parishioners have been working night and day on their projects. If Rafe refuses the use of the inn, we'll hold it in Willa's house or the chapel or in the mercantile, if necessary. You cannot stop us."

Paul looked pained but her husband knew better than to argue unless she was suggesting immoral activities. Heaven forbid that she should ever *suggest* dishonesty. She might indulge in lying, cheating, and deception, but she would never actually *tell* him and strain his patience. He knew that. She'd married him for his perceptivity and his brilliant ability to adjust to being married to someone like her. . . The reason she wished to reward his patience and understanding with a hearty breakfast. Someday. It was the very least she could do.

Damien was the one pacing the drawing room in fury. "We have a killer on the loose! Elton could very well be lurking in the da. . . deuced inn. He could take any of you hostage if he thought it would bring him the orphans. We don't know what he'll do!"

"If he's very lucky, he'll only get himself kicked into next week," Brydie retorted.

Minerva almost snorted at this entertaining turn of phrase.

"We are not helpless infants," Brydie continued, clearly working up a storm of her own. She and Damien had a few issues to resolve before they married. "Rafe and Verity are guarding the helpless in the attic. If it makes you happy, surround the pub with men and swords. We are holding the fair."

And hoping to lure Elton into the open. Verity had yet to push that one past Rafe. The hard part had been convincing Verity, but now that she understood, the inimitable innkeeper's wife would bring Rafe around.

Minerva fastened her redingote. She hated being buttoned up but, for a church event, she needed to be respectable.. "If you really want to be helpful, you'll lock up Lord Chatham. I showed you the Debrett's. He's a *Turner*. And probably a liar and possibly a killer. When he wakes up, ask him how he's related to his supposed solicitor and the orphans. His reaction ought to be telling."

That might protect the orphans. It didn't explain Willa.

"Elton is the one giving orders and hunting for the children. We have no reason to lock up a viscount," Paul warned, not pacifying but offering rationality. "Hunt will have someone outside his door. I'm sure it can all be explained if you'll just have patience."

Her husband liked to believe the good in everyone, even imbeciles. Minerva had reason to be cynical. "Your lordling is a ninnyhammer at best, a killer at worst. We need to identify this Turner person, if he exists, and find Elton, whom we've actually seen." Minerva tied on her bonnet. "Unless you wish to believe Mr. Dryden is hiding in the village as well, I can only think of two men recently arrived who might pass as a solicitor: Mr. Jasper and Mr. Cooper. Neither of them seem likely. The servant may be lying."

"If you leave the manor, we'll have to send men down to

guard you, which means fewer people here to protect the orphans. This is not acceptable!" Damien shouted, ignoring her perfectly rational argument.

Minerva could understand why Brydie had to fight back. An angry Damien was an autocrat of great beauty, tall and strong and straining the seams of his tailoring with muscle—and protective male instincts. Most women would bow to his wishes.

Brydie was not most women. In amusement, Minerva watched the Viking warrior, her cloud of untamed auburn hair escaping its pins, go nose to nose with him.

"*You* cannot tell *us* what is acceptable, Damien Sutter. We are grown women with minds of our own, not slaves. You may suggest and offer aid but you cannot bind us hand and foot and prevent us from going our own way."

Damien clenched his fists and leaned into the argument.

Minerva ignored them when Paul bent over to whisper in her ear. "I will suggest they call the banns sooner rather than later. If they were alone right now. . ."

As they were quite often, Minerva knew. Two passionate people. . .

She intervened before they could lay hands on each other. "Come along, Brydie. There is time for you to make some buns in Rafe's oven, surrounded by servants and church ladies and probably the deacon, since there is nothing he likes more than a good gossip over food. If Mr. Elton shows his face, we shall slam his nose with a skillet. And then you may kick him however you like, although into next week might make him more elusive."

She grabbed Brydie's arm, steered her away, and murmured, "I did not dare mention that Clare and Patience and quite possibly, even the dowagers, are attending. I am quite certain there is another lecture in that."

"We are always arguing," Brydie said with a sigh, tying the hood of her cloak before stepping into the wind. "I am not certain marriage is for me."

Minerva laughed. "It's that or babies without marriage. The

two of you simply need to accept your differences. But not right now. We have a thief to catch."

"And gifts to sell and merriment to be had. I want a real Christmas this year, not another pathetic one where we huddle over coals and warm milk and call it a holiday. We didn't even have a church to attend!" Brydie set down the drive in determination. "I want glorious hymns and carols!"

"I spent last Christmas hiding from His Grace's guests, writing letters in search of a particular tome he wished added to his library. With all those unmarried sons and their friends, his household tends to be very. . . boisterous. I am looking forward to music and greenery and childish excitement." Minerva almost raced toward the village in anticipation. If they must catch killers, it should be done with merriment, which was ridiculous and proved the holiday spirit had infected her wits.

It was early yet. Rafe's kitchen staff had the fire going and breakfast cleared away. Under Fletch's orders, they were mopping and dusting, but he was already gone, having chosen to ride to Stratford for the mail rather than deal with holiday merriments.

"All right, ladies, today we are to be festive," Minerva declared. "Mr. and Mrs. Lavigne will be bringing in greenery for decorating the pub. Are any of the guests about who might be interested in helping?"

"Mr. Jasper's at the hardware store," Miss Butler replied. "Mr. Cooper's been staying over to the bakery. He was here last night looking for a meal but hasn't been in yet this morning. Mr. Fletcher told Parsons to chop firewood, so he's out back."

"I'll talk to Jasper," Brydie offered. "I'll ask him to fetch Cooper and bring hammers and nails as his tithe to the church. He should meet the community if he wishes to sell to them."

While Brydie was hunting for hammers and men, Henri and Patience Lavigne arrived in a cart filled with greenery. This was what Minerva had hoped of her first Christmas in her new home. Forgetting their grim purpose for a moment, she ran out to delight in the fresh smelling evergreens, exclaiming over pinecones and mistletoe as the inn staff joined her.

"I told Paul I'd meet him over at the chapel to finish up some projects. I'll be back to help you hang the mistletoe," Henri promised, kissing his wife.

"Take a few of the wreaths with you." Patience pointed at beribboned holly and ivy entwined in circles.

"My word, you are a saint," Minerva said in awe, watching the beautiful decorations being carried off to adorn Paul's modest chapel. "I should learn how to do that."

"What, be a saint or make wreaths?" Patience dropped a wrapped bundle of holly into Minerva's arms. "I believe you've missed your chance at sainthood. And making wreaths is why you have parishioners." Patience was the daughter of a curate. Unlike Minerva, she knew how a proper church should be run.

As they carried in their festive boughs, the widows and single mothers still living in the village bustled from their cottages, bearing their own contributions. Before long, Rafe's pub smelled of a forest and scented candles. Besides the candles, his tables overflowed with baked goods, crocheted ornaments, knitted infant garments and stockings, and anything else that could be put together with what was available. Minerva crowed in excitement over every addition.

Brought in from his woodchopping, Parsons stood on trestle tables to drape holly over the huge mullioned bay windows. Brydie returned with Jasper, Cooper, and hammers to hang the boughs they were stringing together with ribbons and pinecones.

Once she'd set the men to pounding nails, Brydie cornered Minerva out of hearing of the chattering ladies setting up their tables. "You mentioned Mr. Dryden earlier. He arrived with Elton and works for a solicitor's office, does he not? If Lord Chatham's manservant claims he saw this solicitor called Turner in London *and* Stratford, might Dryden be hiding under the name of Turner?"

Minerva recalled the nervous young man and frowned. "Mr.

Browning says his office does not handle the estate trust, just the sale of the house at the estate's request. And Mr. Dryden is merely a clerk in his office. I cannot feature it, not any more than I can see nice Mr. Jasper or lazy Mr. Cooper. I fear we are being blind and expecting a killer to look like Parsons or Elton or even Gillespie. We cannot believe a gentleman might be a killer."

"Or a woman," Brydie noted with a grimace. "Jealousy might be a motive, for all we know. Willa was asleep. How difficult would it be to stab a sleeping woman?"

"She'd have to be strong enough to crown Cooper and knock him unconscious. I suppose. . ." Minerva wrinkled her nose in disgust. "I hate thinking like this. Let us not for a few hours, or we'll be suspecting every one of these good women selling their wares."

"We'll wait until Verity arrives," Brydie agreed, sailing off to the kitchen to finish her baking.

Minerva's insides clenched at just the thought of the plot they'd hatched. So, she wouldn't think it just yet. She welcomed Paul's parishioners with open arms, exclaiming over beautifully woven wool blankets, glorious currant cakes, jars of honey, and even homemade whiskey. As they'd hoped, everyone was ready for a little cheer after the dark years of war and poverty.

Once the greenery was hung, including a kissing ball over the pub doorway, and the tables set with tempting gifts, the manor staff arrived with cauldrons of hot, spiced cider for the punch bowl. The pub, already scented with pine and candles plus the cinnamon from baking, now smelled of delicious apples.

To Minerva's consternation, the men—in their infinite wisdom —had decided to keep an eye on the viscount's valet by having him serve the punch. Gillespie seemed nervous but quite capable at pouring hot cider into tin cups for the ladies crowding around him. She supposed he was the only person who might recognize Mr. Turner. Minerva held out little hope of a solicitor lingering in Gravesyde, but if they could catch Elton. . .

They'd stationed as many boys and men around the inn's

perimeter as available, then locked all the inn exits except the one in the lobby. As curate's wife and ostensibly in charge of a church fair, Minerva stood at the door to greet their customers. She expected no surprises from the village folk, but Brydie's warning about a female killer had raised her awareness. Most of the local women were elderly, some were very young, but might there be a jealous wife among them?

Half the parish was already inside, hovering over their tables of wares, so it was the manor ladies who arrived as the first customers. Lady Elsa was busy overseeing the kitchen preparations for Christmas dinner on the morrow, but Clare Huntley and Lavender arrived in a sweep of ruffled pelisses and feathered bonnets. Having spent most of her life in a boarding school, Lavender was as excited as a child and swept past Minerva as if she didn't exist.

Clare laughed and watched her go. "She works so hard, it's sometimes hard to remember that she really isn't full grown yet."

"But she's adult enough to have made Boxing Day gifts for all her seamstresses," Minerva said, in between greeting a few of the manor maids arriving next. "I do hope her grandmother has thought of her. Lavender still doesn't believe that the dowager has softened toward the notion of having an illegitimate grandchild."

"The old tabby has been contemplating which jewels she should give Lavender next. I told her the child needed a warm shawl more, so she bought pattern books and, besides the shawl, has knitted booties for Lavender's dog and stuffed a bed for its basket!" Clare let her bonnet fall back on its ribbons to admire the pub's festivity. "I spent last Christmas trying to scrounge enough coins to buy Oliver an orange and a used mathematics book. Not having to pay for the roof over our heads or the food in our bellies is immensely freeing! I am ready to spread the wealth."

She sailed into the pub carrying a basket in which to collect her purchases.

The pub was starting to fill with excited chatter and laughter by the time the manor's grand dames descended in their carriage.

Lavender's grandmother, Lady Marlowe, and Hunt's aunt, Lady Spalding, spurned current fashions and clung to the lower waists and heavy petticoats of their youth. Minerva was amazed the intimidatingly grandiose Lady Marlowe didn't still wear a powdered wig.

The dowagers had been outraged widows when they'd first claimed their share of the manor. But now, they'd made up with their families and actually condescended to visit the village's tiny chapel upon occasion. Minerva hoped they'd tithe generously.

"Did anyone bring mince pies?" Lady Marlowe asked, the mole on her lip seemingly quivering in anticipation. "Elsa refuses to make them."

"Because we do not need all that suet and you refused to try her apple mince." Lady Spalding pecked Minerva on the cheek. Rounder and friendlier than the baroness, she eagerly sniffed the tempting scents. "This will be such fun! I'm glad you girls thought of it."

It would be much more fun if Minerva wasn't watching Verity and Arthur approach with a gaggle of urchins disguised in old shirts, coats, and boys' trousers—and knew two of them were little girls.

THIRTY-THREE

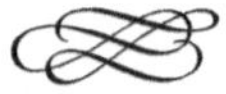

BRYDIE

Brydie almost swallowed her tongue at the sight of Lynly and
Daphne with their hair hidden under boys' caps and wearing
Rob's outgrown shirts with rolled up breeches. Anyone with half
an eye and brain would know they were too clean to be street
urchins. But Verity had lived in London and had an eye for
costume, so they were passable boys.

To her relief, Arthur and Kate had the four younger boys in
hand. They wore similar patched, loose-fitting clothes, even the
heirs. Brydie looked over their heads for Mr. Birdwhistle, but he
wasn't to be seen. His presence would give away the fact that the
heirs were present, she supposed. He probably wasn't far away
though.

Fashionable Verity had garbed herself in what appeared to be
a maid's black round gown and a mobcap instead of her usual
beautiful bonnet. Beneath the cap, her expression was fierce. It
had been her idea to separate the orphans to make it difficult for
kidnappers to recognize them.

In rough cap and clothes, Daphne still looked like a blond fairy angel, but she was quiet, while dark-haired, skinny Lynly bounced and chatted, distracting from the younger girl.

With his curly, fair hair hidden and hot chocolate smeared on his mouth and nose, Daniel looked a little rougher. He clung to Arthur, his big blue eyes round as he took in the pub filled with holiday festivity.

Twelve-year-old Rob swaggered behind Arthur, with the two eight-year-old heirs, pretending he wasn't as wide-eyed and swivel-headed as Daniel. Except for Arthur, all had chocolate on their faces.

Under the protection of Minerva and Brydie, Verity nervously tugged down Daphne's cap and instructed her crew. "Lynly and Daphne and I will go in first. Daniel, you and Rob wait here a moment with Arthur. Oliver and Davey, you need to wait for last and stay with Kate. That way, we won't each see what the other is buying."

And anyone watching wouldn't know which child belonged with whom, without the children understanding they were in danger. Brydie smiled at their excitement. Children ought to feel safe to venture into the world and explore.

For this reason, Brydie would do what she must to capture a kidnapper and killer. She would never be a proper lady thinking like that, but she preferred being useful.

Perhaps Damien felt a little bit like that when he was trying to protect her? She'd think on it, later.

Verity donned a smiling face but her fear was obvious. "We have been ordered to buy currant biscuits, and we are hoping there might be candies."

As if they hadn't spent half the morning plotting this, Brydie gestured at the crowded market. "Good thinking. If you hurry, there may be some left."

The girls dashed eagerly into the pub to examine all the goodies on the three rows of trestle tables. They exclaimed over crocheted angels and pinecone elves in equal excitement. Brydie waited until they were deep inside the high-ceilinged pub before she discreetly followed. Minerva fell in behind Arthur with Rob and Daniel. Kate stayed with the heirs. Mr. Birdwhistle would follow eventually.

The enormous pub had been organized in three rows of tables, six tables long—eighteen tables of delight, plus the bar with cider and nibbles. The children barely knew where to turn.

At twelve, Rob was too old to rein in for long, of course, but he dutifully stayed close to his older brother while casting longing gazes to a table of baked goods. They'd given the children coins and told them to think of others, but Brydie didn't expect them to make wise choices at their age.

She listened to the girls prattle, while searching the face of every man squeezing through the narrow aisles. She'd not met Elton and wouldn't recognize him. But she could identify *almost* everyone from church or around the village or manor. His lordship's valet seemed to be enjoying serving punch and flirting with the women who stopped to have their cups filled. Gillespie had Rafe's convict clerk running back and forth from the kitchen with clean cups. Mr. Jasper from the hardware was picking over a table of lacy collars, presumably for his mother. None of these newcomers even looked up at the arrival of a gaggle of youngsters.

Brydie didn't see Cooper, but that wasn't unusual. She was fairly certain he had pockets to let and only stayed because he had nowhere to go. Perhaps he'd asked his family for funds when he sent his letters. Surely, they'd have a reply soon. Even after learning of the orphaned children, he certainly hadn't shown any concern that they might belong to his distant cousin. He probably wasn't even aware that she'd had children. A family man, he was not.

Mr. Oswald from the mercantile arrived with his wife. A few farmers and laborers from the manor and the stable yard showed up. Brydie wasn't as familiar with these men, but she was thrilled that they'd been drawn into village affairs. Still, she couldn't revel in the fair's success while scrutinizing everyone who might be the man who'd try to kidnap the children and had possibly killed their nanny.

"Should we have asked Rafe and Damien to stand guard?" Minerva whispered, catching up with her. "They're the only ones besides Gillespie and the orphans who might recognize Elton."

"Showing their faces would scare him off. They know that. But they're here, you can be sure of it." Brydie glanced around, searching prospective hiding places. "Rafe won't let Verity and the children out of his sight."

"Ah, that's how Kate became involved. Damien sent her." Minerva did the same as Brydie, hunting hiding places.

"There's a place on the lobby stairs where we can see anyone entering the pub. One of the men will be there," Brydie concluded. "Rafe may be patrolling, hoping to prevent Elton from entering."

"It would be most excellent if he were captured before disrupting the fair." Minerva smiled in satisfaction at the bustling scene. "We might even earn enough to buy fabric for altar cloths."

"The chapel needs cushions more. We should write wealthier churches, ask if they have any old altar cloths in their closets that they're not using. The sewing ladies can fix anything."

A half dozen men garbed in old army coats sidled in, uncertain of their welcome. Until recently, they'd lived in a camp by the river, homeless and unemployed. Hunt gave them what work he could and a roof over their heads when they wanted it.

"Oh, a chance to persuade them to church." Minerva perked up. "Paul will be proud of me." She abandoned Brydie and wove her way through the crowd.

It was almost impossible to keep track of all the people in the room now. The aisles were packed. Uneasily, Brydie worked her way closer to Verity, who had the girls. The boys were everywhere. She spotted Daniel at a table in the aisle by the bar and kitchen, watching one of the market women work a carved puppet on strings. Arthur hovered nearby, pretending to admire fine handkerchiefs. With Damien as an example, her nephew would grow into a strong, brave man someday.

Brydie would buy the children everything they wanted, if she could, but her purse was nearly empty after handing out coins to her nephews and niece.

Daniel turned to Arthur, pointing at the puppet in excitement. Assuming he was well in hand, Brydie almost turned away—until the boy's smile suddenly shut down. She followed his gaze to a burly soldier in an overlarge greatcoat, wearing a cap pulled down over his forehead, in the aisle farthest from the mob at the bar. He blended well with the other former soldiers. Brydie didn't recognize him, but then, she didn't recognize his companions either, except by their army coats. They hadn't expected the soldiers to attend.

Besides Damien and Rafe, the orphans and Gillespie were the only ones who might recognize Elton. Did she have time to look for the men? Not if she was the only one who had noticed Daniel's reaction. The aisles between tables were too crowded for her to navigate easily. Looking for what was in reach, she grabbed a candle and flung it at Arthur's shoulder.

He jumped and glanced around in surprise. She gestured for him to take Daniel out. She prayed he'd fetch Damien at the same time. Once assured they were easing their way toward the kitchen. . . *smart choice, Arthur*. . . she studied the situation.

Verity and the girls were on the far end of the room, nearly invisible with all the big men towering through the crowd. The suspect stood between Brydie and the girls.

A table of cakes separated her from the blond, burly man in haphazard uniform. The beautifully decorated cakes were the prizes everyone hoped to purchase at the end of the day, for the benefit of the church. The soldier was in the middle of the pub, studying the mob but not looking in the direction of Daniel and Arthur slipping out.

Brydie hated to be the one who cried *Wolf* but she couldn't reach Daphne and Verity to warn them. Children first, humiliation later. Heaven only knew, she'd embarrassed herself sufficiently for everyone to expect it of her.

She yanked off a glove and put two fingers to her lips and whistled the way she had once done to call pigs, back when they still had pigs. The result was effective. Every head in the room turned to her.

"Ask his name," she shouted, pointing at the burly soldier on the other side of the cake table.

She didn't even have to explain. Everyone in the village knew they were hunting a killer. At her whistle, Damien burst in from the lobby and elbowed the crowd out of his way. Clare and the dowagers directed the women toward the walls, blocking doors and windows. Men eased between the tables to the center, where she pointed. Brydie prayed they wouldn't be furious if she'd marked the wrong man.

Verity lifted Daphne into her arms. With the aid of Clare and the ladies, she and the heirs navigated around the far end of the room toward the kitchen. Brilliant Verity had her exit prepared.

Surprised and relieved at how swiftly everyone reacted, Brydie tried to guard the cakes from whatever happened next. The crowd had eerily silenced. The inhabitants of a village this small knew everything and everyone. They were protecting their own.

Surrounded, caught by surprise, the blond soldier sought the weakest link in the circle, and attempted to shove past the deacon's elderly wife at the cake table.

Small, round, motherly Mrs. Jones slammed his midsection with the bulbous head of her walking stick, then swung at his head. He ducked and dodged under the table. Not bright at all.

Brydie crouched down on the other side. "Hey there, big boy." Before his surprise could even register, she grabbed the cape of his wool coat. She didn't think the heavy oak trestle table would move if he surged upward but she wasn't taking a chance of losing all their hard work.

She couldn't haul him out, but she could punch his snout. Repeatedly. He was still howling and trying to wriggle free when Damien joined her. Getting down on his hands and knees, her beloved grabbed the man's head in a lock hold and hauled him out. With Brydie on one side and Damien on the other, they let the culprit scramble to his feet and wipe his bloody nose. The dunce tried to dive past Brydie. She punched him again and Damien wrapped his arm around his throat, jerking his head back.

Brydie winced. One wrong move, and she feared Damien would snap his neck.

Mrs. Jones and half a dozen other people guarded the table of cakes while Damien tussled with the soldier and dragged him into the relative safety of a broader aisle.

While the men struggled, tiny Minerva arrived with a carved wooden spoon and shoved the handle into the soldier's back. "Hands up, soldier, you're under arrest."

Brydie snorted in laughter. The entire crowd began to snicker at the curate's wife saving the cakes with a spoon.

At the crowd's mirth, the soldier gave up without asking why he was being arrested. While one of the farmers held his arms behind his back, the prisoner just glanced at the bar where Mr. Gillespie stood in shock and shouted, "Find Turner!"

The men would be waiting for him in the lobby if Gillespie tried to escape.

Damien hugged Brydie, and she nearly melted in the aftermath of fury and shock. "Elton?" she asked, knowing he'd recognize the thief.

"Yes. Will you teach me to whistle like that? You promised you would but never did." He cuddled her against him, letting her choke on a laugh while crying into his broad, wool-covered shoulder.

For just this one moment out of time, Brydie clung to the security of Damien's embrace. She had no idea what they'd done, but she prayed this was over.

"I love you, even if you bully me," she murmured, pressing a kiss to his stubbled jaw. "But I think I understand why you do it now. If you can learn to pig whistle, let's get married."

He roared his mirth and led her through the excited, chattering Christmas crowd returning to their shopping.

THIRTY-FOUR

VERITY'S HEART SWELLED WHEN RAFE STORMED INTO THE KITCHEN, observed the frightened inhabitants and weeping children, and swept up Daniel and Daphne to hug and reassure them. She knew her husband ached to be with the other men, apprehending and questioning their would-be kidnapper, but the wonderful soldier she'd married understood that little ones needed to feel safe first. When he sat calmly at the kitchen table and balanced them on his lap, she thought her heart might explode with joy, and tears slid down her cheeks.

She may have chosen this man in haste, but she had chosen well.

"Do you know that man Miss Calhoun yelled at?" Rafe asked the children. "I know it's hard to recognize faces when people are dressed differently."

Daphne nodded silently. Daniel spoke for them both. "He's Mr. Elton. He's mean. He wouldn't let us bring our toys when he told Nanny to take us away."

"You are both very, very brave to come to us for help. Mr. Elton can't take you or your toys away anymore. Do you want to go back to the fair? I'll come with you." Rafe held them, waiting for an answer, not forcing them to do anything if they were still afraid.

Verity didn't think she could ever love this giant of a man more than in that moment. He had terrified kitchen staff wringing their hands, waiting for orders, a magistrate at the manor wanting explanations, and a dangerous prisoner to question—and he made them all wait so two orphans could enjoy their first Christmas Faire.

Wiping hastily at their eyes, Daphne and Daniel scrambled down from Rafe's knees. They took his burly hands and led him eagerly toward the chaos his once orderly pub had become.

"Daniel would like that puppet," Verity stood on her toes to hug him and whisper in his ear before he could pass her by. "And a lace collar for Daphne, please."

He raised a questioning eyebrow. "And you?"

"I only want you. I'll stay here for a bit to see about dinner. Surely it will be safe to sleep here tonight?"

He pressed a kiss to her cheek since the mobcap covered her hair. "I'll try to make it so."

He didn't seem to care that she looked like a ragamuffin. Verity hastily threw aside the ugly cap after they left, collapsed on a chair, and took the strong cup of tea Miss Baker offered. "Thank you. Thank all of you for staying and keeping the kitchen running. I don't think I could have done this without your brave examples. I know I am awkward and backward and not a proper anything, but if you can bear with me, I hope to learn to be what Rafe and the inn needs."

And the mother the children needed, but she did not dare express that wish aloud.

Arthritic Mrs. Hatter scoffed. "You are a lady, anyone can see that, even in those rags. You should go out there with the other ladies, buy the pretties you want so others can buy cakes. We'll bake the finest cakes you'll ever want right here."

Verity hid her smile. The old women were still learning their way around Rafe's medieval kitchen. He'd be doing any cake baking. But the kind words stiffened her back bone. "You're right, I need to go back—as soon as we decide on a dinner menu for our hungry guests. Rafe is likely to be at the manor. Do we have ingredients for stew?"

She wasn't of great use in the kitchen either, but she did have the long-ago experience of listening to her mother talk to their cook about menus. She'd learn her place here eventually.

"Tatties, carrots, good mutton. No one will go hungry. You go on. We can manage stew." Mrs. Hatter shooed her out.

Stew, perhaps, because it just needed a fire. Not rolls, Verity thought as she returned to the still-busy fair. Perhaps one of the tables held baked goods. Brydie would be a perfect village baker. She hoped Fletch returned with mail letting them know who had authority over Willa's cottage, but that would most likely take months.

The punch bowl had been emptied. Mr. Gillespie was gone, presumably to identify Mr. Elton. Rafe had Arthur trailing after him, picking up items he or the children wanted and doling coins from his purse. Rafe's purse never had much in it, but his generosity knew no bounds. They'd never be rich, but with any luck, the goodwill he generated would pay him back someday. She'd been wealthy once. Love was better.

Mr. Birdwhistle had taken the manor's heirs in hand now that the danger had passed. Oliver and Davey were normally silent, scholarly sorts, but even they were gleefully spinning tops and crunching candy, behaving as the children they were for a change.

Kate had Rob and Lynly. Verity knew the family had few coins to spare, and because Kate spent all her time sewing for others, she didn't have a table to display her goods to earn more. Lynly lingered at the cake table, gazing longingly at a small fruit cake adorned with dried cherries. It had been so very long since Verity had given or received gifts—she couldn't resist.

She leaned over Lynly and whispered, "Do you think your mother likes cherries?"

The child nodded eagerly. "She said my grandma used to make fruit cakes with cherries. I never knew her and our cherry tree died." She held out a penny. "Do you think they'd sell slices?"

Verity gestured to the church ladies working the table, indicating the fruit cake. She knew the cakes were selling well below cost for charity. Motherly Mrs. Jones smiled at Lynly's eager face and held up three fingers. Before Lynly understood, Verity pressed two more coppers into the child's palm. "That's how much it costs. Your mother should have a merry Christmas."

Joy illuminated her plain dark face. Lynly would never be a beauty. None of the Calhouns were. But they made up for it with the beauty of their souls.

Brydie returned from whatever errand she'd been on. Verity signaled her to take Lynly and her gift in hand so the cake didn't get jostled by the crowd.

The pub was starting to clear out a bit. People had suppers to prepare. Rafe had released Daniel so he might admire the puppet show. Gleefully tugging at Rafe's riot of red curls, Daphne was riding on his shoulders, high above the crowd.

They might not have caught Willa's killer, but Verity assumed he was long gone by now. Elton had undoubtedly been the villain who gave the children's nanny the pills. Whether or not it had been intentional, he would hang for her death. Not a joyous thought for the season. But now that the danger was gone. . .

Christmas. They might finally experience the full joy of the season. She'd pray fervently in church tomorrow and tithe all her coins in gratitude for this moment of happiness.

Studying a sad young woman's misshapen biscuits, Verity reached for her coin purse. The biscuits scarcely looked edible, but the seller had obviously tried her best. As she set down a shilling, a high-pitched shriek curdled her blood.

So much for that moment of joy.

Swinging around, she saw Daphne trying to burrow into Rafe's arms, while screeching frantically. Had she been hurt?

Shrieking wasn't the behavior of a hurt child. Rafe sent Verity a look as frantic as the child's screams.

Terrified, she scanned the crowded room for any perceived threat.

Lazy, easy-going Mr. Cooper was leading Daniel past the cakes, toward the front and the puppet table. Not alarming—until Daphne finally used her words and shouted, "Bad man! Bad man!"

And Cooper glanced up with a guilty expression.

Verity had survived some terrible ordeals, but she'd never experienced such terror as fear for a helpless child.

In her patched maid's skirt, her frizzy hair escaping its pins, Verity was no prepossessing giantess, but she may as well have been as she impolitely carved a path past startled manor ladies and puzzled farmers, bearing down on Cooper with the momentum of a ship in full steam.

When Cooper saw her coming and scooped up Daniel, Verity shrieked at the top of her lungs like the worst fishwife. "Stop him! Stop him! Daniel, darken his daylights! Plant him a rammer! Scuttle his daylights!" She'd evidently spent too much of her idle youth teaching London's street urchins.

The boy started swinging fists. Bless Daniel's heart, he listened to *her* and not whatever promises Cooper made. Cooper! It was hard to believe the lazy gentleman might stir a muscle.

Carrying a sturdy eight-year-old was no mean feat. Carrying a struggling one required Cooper catching him in both arms before the boy wriggled loose. The villain raced for the exit, knocking over tables and shoppers in his rush.

Daniel continued to struggle and kick.

Finally understanding what was happening, ladies trapped between tables screamed for someone to stop him. Trapped in the back of the pub, Rafe roared in fury and frustration. He handed Daphne to a startled onlooker, then fought his way through narrow, crowded aisles.

Bewildered, the few male shoppers tried to grasp what needed to be done. None of them knew Daniel or Cooper. They saw only a small boy having a tantrum. They didn't understand.

Verity finally fought free of the crowd and threw herself at Cooper's back, grabbing his greatcoat capes and clinging helplessly. He tried to shrug her off as he shoved his way into the less busy lobby.

Fletch, carrying a heavy mail pouch in the front door, roared at the sight of Cooper carrying the struggling child and dragging Verity. Rafe's silent, angry friend didn't waste time with questions. Dropping the pouch, he crossed the room and swung a massive fist at the gentleman's jaw—with the rage that he'd most likely kept pent up all week.

Cooper had been in Willa's house. . .

The kidnapper staggered. Verity clung to his capes and tugged, keeping him unbalanced. Daniel kicked and wriggled.

And Parsons, Willa's felonious brother, ran from behind the lobby counter to clout Cooper's ear, shouting, "*You*! I knew it was you—" His shouts descended into epithets unfit for anyone's ears. Convicts learned strong language.

Another powerful blow from Fletcher, and Cooper dropped Daniel. Crying in relief, Verity released Cooper's capes and crouched to catch the boy. Fletch unthinkingly did the same, leaving Cooper to shove Parsons, who fell backward over Fletch and Daniel.

In the resulting melee, the villain ran for the door, Fletch and Parsons on his heels.

By this time, the lobby had filled with onlookers anticipating a fight. Men and women alike blocked all exits, surrounding the brawl as if the lobby were a boxing ring.

Verity hugged weeping Daniel as Fletch grabbed Cooper's coat and flung him backward at Willa's brother.

While fists flew, Kate finally fought her way through the crowd to Verity's side. She held a terrified Daphne and kept a hand on Lynly's shoulder. "Arthur and Mr. Birdwhistle took the boys into the kitchen," she murmured, blocking Verity and Daniel from the fight.

If Kate had Daphne. . . Rafe wasn't far behind. Verity glanced past her.

Head taller than most, Rafe stalked through the now-shouting mob without a word. Rather than wasting time on fisticuffs, he wrapped a massive arm around Cooper's neck and jerked his chin up until the. . . bastard. . . fell limp. Thank all the heavens Rafe had stayed with the children when all the proper gentlemen had left for the manor to interrogate Elton.

Verity fell to her knees and hugged her poor, weeping babies.

"He's the one what killed Rose!" Parsons shouted over the commotion. "It was him in her house that night! I coshed him so he couldn't get away."

THIRTY-FIVE

RAFE

Sitting in Captain Huntley's small study—the old one, not the spacious new one—Rafe sprawled in one of the sagging leather wingbacks and rubbed his weary brow. All he wanted to do was go back to his family, see they were safe, hug and feed them. . .

But for everyone to be safe, he had to have the danger locked up, which meant convincing Hunt to do so. "Parsons swears *Cooper* killed his sister, but he's a felon and a coward and may have done it himself, for all we know, which is why he didn't say anything earlier. Except—Elton and Gillespie both agree that the man we call Cooper also calls himself Turner and works for Lord Chatham's solicitor. They're sniveling mongrels, as far as I'm concerned, but that's three people attesting against Cooper. Elton swears that Turner, as the solicitor's representative, told him the children were bastards to be taken to an orphanage. He gave the nanny the opium candies to shut them up, so that's two murders of which he stands accused, even if the nanny's death might be ruled accidental."

Squirming uncomfortably in his chair, Fletch laid the letter on

261

Hunt's desk that he'd purloined from the mailbag. "It's addressed to *Cooper Turner*, Esquire. I opened it. Arrest me, if you will, but read it first."

Both names, proving some of their pathetic witnesses told the truth.

Not wearing the reading monocle for his one good eye, Hunt handed the letter to Walker, his steward. "Why did you think to open it?"

"Because I owe Willa the justice of having her killer caught. Parsons is terrified of authority and won't speak to Rafe, but I got him drunk enough last night to spill his story."

Hunt scowled but gestured for Fletch to continue.

Looking uncomfortable, Fletch leaned back in his chair and glared at the shelves. Rafe knew his friend had difficulty gathering words, so he waited patiently.

"Her brother is a coward who's been lingering about for a week, too afraid to confront his sister." Fletch wriggled uncomfortably but when no one interrupted, he continued. "When he saw a horse ride up her drive, he grew concerned. Parsons doesn't trust gentry any more than authority. When he smelled rubbish burning, he panicked and feared the worst. He swears Willa's front door was unlocked and half open. He's a jittery chap so he pulled his cudgel and entered without knocking. Thinking to catch a thief or arsonist, he saw Cooper rifling through the desk. He did what a coward always does, strikes first. After flooring Cooper, he found his sister dead, and he fled, like he always does. He's not completely stupid. He knew we'd suspect a convict long before we'd suspect a gentleman."

"*Parsons* cracked Cooper's head? And claims Cooper killed Willa?" Hunt leaned back in his desk chair and rubbed his brow just the way Rafe was doing. "Why?"

"If you'll read the letter, it becomes more clear," Rafe said wearily. "These are not matters I understand. You will need to question Lord Chatham. But it appears Willa had information that would endanger Lord Chatham's inheritance to the title and fortune. I've tried to question Cooper, but he refuses to talk. If he truly is a solicitor, he knows better."

"Can I just send them all to assizes and let a judge straighten this out?" Hunt reached for the brandy decanter and refilled his glass, offering the bottle to others.

Rafe had no taste for the stuff. After his exercise in speaking, Fletch accepted a glass.

Rafe eyed the mantel clock and wondered if the captain would mind distracting a tense Fletch with the timepiece before he drank more.

Walker returned the letter to Hunt. "Talk to his lordship. Taking the viscount to court might be hasty unless we know how involved he is. The letter to Cooper is from the late Lord Chatham's estate solicitors, advising him that they are delaying the transfer of funds and property until they have communicated with a Beatrice and Bronwen Bartlett of Bath."

Bee and Boo, Rafe recalled wearily. The letters from the orphans' mother to Willa talked about Bee and Boo in Bath. Willa had just received a letter from *B and B* in Bath saying they were delayed. He didn't see the picture yet, but pieces were falling in place.

Walker explained. "The late viscount's solicitors are notifying *Cooper Turner* that he might have been ill-informed. The Bartletts are claiming that their grand-niece properly married the Honor-able Thomas Turner, younger son of Viscount Chatham, in Bath, and the Beanblossom trust was part of the marriage settlement. Before Margery Bartlett Turner's parents sailed to Virginia, they left copies of the marriage documents with Willa, and there should be records with the church."

Walker gestured at the letter. "Apparently, as a representative of Major Thomas Turner's estate office, Cooper must have informed the late Lord Chatham's attorneys otherwise. Because of the Bartletts' intervention, the viscount's solicitors are now searching for Major Turner's marriage documents, settlements, and a more recent will. I'd say they have grown suspicious."

The curate, who had been sitting quietly in a corner, spoke up. "Minerva has read the Debrett's entry. The late Viscount Chatham had two sons. The elder died without issue. The younger, Thomas, was listed as an officer in the cavalry, a regiment which Minerva says fought at Waterloo. Our Debrett's is out of date. The older brother's demise is recorded but not the younger's marriage, offspring, or death. The late viscount's title and estate would legally descend to his sons. If they both die without legitimate male issue, the title and estate descend to the next in line— their cousin, son of the late viscount's younger brother, the gentleman currently calling himself Lord Chatham. But if the birth records in Stratford are legitimate, Major Thomas Turner dutifully produced a male heir, Daniel."

Rafe sank deeper in his chair. He'd left his rural home at eighteen, spent a lifetime at war, and never had interest in the ways of aristocracy. He was out of his field when it came to titles. But human nature, he understood. "So if Daniel is declared legitimate, he is Lord Chatham, heir to an estate? And if the marriage papers are destroyed, there is no proof of his legitimacy? And the cousin inherits? Can we arrest him for that?"

He knew the answer, but he was tired and wanted to go home to Verity and worry about this tomorrow.

The curate and Fletch inhaled loudly at his conclusion but blessedly refrained from commenting. The thought of Daniel as a viscount. . . gave Rafe a head pain.

Hunt tapped his pencil up and down against his blotter. "We need, at the very least, the marriage documents, which—if we are to believe Parson's story—Cooper may have burned, along with his bloody clothing. Which means we have to wait until the estate solicitors find the official records, which won't happen over Christmas. I'll question his lordship, if I can do so discreetly."

"Have Damien question Cooper Turner first," the curate suggested. "How is he related to the viscount's family? Minerva didn't notice anyone else in the line of succession."

Hunt nodded. "We need more information before we hold a

trial. We can blame the season for the delay, leave Cooper and Elton to rot, unless they're inclined to talk. Unless Cooper wants to press charges against Parsons, we have nothing on him. Looks like we might be grateful for his cowardice."

Rafe wanted to lock up the possibly fake viscount as well, but he knew better than to ask. One did not imprison aristocrats based on nearly no evidence. After all, the new lordling was incompetent enough to be a pawn.

No one objected to the captain's command. The ladies of the manor would never let a prisoner rot. They'd be well fed while moldering in the monks' crypt. Leaving Fletch to haul prisoners around, Rafe lumbered to his feet, eager to return to Verity and the children, hoping Daphne had decided to talk.

"I hear the carolers are expecting a wassail bowl at your inn tomorrow?" Hunt asked as they left the study.

"So I have been informed. A Christmas Eve tradition? We are apparently keeping some of the elderly singers from having to climb the manor's hill at night. Will you be there to greet them?" Rafe took the coat the butler handed him. He was becoming accustomed to *butlers*.

"We all hope to be there. I don't suppose a little extra ale might be added to our noble viscount's cup so I might question him while he's merry?"

"*All?*" Rafe tried not to stagger. "The marquess? The viscount?"

"The dowagers." Hunt grinned. "I'm stuck with them the rest of the time. I may spirit Clare away early for a little quiet."

"Right." Rafe left the captain smiling and trudged home trying to imagine how to entertain a marquess in a medieval pub that barely had *benches*. Being a mess sergeant had been simpler.

But not as satisfying, he admitted, as he entered his kitchen to the rich aroma of mutton stew. He'd been planning on making shepherd pie but having food waiting was so unusual that he felt as if a ten-stone rucksack had dropped from his shoulders.

He felt even lighter when the children raced toward him,

hugging his legs and chattering. *Chattering.* Daphne was talking again. Not well or sensibly, but enough to have everyone in the kitchen smiling for a change.

"Merry Christmas," Verity murmured, taking his coat. "She hasn't stopped talking since you hauled off her *bad man.*"

A child would not be allowed in court as a witness. What had she seen?

"Has she said anything useful?" It would be Christmas miracle if so. The child was currently questioning how the currants got into the bread. Apparently one of the ladies knew how to make soda bread over a fire.

"She cries if I ask anything about her mother and Beanblossom. So we're talking about the fair and Christmas dinner and singing." Verity shooed the children toward their room. "Let Mr. Rafe eat his dinner while we read a book, shall we?"

"She'll be a wonderful mother," Mrs. Hatter said as she set out a plate for him in the kitchen instead of the private dining room.

Rafe didn't care where he ate as long as he had food. He'd gone without far too often. "Verity is a good teacher," he agreed proudly.

Motherhood—might be problematic.

If Daniel was actually *Viscount Chatham,* he'd be ushered off to some grand estate, surrounded by guardians and servants and a dozen tutors.

How the devil could he tell Verity that? She was the happiest he'd seen her in weeks.

CHRISTMAS EVE

DECEMBER 24, 1815

THIRTY-SIX

MINERVA

"Do I sing for my supper with the village folk or stand as a representative of the manor?" Minerva asked, hanging on to Paul's arm as they took the short path from the parsonage to the inn. It was already dark at this hour and starting to sleet. After Sunday services, she'd spent the afternoon nobly visiting the housebound. She'd left Patience decorating the chapel for tomorrow's Christmas mass and hadn't had time to nibble her way through whatever feast Elsa had prepared for tonight's festivity.

"You have a lovely voice. Sing," Paul ordered. "It will be good practice for tomorrow, where I trust you will sing prayers and not *God Rest Ye Merry Gentlemen.*"

Minerva laughed. "Patience's pagan greenery might warn of local preferences. She even has mistletoe, if you look closely."

To welcome his noble guests, Rafe had illuminated the inn yard with every lantern and candle he possessed. A barouche and curricle indicated the manor inhabitants had arrived. Minerva sighed her pleasure at the festive sight. "It feels so good believing we have the criminals locked up and may truly celebrate. Please do not tell me otherwise."

"Hunt has Cooper in the crypt. The scoundrel is in a state, threatening to bring charges, demanding that he see a lawyer and Lord Chatham. Damien has explained there won't be any trial until after Boxing Day. His legal services have been refused," Paul added wryly.

"Brydie sent her first batch of hot-cross buns to the prisoners because she didn't like the way they turned out. I assume that didn't sweeten their dispositions." Seeing Patience and Henri approaching, Minerva halted outside the inn door to greet them.

"I've asked our carolers to gather in the stable. Shall we join them?" Patience asked, clearly planning on singing for her supper, despite also being one of the manor owners.

Delighted to have company, Minerva sent Paul inside with Henri. Her brilliant husband sang like a croaking frog.

"Is Brydie coming? I brought Willa's recipe book. She thinks it might have a better recipe for buns than she's found. We really need to have it copied out and perhaps sent to a printer as a memorial to Willa and her bakery." Minerva trailed behind the statuesque gardener, while fumbling in her cloak pocket for the tattered volume.

"Clare knows printers. Who has a fair hand for copying?" They halted in the stable doorway to admire the gathering crowd of eager revelers.

Even Verity and the orphans had joined them. The orphans clung to Verity while all the other young ones raced about in unbridled excitement. Fletch towered over the corridor leading to where the horses were stabled, blocking the valuable animals from mischief.

"Do you know anyone with a fair hand for copying Willa's recipe book?" Patience was asking Verity.

"I have a fair hand, and Mr. Birdwhistle, but we don't have much time with school starting in a week. If you want it soon and are willing to pay, Mrs. Mayfield has been copying out Rafe's tattered notebook of recipes. She might like the extra coin."

Minerva handed over the thick volume. "Talk to Mrs. Mayfield, please. This past week has been so busy, I haven't had the time to even look for the recipe Brydie wants. The handwriting is execrable." Minerva knew, as a librarian—not a cook—she was being uppish over a tattered and handwritten old recipe book. It held no value to her.

Wearing warm wool and an apron instead of her usual fashionable attire, Verity worked the book into her capacious apron pocket. "Rafe might like to see the recipes, thank you."

As official leader of the church ladies, Mrs. Jones clapped her hands. "I think we're all here now. Shall we start with *God Rest Ye Merry Gentlemen*?"

Minerva snickered. This would definitely be a merry evening that would leave half the parish hung over for Christmas services on the morrow.

"I'll take Daphne and Danny back inside. We only came out so they wouldn't be afraid when a mob shows up at the door." Verity ushered her charges from the stable ahead of the singers, slipping in through the inn's kitchen door.

Knowing what she did of the orphans' parentage, Minerva worried for her friend. But this was Christmas Eve and they had much to celebrate.

With the newly-formed choir to hold the tune, the motley group paraded through the inn yard singing. By the time they reached the inn's front door, Rafe was there in his best uniform coat to welcome them. A reception line of finely-dressed ladies and gentlemen ushered the carolers into the pub as if this were the manor and they were the hosts.

The children broke rank first, racing to admire the treats set out. Under the direction of Patience and Mrs. Jones, the rest of the carolers ran through their practiced tunes, with everyone joining in on a final *Deck the Halls*. The Huntleys made a brief welcome speech and the dowagers actually handed out the first wassail cups, enjoying the opportunity to play ladies of the manor again.

"Verity should be here, enjoying this," Minerva murmured to

Paul when she realized Rafe was here but his wife was not. "Let me see if she'll trust the children with me for a bit."

Paul scanned the crowd. "Brydie and Kate aren't here?"

"They wanted to spend Christmas Eve at home, out of the weather. So much has happened. . . they need their routine. Besides, their chickens need feeding." Minerva grinned and gestured at Rafe. "Verity stole Willa's hens and rooster, with Brydie's aid. Damien and Rafe have to decide if they must pay Parsons for theft."

Paul laughed. "Now that Cooper is out of Willa's cottage, Parsons has moved in, says he's guarding it. We're still trying to determine who owns it. Go, help Verity."

Minerva kissed his freshly shaven jaw. "I am glad you are not a curmudgeon about commandment breaking."

He shrugged. "Chickens would have starved or been eaten if left alone. Verity will take care of them and Rafe will feed the hungry with their eggs."

"I love your pragmatism." Minerva left him to his parishioners while she traversed the hall to the Russells' private quarters. She could hear the children giggling in their room and knocked on that door.

Verity answered, holding an iron poker at her side. "Is anything wrong?"

Her anxiety was so strong that Minerva wouldn't have told her if there had been. "Everyone is having a wonderful time. As the curate's wife, I shouldn't be indulging in punch, so I thought you might like to enjoy the festivity for a while. Will you trust me with Daphne and Daniel?"

Verity bit her lip, cast a glance to the pair bouncing from bed to bed in some game, then down at her faded attire. "I should, I know. But Daphne is finally talking and I—" She gestured helplessly.

"Ah, then might I join you? If we could have them talk a little about that day, it might help the captain to ask questions later. Then you can put them to bed and I'll read to them while you take a look at Willa's recipe book to see if it might be copied." Minerva knew she was manipulative, but sometimes, people needed a little shove.

Verity nodded and let her in. "They're playing some game their mother taught them, but it's time for them to settle down. You're good at questioning. I'll see if the book is legible enough for copying. The ink looked terribly faded."

Should Minerva and Paul ever have a child, they could learn a lot from Verity's calm authority. She watched in awe as Verity persuaded the excited duo into their night clothes. They brushed their teeth in the wash basin and wriggled beneath the covers, still giggling and hiding under sheets. They were a joy to behold after this week of tragedy.

When Minerva sat on the chair between the beds with their book, their heads popped out to listen. As a librarian, she approved. Books were a form of magic.

Verity settled at the small school desk Rafe had brought down from the manor attic. She lit a candle to better study the battered ledger. But the instant she set the leather tome on the desk, Daphne cried, "Mama's book!"

"Is not," Daniel said in scorn. "Mama's is prettier."

Minerva exchanged a glance with Verity. They had only brought children's books from their home, until the disposition of the estate was settled. She hadn't noticed a thick leather ledger like this one, but then, she had been looking for documents.

Verity rose with the recipe book in hand. Minerva set aside the fairy tales. Did they dare hope the orphans were ready to talk?

Settling on Daphne's bed, Verity showed them the heavy notebook. "Your mama had a book like this?"

Daphne nodded uncertainly, wrinkling her nose. "Mama's had pretty drawings. That's nasty." She picked at the peeling leather.

Drawings instead of recipes? Possibly a journal or family tradition?

"Told you." Daniel sat up against his pillows. "Mama's had shiny gold letters with her name. It had pockets inside."

Pockets? Minerva studied the cover. It did, indeed, seem to have hints of gold lettering. The darker leather where the letters had once been might have spelled Bartlett, which made sense, if this contained the bakery's recipes. Willa hadn't been able to read it, so she'd thrown it on top of the cabinets, out of her way—because Willa never threw anything away.

She opened the pages—yellowing vellum, wrinkled and stained from decades of use, with nearly indecipherable scribbling. But the journal had once been lovely and expensive.

Daniel leaned over to examine it. "There." He pointed at the thick cover. "Mama kept Papa's letters in there. She read them to us sometimes."

Heart breaking as she imagined the loving mother attempting to teach her children about the father they'd never known, Minerva ran her fingers over the brittle edge. She hated disturbing the binding, but there did seem to be extra padding and a slit on the edge. There might once have been a gold edge to protect it but that was long gone.

"Do you know where your mama kept her book?" Verity asked as if she were just keeping the conversation going, while Minerva pried at the opening.

"In the wall, by her bed," Daniel reported matter-of-factly.

"Where the bad man couldn't find it," Daphne added in satisfaction. "She said not to tell the bad man."

"Well, we're not men and we're not bad." Verity tucked the blankets round them more securely. "So you did the right thing by telling us. We'll find your mama's book and give it back to you. Did you ever see the bad man, Daniel?"

Minerva pried loose pages from the slit.

Daniel shook his head.

"I did." Daphne wrinkled her whole waif-like face into a frown. "He was mean. He yelled at Mama. She cried and called for Elton, but he didn't come." A tear streaked down her cheek.

"I wasn't there or I'd hit him, like I did yesterday," Daniel said fiercely. "I'd have beat him up."

"You are both very, very brave, and we're all proud of you," Verity assured them, hugging Daniel. "Did the bad man leave after your mama yelled?"

Daphne shook her head tearfully. "He put a pillow on Mama's face and she went to sleep. Then he opened her desk. We were never ever to touch her desk, so *I* yelled at him."

A pillow? Minerva exchanged a horrified look with Verity. "Is this the same bad man who took Daniel yesterday?"

Daphne nodded emphatically. "He said if I talked, he'd put a pillow on my face too. I don't want a pillow on my face." Then she sobbed and threw herself into Verity's arms.

Mrs. Turner hadn't died of her illness. Cooper had smothered her.

Shaken, Minerva finally pried the papers loose from where the years had stuck them to the leather binding. Unfolding them, she stared wordlessly, then handed them to Verity.

The marriage documents the Bartletts had sent to Willa for safekeeping.

A choir of half-drunken singers in the pub broke into a rousing rendition of *Joy to the World.*

BOXING DAY

DECEMBER 26, 1815

THIRTY-SEVEN

RAFE

Christmas Day had been more satisfying than any day Rafe could remember, even as a child. The highly improper church services with pagan hymns and greenery and the entire village cheering the curate's message of love had set the mood for the remainder of the day. A dash of snow to dazzle the evergreens had added to the festive spirit.

At home, Verity had crowed in delight over the blue dinner gown he'd asked Lavender's ladies to make for her, which relieved Rafe no end. He was never certain what women liked.

The orphans opening gifts of new books, dolls, and puzzles brought smiles to everyone's faces, including the dour old women in the kitchen.

This morning, wearing the formal green, tailed frockcoat Verity had commissioned, Rafe had left his small staff singing, delighted with their bounteous Boxing Day gifts and planning their day off.

But now Rafe grew impatient for justice.

Hunt, as magistrate, had left the prisoners locked up until after the Christmas festivities. The mail was slow and they needed more information. But Fletch had brought a mail pouch today, and the time had come to settle the prisoners' fates.

Leaving Hunt's holiday undisturbed until they had answers, Rafe hauled Elton from his cell and borrowed the manor's study for his interrogation. The curate agreed to sit in as witness—and to keep Rafe from punching the scruffy lout if he didn't cooperate.

Looking well-fed but even grubbier than usual, stout, balding Elton glowered resentfully at the book-lined study and Rafe looming over Hunt's old desk. Rafe knew he was a peasant like Elton, but he'd worked hard to earn his place at the table. He had his doubts about this thief working hard at anything.

Rafe settled back in Hunt's comfortable chair as if he were lord of the manor. "You're the gent who looked after Mrs. Turner and her children, are you not?"

"That was me," Elton replied stiffly and warily. "Did what I was paid to."

"And who hired you?" Rafe asked, starting with simple questions, the way he used to do in the army, with thieves who raided his food supplies.

"Solicitor, said I was to give him the doc's reports. She was wasting away and he didn't want the children left alone," the footman said self-righteously.

"And the solicitor's name?" Upton asked.

"Turner, said he was related to the late master's family. But people here been calling him Cooper."

Rafe bit back a snort. Liars and thieves abounded. "Where were you when the lady died?"

"Weren't no lady," the servant insisted. "Just a rich man's doxie. His lordship was generous to let her stay."

"Did the lady have anyone else looking after her?" Upton asked, not showing the fury Rafe felt, although the curate's jaw twitched.

"Solicitor hired her too. Called herself Nanny Smith, but she weren't no nanny. She cooked a bit. Helped with the brats. Dusted some. But things went missing when she was about."

Probably went missing when Elton was about, also, but innocent until proven guilty, Rafe reminded himself. "This the woman you claimed was your sister?" Rafe showed Elton the sketch again.

The balding servant shrugged. "Turner told me to say that. Said it would get the brats back faster. Yeah, that's her."

Rafe sat back in his chair. "Tell us what happened the day Mrs. Turner died."

Elton shifted uneasily, no doubt looking for the best way to present himself. "I sent word to Mr. Turner that the physician said she didn't have long. She was writing her family to fetch the childern." He parsed his words carefully. "So Mr. Turner came early one morning and was there when she died."

"You weren't in the room when she passed?" Rafe wanted it on record, if only to determine how much Elton lied. He'd believe Daphne before this lout.

"No, I warn't."

Well, at least that part was truth. Rafe watched for tics that might give him away. "What day was this?"

Elton wrinkled his brow. "A Friday? Cause we was to go to market and couldn't with her dead."

"So Cooper tells you the lady passed. What did he do then?"

"He said he needed to arrange burial and all. He took some of the silver with him. I knew it was the end then, and me and Nan would have to look to ourselves."

"Smart thinking." The curate scribbled in his notebook. "Is that when you began boxing the silver?"

Elton crossed and uncrossed his legs. "That was our orders, sir. But the little girl was a'weepin' somethin' awful and the boy came home from school and had a right fit, and there warn't time for boxin' much."

Consoling distraught children should have come first. Rafe hid his impatience. "So when did you see Mr. Cooper Turner next?"

"On the Saturday, early, he came in a fancy coach and has the corpse takers with their cart. He wouldn't let us go to the funeral.

'Stead, he has Nan lock up the childern and takes me into town in his fancy coach, sells some silver, and tells me to buy an old cart with it. Then he leaves me at the inn, takes his horse, and says he's a'ridin' back to the cottage to start closin' it up, and I was to hurry."

"When did you see him next?" As far as Rafe could determine, all this agreed with what he'd learned from Gillespie, the viscount's valet, so Elton got points for sticking to the verifiable parts of the story.

Elton wrinkled his brow as if it was an effort to think. "Took me some to find a vehicle for what little he gave me. Needed a nag too. Finally found an old lady wanting to be rid of her buggy."

Rafe feared it may have been stolen, but he didn't interrupt, just nodded encouragingly.

Relaxing, Elton fell into the rhythm of his tale. "Got back to the cottage maybe a bit after noon? Brats were crying and yelling and bein' obstreperous in their rooms. Turner was there, ordering Nan to take them away, refusin' to let her take their things, rightly so. Couldn't have nice things at no orphanage. He gave Nan some candies to quiet 'em down. Ordered her to take the buggy and haul them to Birmingham once she got done boxing the valuables. He had me filling a cart with the boxes, for safekeeping. Don't know why he had me hunting for a cart when he already had one. He coulda just waited until Nan got back."

Except the nanny hadn't come back and Cooper planned to be long gone with the silver? Made horrible sense but not Rafe's immediate concern. He needed evidence, not speculation. "And then what?"

"Turner was a'cleanin' out the lady's personal papers, found a letter of some sort, and come out in a temper, yelled at us to finish up and close the house. Nan said it was too late for travel. Mr. Cooper said give the brats candy and let them sleep in the buggy. That was maybe middle of the afternoon cause it weren't dark yet."

The letter Willa had sent, no doubt, saying she'd take "them." Cooper hadn't known of Willa's existence until then.

"But Nan was looking after herself, like you said, right?" No wonder the children had been terrified, Rafe thought. Monsters surrounded them.

Elton looked for a way to deny it but finally nodded. "She took the coins Turner gave her and told me she knew someone who would pay to take the brats. She figured the buggy and horse would sell too. Turner didn't seem to care what happened to them. Warn't none of my business what she did."

Hiding his rage, Rafe studied his notes. "So, on Saturday, the funeral was held, Cooper ordered the house closed up, and after reading a letter, rode off. He simply left you with the valuables in the cart, and Nanny Smith with the children and the buggy. Nanny left late in the afternoon with the children. What did you do then?"

Elton shrugged. "I loaded the cart, as told, fixed myself a bite, and enjoyed the evening with the brandy nobody said nothing about. Nanny took the horse, so I didn't have none for the cart. I waited to see what happened."

"And what happened?"

"Turner didn't come back. Nobody did, until a lawyer fella turned up a few days later with a lady and gent. I hid and listened and heard about Nan dying and thought mebbe I could learn who she meant to sell the childern to. So I cleaned up and presented myself to the lawyers."

By way of what silver could be carried in his pockets, Rafe surmised.

But the real crime here, if Elton were to be believed. . . Cooper had almost murdered the children as well as the nanny with opium pills. And if Daphne were to be believed, he'd smothered their mother as well.

Rafe was feeling a bit murderous himself.

NEW YEAR'S EVE

DECEMBER 31, 1815

THIRTY-EIGHT

SUNDAY, NEW YEAR'S EVE, VERITY SMOOTHED THE LOVELY SILVER-blue silk gown that Rafe had given her for Christmas. It went beautifully with one of the Kashmir shawls from her mother's trunk. She fingered the pearls at her throat for good luck, praying her parents watched over her. She was hoping for a miracle, here in Gravesyde, where anything seemed possible.

They weren't attending a party to welcome the new year—although the children were bouncing in excitement as if they were. They loved the attention.

Lavender hadn't been able to tailor Rafe's frockcoat, but at Verity's request, she had taken his measurements from his dress uniform and sent them to a tailor Damien had recommended. Rafe had been shocked when he'd opened the elegant gift, but he wore the dark green superfine proudly now. It went well with his red hair. Her husband was a magnificent gentleman. She could never find one finer.

Armored for battle, they followed Minerva and Paul into the manor's library where all the officials had gathered. Apparently solicitors did not observe the holy days or even New Year's Eve.

Verity had hoped to meet the Bartletts, the orphans' only remaining maternal family in England, but Bee and Boo were apparently elderly and unable to travel the distance. They'd never met the children and had only stepped in when they heard rumors that injustice had been done to the family name.

Swallowing nervously, Verity worried about the solicitors' disregard to their families, but she supposed the viscount's estate paid well. And Captain Huntley had been rather forceful in his demands, now that they finally had reliable evidence.

After Damien rode to Stratford and showed the marriage documents from the recipe book to Mr. Browning, the lawyers had searched Beanblossom. Once they'd found the leather notebook with original documents and the late Honorable Major Thomas Turner's letters, right where the children had said, Browning's firm had backed Hunt in demanding a meeting with Chatham's solicitors.

Verity touched Daphne and Daniel on their shoulders. Dressed in their finest, their hair neatly trimmed so they resembled blond angels, they seemed more interested in the manor's recently-installed gaslight and the bonging floor clock than anxious about the proceedings. "You are to make your bow and curtsy, then go with Brydie, understood?"

"Will our cousin be there?" Daniel turned his gorgeous, deep blue eyes to them.

"He should be." The former—or was that the false?— Lord Chatham had thrown the mother of all tantrums after being confronted with the facts. That he'd turned his rage on Cooper and not the children spoke well of him, Verity prayed.

Rafe had not been able to pry a word out of Willa's killer. They'd had to patch together his treachery by interviewing everyone Geoffrey Cooper—he did not have a legal right to the name Turner—had bamboozled. Major Turner's letters to his wife had also been revealing. He hadn't trusted his impoverished cousin, Laurence, or his illegitimate cousin, Cooper, which was why he'd tucked his family out of harm's way.

They'd learned that Geoffrey Cooper was Laurence Turner's half-brother, a by-blow of his father. After Major Turner's death at Waterloo, followed by the death of the old viscount, Cooper had presumably hoped to ride his half-brother's coattails to title and wealth.

Verity squeezed Rafe's arm for comfort as they entered the enormous library. Solicitors stood at their arrival. Laurence Turner, formerly known as Lord Chatham, prodded by his new solicitor, reluctantly rose from his sprawl in a wing chair. Fair-haired, not overly tall, and well-dressed, Turner bore a vague resemblance to his cousin's offspring, although his eyes were a washed out blue.

The children behaved graciously upon being introduced to this unknown relation, staring only a little as they curtsied and bowed. Neither of them shrieked in fear or even cried out in recognition, which was a relief. Not realizing how tense she'd been until Brydie led them away, Verity nearly melted into the chair Rafe pulled out for her. He squeezed her bare shoulder reassuringly.

Even though Verity knew they debated their future, the lawyer talk passed over her head. She studied the pouting, rather young Mr. Turner who returned to sprawling in a side chair, already dismissed as no longer relevant to the discussion. She compared him to Hunt's friend, the dowager's stepson, the Marquess of Spalding. Older and more elegant, the marquess was slender and blond, too, but muscles instead of padding filled out his coat shoulders.

She was glad she and Rafe had worn their finest wardrobe so they would not shame the nobleman prepared to stand up for them and the children.

Damien and the manor's solicitor, Mr. Browning, presented all the documents they'd located and made their case. There didn't seem to be any doubt that Daniel was the heir to a viscountcy. The devil was in the details. That's why Verity and Minerva were there, despite gentlemanly disapproval.

The late viscount's solicitors from Bath had folders and documents of their own. They presented his will for Mr. Browning and Damien to read. The hidden journal had provided enough information to locate where the late Major Thomas Turner had left *his* will—not the old one the lying Cooper had showed them.

With marriage and birth documents secured, the legal part was all clear and aboveboard. Daniel was the new Lord Chatham, heir to a modest estate and fortune.

Verity threaded her fingers together in her lap and prayed as they began discussing schools and guardianship. In a pause in the discussion while Hunt brought out the brandy decanter and a maid delivered tea, she finally spoke. "The children need a mother, not some distant guardian who won't be around to wipe their tears. They have been terrorized to the point of not speaking. They cannot be given over to strangers who treat them only as a means of making a living."

She'd practiced that small speech all day. She'd be quaking in her shoes had she stood. She wasn't shy. She simply wasn't accustomed to standing up to men.

"In an ideal world, Mrs. . ." The solicitor from Bath couldn't even remember her name.

"Mrs. *Russell*." Rafe provided it emphatically.

"No one can bring their mother back. We'll find a good nanny for the little girl." The solicitor continued with impatience.

"Daphne," Verity inserted, imitating Rafe's irritation.

"For Daphne." The solicitor was a little more annoyed at her interruption. "But Lord Chatham needs to be in a school where he will meet others of his rank who will help him become the man he needs to be to run our great country."

A few cynical snorts followed that declaration, and Verity waited for the American Hunt or the political marquess to wade into the fray. Amazingly, they didn't. They allowed her to state her case.

Filling her lungs and finding her courage, she glared at the solicitor and continued in a firm voice. "Of course Daniel should have an education, as should Daphne. I am a teacher. I respect that they'll have enormous responsibilities in the future and should be well educated and prepared accordingly. Right now, however, they are terrified babes who have just lost both their parents. All they know is a small cottage and a very limited world. You cannot begin to imagine how brave they were to walk the woods at night in search of a church and help. They are *amazing* children."

She was in danger of rambling. She caught her breath and Rafe reached over to squeeze her hands.

"They'll adapt, as children do," the solicitor said with a dismissive wave. "The main concern is the guardian responsible for the estate—"

The bored former Lord Chatham abruptly sat up straight.

Enraged, Verity discarded any remaining timidity and pushed to her feet to lean over the table. "*NO*. It is *not*. I—" She swung her hand to indicate everyone at the table. "I and everyone in the Priory can tell you from *experience*, that money is the *least* important part of growing up secure and happy. Children need a circle of family and friends who will provide love and understanding and support so they can grow up to be the very best they can be. Money is nice. People are *necessary*."

Shaking, she sat down before she fell down.

Before the lawyers could find their tongues after that outraged speech, Minerva rose. "I and almost everyone in the Priory are descendants of the late Earl of Wycliffe. Between us, we are related to, have gone to school with, and have married into half the aristocracy, at the very least. Yes, eventually, Lord Chatham must have the same education as the earl's great-grandsons, who are currently being tutored upstairs by an educated gentlemen the Duke of Castlefield recommended. But right now, they're too young, as is Daniel. He needs to know he has a family and people he can count on first. He can do that here, under the tutelage of Mr. Birdwhistle and Mrs. Russell, forming the friendships he'll need to survive the rigors of boarding school and university."

Rafe chuckled. Damien, Hunt, and Paul grinned broadly. Even Mr. Browning, the manor's solicitor, hid a smile.

Verity offered a prayer of gratitude and relief for this wonderful home she had found.

Clutching her hands and not standing this time, she used her best schoolteacher voice. "Rafe and I only wish legal guardianship so we might act as their mother would have. As I understand it, she has been raising them on the limited funds of their father's trust, without anyone's aid, and has done a fine job."

She took a deep breath to settle her nerves. "I have my own money. Rafe has a business plus a salary. We have a home. We don't need as much she did. We can send the invoices for their tutoring and clothes directly to you. Money is not the *point*. We will love them as their mother did. We will raise them in a community that wants the best for them. They will have more nannies and governesses and tutors than any fortune could pay for. If you must think about trust funds and estates—look at Mr. Turner. He probably needs our help too, but he's of age and Daniel's heir. Unless you wish him to fall into debt and drunkenness, shouldn't he receive an education in how to run an estate and be given an opportunity to marry well? Had that been done in the first place, none of this needed to have happened."

Hunt clapped. Verity blushed and shut up.

Rafe pushed his chair back so he could hook his fingers in his waistcoat over his massive chest, as he liked to do when he wanted to intimidate. Then he used his best boarding school accent. "My wife is the granddaughter of Lord Higginbottom, the daughter of a wealthy shipping magnate and financier, an excellent teacher, and to my eternal gratitude, a brilliant keeper of accounts. She can probably teach the boy—" He cast the now upright and listening Mr. Turner a glance. "—*boys* more than any school. Greek is all very well and erudite for lounging about London, but learning how to run an estate is essential for prosperity. No school can teach that."

Blessedly, Damien pushed official-looking documents toward

the Bath solicitors. "We have drawn up simple guardianship papers for your perusal. If you mean to appoint Mr. Turner as guardian of the estate, you'll need to draw those up separately. The Russells are only concerned with the well-being of the children."

Young Mr. Turner was on his feet and pounding the stiff-necked solicitors on the back. "I wholly approve. I'm not good at monitoring minors, but I have that education you claim the heir needs. I have friends. I can keep my uncle's estate running until my cousin comes of age. Just try me!"

He was just as likely to run it into the ground unless they tied his hands, but that wasn't the point either. Verity fought back tears, terrified they'd have to fight this all the way to the highest court when the solution was so simple.

The Marquess of Spalding lazily unfolded his slender frame from the library chair. "Most excellent decision, gentlemen. My friend, Mr. Sutter here, has the approval of the Duke of Castlefield as well as mine. He can help you draw up the estate papers, if needed. Your heir is in most excellent hands. I understand the ladies have an entertainment prepared to welcome the new year, if you'd care to join us."

Verity's jaw dropped. Rafe nudged it shut and offered a hand to help her up. A marquess and a duke defended her? A viscount's solicitors wouldn't stand a chance against such powerful men.

"They're mine?" she whispered.

Rafe shrugged his now finely-tailored shoulders. "As much as any young ones can be, I reckon."

She thought she floated out of the room in the company of the others. She was a *mother*. She'd never even thought to marry and now she was the mother of two beautiful, extraordinary children. She would teach Daphne as her brilliant governess had taught her. Daniel would go to school with Oliver and Davey and maybe Rob and Arthur and have an army around him. They...

The ancient floor clock on the landing began its deep, sonorous bonging. The men glanced at their pocket watches. Was it really midnight? Better yet, was the clock actually correct and ringing in the new year?

In answer, a pianoforte melody rang from inside the great hall, accompanied by Patience's beautiful voice. As if by magic, couples emerged from the drawing rooms and down the stairs. Before Verity could even fully register her joy, Rafe bowed and offered his arm, and swept her into the row of dancers forming down the wide corridor.

Laughing in delight at this impromptu ballroom, even as the clock kept insanely chiming, Verity danced her very first quadrille.

Over her head, Rafe shouted at Hunt, who had his own lady in line. "Better fetch Fletch. He's as berserk as your clock and never saw one he couldn't fix."

The clock stopped, the music was joined by a violin, and the dancers welcomed the new year.

∽

Much later, clinging to Damien's arm as they drove toward home, Brydie whispered, "We can always run off to Gretna in your lovely purloined carriage." Still dizzy from the dancing, she didn't want to go back to her lonely bed.

Her beloved lawyer grinned down at her. "We've declared our first banns. We'll only be anticipating our vows a little. Kate will think you stayed at the manor."

Overjoyed that he was willing to be as improper as she, Brydie threw her arms around him and covered his jaw with kisses. "Happy Brilliant New Year!"

She'd put fresh linens on his new bed in his new house, hoping for this opportunity.

Besides, if Damien could purloin a carriage, she might kidnap a bakery. They had much to celebrate. The year 1816 promised a whole new story for the village.

~

Minerva snuggled under Paul's arm as they walked down the drive to the parsonage. "Did Hunt decide Parsons might have Willa's trinket collection?"

"He's doling them out in portions, based on good behavior and hard work. Parsons appears to be grateful simply for a roof over his head and food in his belly. Rafe is delighted to have a new employee and happy with him so far. It's a good way to start the new year."

Minerva finally admitted her own failure. "I am very sorry I spent my coin on bread all these weeks instead of saving for your new shirt. I will learn to bake bread, I promise, and use my salary for better purposes."

"Bread?" Paul laughed in surprise. "My mother bakes bread, if we need it. Elsa and Brydie bake it. You, my brilliant wife, keep Mrs. Jones and her ladies out of my hair, organize fairs to feed my parishioners, and stand up in front of officious idiots when they're being idiotish. Along with solving mysteries that save innocent children from those same idiots. I do not need bread when I have you. The shirt however. . ."

She tickled him under the arm and ran off laughing. He'd have his shirt by his birthday.

COUPLES

GRAVESYDE VILLAGE MYSTERIES

The Villain's Fatal Plot
Book One

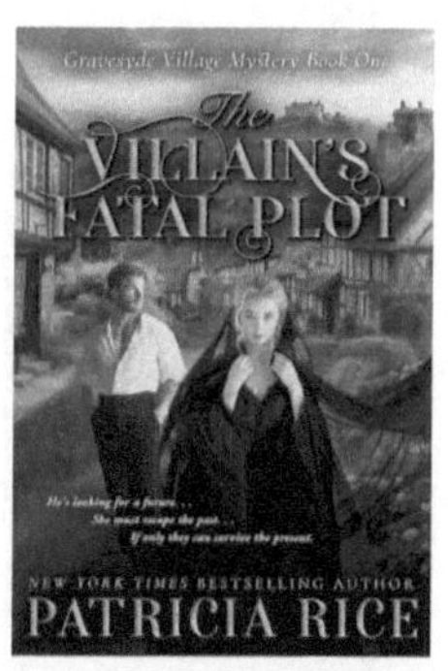

Bestselling author Patricia Rice brings you another small-town mystery in Regency England. . . He's looking for a future - she must escape the past. . . if only they can survive the present.

In the derelict village of Gravesyde Priory, newly-arrived Verity Palmer discovers her beloved former governess poisoned, her dying breath a whispered confidence. Shaken and alone, cautious Verity fears trusting total strangers with a dangerous secret.

Seeking work and a roof over his head, bluff ex-mess sergeant Rafe Russell accepts the position of bailiff, tasked with uncovering the truth about the governess's untimely demise. Caught in a web of suspicious characters, he discovers an unexpected ally in his best suspect, perspicacious Verity. She possesses a sharp mind that cuts through nets of intrigue, while hiding behind a cloak of mystery.

With no choice but to share a cottage—and a kitchen that quickly becomes his, not hers—Verity and Rafe piece together clues to save lives, including their own. As violent incidents escalate, Verity has to confront her own past and learn to trust if they are to expose the shadowy villains stalking their every move.

If they're to have any hope for a future, they must unveil the truth before the killer strikes again.

Buy The Villain's Fatal Plot

The Scoundrel's Deadly Deed
Book Two

"Patricia Rice writes stories with so much attention to detail the characters truly seem to come to life." *Booklist*

The past rarely gives second chances—and neither do killers

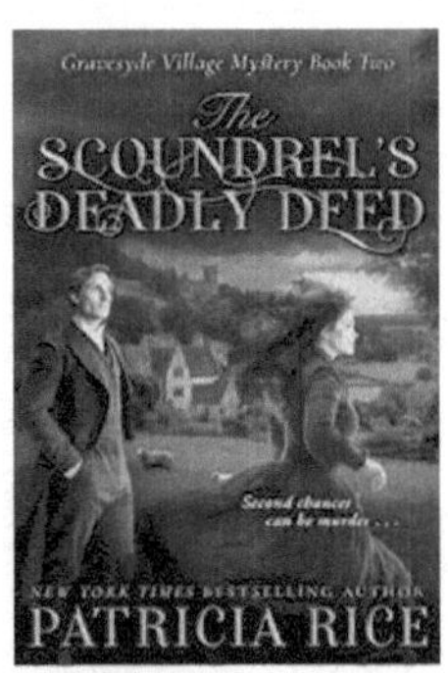

Damien Sutter fled his abusive family and the decaying village of Gravesyde at age twenty, abandoning his first love without a second look back. Fifteen years later, he's a respected solicitor, returning only to sell his inherited property, never expecting to find the best part of his childhood still unmarried—and believing him capable of treachery.

Despite her humiliating spinsterhood, fiery Brydie Calhoun refuses to marry any man who doesn't appreciate her spirited temperament. Nor should she be forced to pair with someone possessing fewer wits than her own. But when her childhood sweetheart returns, Brydie is forced to deal with the devil... and his troubled past.

Alarmed that a traveling camp of political and religious zealots will cause difficulty in selling his inheritance, Damien approaches them, only to watch in horror as his estranged mother is shot before his eyes. After another murderous attack on a prominent citizen, it becomes clear that the town he despises is under siege. With Brydie in his reach again—and possibly in danger—he can't walk away this time.

Damien and Brydie must unravel a tangled tale of rivalry and greed before tragedy strikes again. Can they confront his past and stop the killer before it's too late for reconciliation--or even survival?

Buy *The Scoundrel's Deadly Deed*

The Madman's Dangerous Delusion
Book Four

Menaced by a madman, a widow and a soldier seek safety. . . and discover so much more.

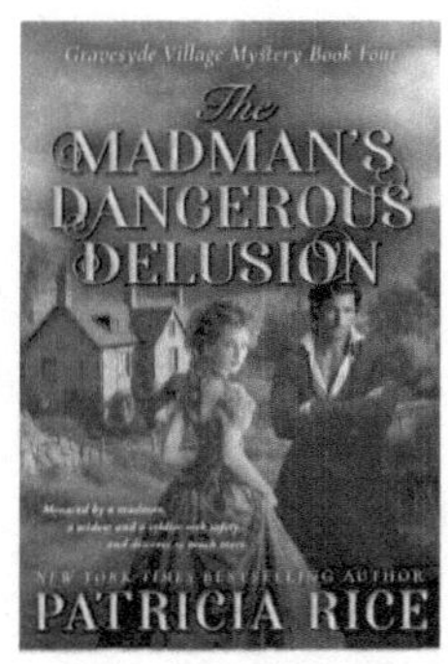

Recently widowed Kate Morgan supports her family as a seamstress in Gravesyde Village. She needs a husband to farm her land but is losing hope of finding love. With her insane brother-in-law claiming her home, she might even lose that.

Battle-worn and bitter, Sergeant Major Fletch Ferguson returns from war with a single goal: fix clocks, not lives. But when the widow's lunatic relation threatens her, Fletch's fighting instincts ignite. The resultant battle leaves him temporarily disabled, Kate terrified, and a madman on the loose.

When a cousin who resembles Kate falls to her death, Fletch refuses to believe in coincidence and insists on moving in to protect her and her children. Terrified, Kate has no reason to deny the surly ex-soldier's offer, especially after a string of suspicious accidents and deaths involving her fellow seamstresses follows

Can one madman really be behind all of the dangerous incidents? Fletch would far rather deal with the manor's eccentric case clock than lunatics and killers. But with women and children endangered, he and a furious Kate must stop the villain before anyone else must mourn a loved one.

Anne Gracie, author of the bestselling Heiress's Daughter, praises Rice's mysteries as "wonderful, fun, gothic. . . with a cast of quirky characters and a heartwarming romance as well. Pure entertainment."

Buy The Madman's Dangerous Delusion

GRAVESYDE PRIORY MYSTERY

The Secrets of Wycliffe Manor
Book #1

Be wary of what you wish for. . .

In Regency England:

The descendant of adventuring—dead—aristocrats, Clarissa Knightley supplements a modest inheritance by penning gothic novels that cost more than they earn. Upon learning that she has mysteriously inherited a share of an earl's estate, she rashly packs up her household. In remote Gravesyde Priory, she hopes to find a safe haven and family who will welcome her and her young nephew.

Instead, she discovers a drunken American army captain, his African servant, and ancient, surly caretakers. Terrified, prepared to flee, Clare is lured to linger by the prospect of secret diaries, hidden jewels, and an increasingly intriguing man. Then a killer strikes.

The crumbling manor's ominous and baffling history offers

fascinating fodder for Clare's horror novels—if only she can survive real-life madmen and a spectral murderer who may seek the jewels at any price.

Buy The Secrets of Wycliffe Manor

The Mystery of the Missing Heiress
Book #2

Wycliffe Manor, a magnet for murder...

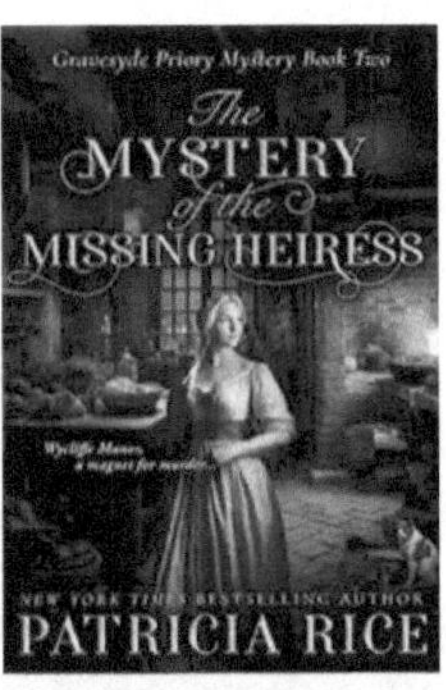

On a long-delayed errand to remote Wycliffe Manor, ex-Lieutenant Jack de Sackville stumbles across the murdered body of London dandy, Basil Culpepper, in the hedgerow, a long way from his usual haunts. To Jack's dismay, he discovers the earl's daughter Culpepper ruined hiding in Wycliffe's kitchen.

Disguised as a lowly cook, Lady Elspeth Villiers may have liked to shoot Culpepper for ruining her life, but she dropped out of sight for more immediate reasons than an old scandal —her wealth has become the focus of greedy men. The arrival of Jack, the man she's adored since childhood, along with Culpepper's corpse, mean her hiding place is no longer safe.

But once Lady Elsa reveals herself to the unconventional inhabitants of Wycliffe Manor, they become the protective family she has never known. Outraged to learn the beautiful woman he once loved and lost has become a target of greed, Jack joins the investigation into Culpepper's death.

With a murderer on the loose, the amateur sleuths must unravel a deadly tangle of kidnappers and counterfeiters or the

Manor's eccentric inhabitants will be in as much danger as their cook.

Buy The Mystery of the Missing Heiress

The Bones in the Orchard
Book #3

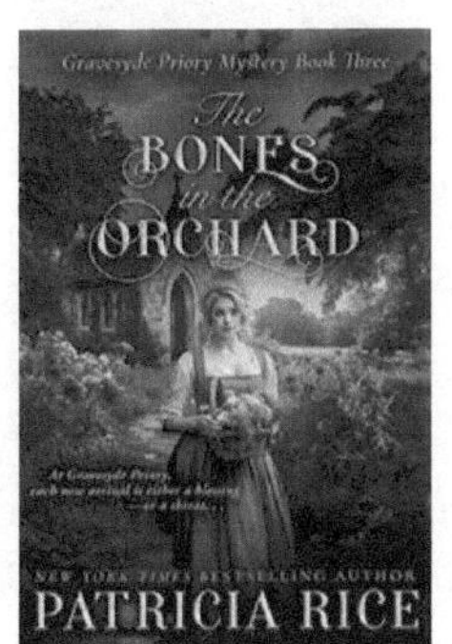

At Gravesyde Priory, each new arrival is either a blessing—or a threat. . .

Wycliffe Manor has been neglected for decades. Its new heirs are determined to create a welcoming home. Yet soon after the latest family moves into the nearby parsonage, bones are uncovered in the orchard. . . and odd strangers arrive.

When her curate father returns his family to Gravesyde for the marriages of the manor's heirs, gawky spinster Patience Upton has high expectations—until her father is murdered. Shock at learning her father had a mysterious past, leads to alarm that the killer may have been after his notebook, which she now possesses.

After the chapel is ransacked and a witness killed, it's clear the murderer isn't done. Desperate to find the truth, Patience accepts the aid of Henri Lavigne, Wycliffe Manor's smooth-talking rake. Intent on saving his new home and family from danger, Henri is drawn to the clergyman's guileless daughter but wonders if she hasn't reason to conceal the killer's identity.

Before there will be any courting, much less marrying, the inhabitants of the manor realize if they want a chance at a future, they must hunt the killer themselves. But are they hunting one murderer. . . or more?

Buy The Bones in the Orchard

The Question of the Wedding Pearls
Book #4

Will death ruin the perfect wedding?

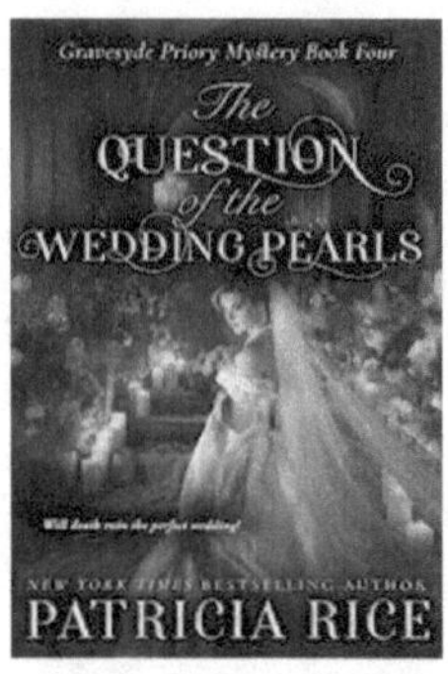

Bestselling author Patricia Rice brings you another haunting country house mystery in Regency England. . .

Spinster and secret novelist Clarissa Knightley and her gruff American engineer, Captain Huntley, along with their friend and cousin, the Honorable Jack de Sackville and Lady Elspeth, are to wed at last! In anticipation of the double wedding, friends and family are gathering at moldering Wycliffe Manor—until a dying stranger is discovered on the neglected grounds.

Despite the tragedy, aristocratic wedding guests, and their retinues, foreign and domestic, continue to arrive, not all by invitation. Compounding the bedlam, tales of missing pearls and ghostly encounters precede a second alarming death. Fearing that a killer lurks inside the manor walls, Clare and Hunt are swept up in a whirlwind of secret bigotries, deceit, and increasing peril. Before their family's joyful plans veer into heartbreak, can they put an end to mayhem and catch a killer?

Buy The Question of the Wedding Pearls

The Case of the Purloined Pages
Book #5

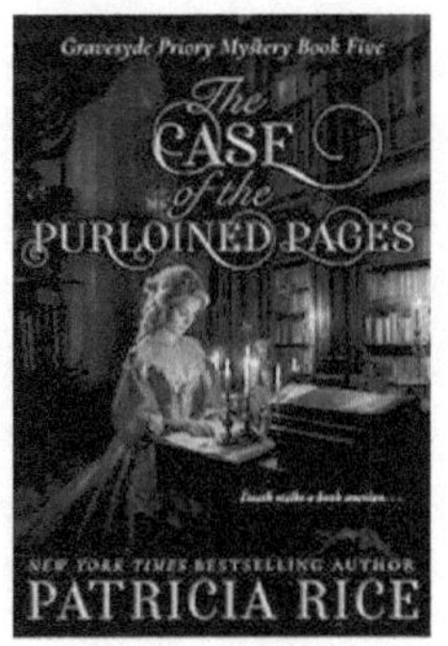

Death stalks the library. . .Bestselling author Patricia Rice brings you another haunting country house mystery in Regency England. . .

Minerva Peniston, intrepid spinster and booklover, is determined to capture the villain who tried to shoot a duke at a book auction— imperiling her father's position and the only home she's ever known. And now the same wealthy bibliophiles are gathering at Wycliffe Manor. . .

Paul Upton, over-educated and impoverished curate, has volunteered to assist the residents of Wycliffe Manor in preparing for a book auction to save the village and the manor's future. When an intriguing wallflower drags him into aiding her quest to find a potential killer, he agrees for her safety, and to keep trouble from upending the long-awaited nuptials of the manor's owner.

Despite their efforts, Minerva's chatty book-collecting friend is strangled before the auction begins. A killer on the loose threatens to upend both sale and wedding. Paul and Minerva must determine what secrets the garrulous victim revealed. . . and to whom. . . before the murderer strikes again.

With valuable manuscripts at risk and a half dozen more potential victims on hand, only an unlikely white-knight and mousy spinster can save the auction and the wedding. As much as Minerva adores books, even she knows they aren't worth dying for.

Buy The Case of the Purloined Pages

∼

The Dilemma of a Dead Scholar
Book #6

At Wycliffe Manor, a legendary pirate treasure draws danger... .Bestselling author Patricia Rice brings you another haunting country house mystery in Regency England. . .

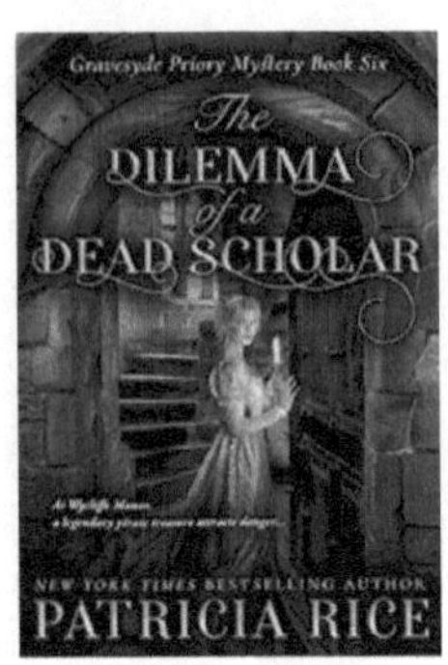

An heiress haunted by ghosts, Dotty Dorothea knows her family believes her mad. Fearing fortune hunters who would lock her and her awkward little brother in an asylum, she flees behind the ancient walls of Wycliffe Manor.

A French artist and émigré, his soul bearing scars from a French prison, Comte Arnaud Lavigne has lost everything to war. His only foreseeable future is restoring bad artwork in his cousin's decrepit manor. Mad heiresses aren't his concern, until the day a mathematical scholar is murdered. The deceased leaves a coded journal that might lead to Wycliffe Manor's lost treasure—inside the sealed tower the terrified heiress swears is haunted.

Ghosts don't exist as far as Arnaud is concerned, but killers and thieves are real, especially when stolen treasure is involved. How is he to work with the dotty heiress when neither of them trusts the other—or themselves? But the inhabitants of Wycliffe Manor, young and old, are in peril unless a heartless killer and thief is caught. . .

Buy *The Dilemma of a Dead Scholar*

BOOK VIEW CAFE

ABOUT THE AUTHOR

With several million books in print and *New York Times* and *USA Today's* bestseller lists under her belt, former CPA Patricia Rice is one of romance's hottest authors. Her emotionally-charged contemporary and historical romances have won numerous awards, including the *RT Book Reviews* Reviewers Choice and Career Achievement Awards. Her books have been honored as Romance Writers of America RITA® finalists in the historical, regency and contemporary categories.

A firm believer in happily-ever-after, Patricia Rice is married to her high school sweetheart and has two children. A native of Kentucky and New York, a past resident of North Carolina and Missouri, she currently resides in Southern California, and now does accounting only for herself.

ALSO BY PATRICIA RICE

The World of Magic:

The Unexpected Magic Series

MAGIC IN THE STARS

WHISPER OF MAGIC

THEORY OF MAGIC

AURA OF MAGIC

CHEMISTRY OF MAGIC

NO PERFECT MAGIC

The Magical Malcolms Series

MERELY MAGIC

MUST BE MAGIC

THE TROUBLE WITH MAGIC

THIS MAGIC MOMENT

MUCH ADO ABOUT MAGIC

MAGIC MAN

THE MAGIC MALCOLMS BOXSET

The California Malcolms Series

THE LURE OF SONG AND MAGIC

TROUBLE WITH AIR AND MAGIC

THE RISK OF LOVE AND MAGIC

Crystal Magic

SAPPHIRE NIGHTS

TOPAZ DREAMS

CRYSTAL VISION

WEDDING GEMS

Azure Secrets

Amber Affairs

Moonstone Shadows

The Wedding Gift

The Wedding Question

The Wedding Surprise

School of Magic

Lessons in Enchantment

A Bewitching Governess

An Illusion of Love

The Librarian's Spell

Entrancing the Earl

Captivating the Countess

Psychic Solutions

The Indigo Solution

The Golden Plan

The Crystal Key

The Rainbow Recipe

The Aura Answer

The Prism Effect

Historical Romance:

American Dream Series

Moon Dreams

Rebel Dreams

The Rebellious Sons

Wicked Wyckerly

Devilish Montague

Notorious Atherton

Formidable Lord Quentin

Urban Fantasies

Writing as Jamie Quaid

<u>*Saturn's Daughters*</u>

BOYFRIEND FROM HELL

DAMN HIM TO HELL

GIVING HIM HELL

ABOUT BOOK VIEW CAFÉ

 *Book View Café* LLC (BVC) is an author-owned cooperative of professional writers, publishing in a variety of genres including fantasy, romance, mystery, and science fiction — with 90% of the proceeds going to the authors. Since its debut in 2008, BVC has gained a reputation for producing high-quality ebooks. BVC's ebooks are DRM-free and are distributed around the world. The cooperative is now bringing that same quality to its print editions.

BVC authors include New York Times and USA Today bestsellers as well as winners and nominees of many prestigious awards.